ROCKED

~ by M.J. Schiller

Published By Kissmet Publishing

CHAPTER ONE

Zane

There was a difference between having a life and living a life, and I really wanted to discover what that difference was. I had a life. Most would say it was a good life. But for me it seemed like all I was doing was chasing the second hand on a clock. I would move forward through the day, but at the close I had nothing to show for it other than the passage of time. At the ripe old age of twenty-six, I was tired beyond belief and walking through my days and nights like a zombie.

But the people who had been filling the stadium for the last hour and a half were not here to see the walking dead. They were doctors, lawyers, garbage men, seamstresses.... They came from small towns and cities, ghettos like those I grew up in, and plush estates like the ones I lived in now. I had come to know the people behind those gilded doors had their own kinds of problems. But all of these people occupying seats in the heart of this building or swaying drunkenly on the floor, they worked, sweated, and stressed to earn the money to buy the tickets to this concert and listen to my music. I wouldn't let them down.

After all, I was one of them once. I even sold my ten-speed to purchase tickets to see my idol, Colton Remkus, who was one of our openers tonight. Because of that, I vowed to sing the hits I'd sung a biljallion times before like I recently released them and they were still fresh. As Colt did for me. Though I didn't feel like I had the heart for it, I would bring the vitality of the damned Energizer Bunny if it killed me.

Knuckles rapped on my dressing room door, and Richard Belamont, our manager, swung it open, holding onto the knob as he stuck his head in. "Five minutes, Zane."

I nodded. "Coming."

My bandmates would already be backstage. Waiting in the wings with them and their chatter always ramped up my anxiety, so I preferred a last minute entrance. I stood and swung my gold sequined jacket from a chair at my dressing table and glanced into the mirror above it. I adjusted my tie to the right, then decided it was fine in the first place and moved it to the left. I didn't fit the dress code of the average rocker, but I was okay with that. I didn't even own any concert T-shirts or ripped jeans, but I had blazers that would blind the sun with their brightness, and a shitload of suspenders, hats, ties, etc.

The jacket hooked on a finger and slung over my shoulder, I left the room, not bothering to turn off the light. The clicking of my boots across the concrete floor was somehow reassuring. The waiting was over, at least. Now that I could do something, now I was actually moving forward along the hall, the tightness of my body released in motion, I felt better. Once I hit the stage and my bandmates made their instruments sing, I would feel completely at home and in my element. I wished I didn't get so uptight—and I was better than I used to be, for sure—but it simply was the way it was. I learned to live with it, and thankfully, the others seemed to respect my sometimes moody and erratic behavior. I continued my solitary stroll to the footlights to meet with the other members of Just Short of Chaos, adrenaline surging through my bloodstream, the oil that loosened my insides and made it easier for me to breathe.

As I got closer to the auditorium, the walls seemed to vibrate with the sound of the crowd. I casually passed my hand across the cinderblocks. They were actually throbbing with the excitement of the audience, the tremors running along my fingers and throughout my arm. We had a lively bunch tonight. After Midnight did a great job of igniting the crowd, and they were followed by Colton Remkus and his band, who whipped the place into a frenzy. I hoped Just Short of Chaos could live up to our headliner billing after that. I still couldn't believe Colton Remkus was opening *for us*. I scratched my chin. It was unbelievable. But Colt was so easygoing and down to earth. Funny even, though squeaky clean for a rock star, which at times was uncomfortable, seeing as we were far from it.

Pressing against the release bar, I pushed through the metal doors at the end of the hall. A twinge of apprehension stirred when people were hanging inside the hall beyond the door, leaning against the walls and talking. Not for my safety, but because I might need to make conversation or act in a socially acceptable way. I took a deep breath in through my nose.

These are my people. I nodded. "Hey."

They bobbed their heads in return. "Good luck," someone offered.

I forced myself to make eye contact with the speaker, and managed a small, genuine smile, laughing inside at my own unease. "Thanks."

Jericho and Rafe were standing, holding shots, when I stepped around a curtain and over electrical cords weaving across each other like the snakes in the pit in that Indiana Jones movie. Dex had one butt cheek resting on top of an upturned crate, but he hopped to his feet when he saw me and snatched two more shots from the end of another storage case to his left, handing one to me. Without fanfare we raised the glasses for an instant, then threw them back. Whiskey. Must have been Rafe's turn to pick. Stuff tasted like lighter fluid. Not that I'd drank lighter fluid before. At least not from what I could remember. I could never be sure. Not remembering what I did the night before scared the shit out of me at first, but now it was a matter of course.

I flipped the emptied shot glass upside down, setting it on the crate Dex abandoned with a sharp ring. The noise accompanied an exclamation that was part exhale, part gasp, as my breath was stolen away by the burn of the alcohol, which seemed to blast a fire into my mouth, along my throat, and throughout my nasal passages.

"Holy shit!" Dex let out.

I decided the newest member of our band needed to attend what we affectionately termed, "Drinking Camp." Although we swore off drugs since our former drummer, Devin's overdose, we didn't consider alcohol a drug and abused it more heavily than ever before. If Dex was gonna make it with Just Short of Chaos, he needed to be more than a casual player in our game.

I willed to life the shit-eating grin I was famous for, super-gluing it on. I shrugged into my jacket, then yanked on the lapels so the fabric fell right. Tugging each cuff down in turn, I looked at my three cohorts. "Let's do this." We lined up for our entrance, listening to the countdown music Rafe put together. Ten, nine, eight.... It raised the buzz of excitement to a feverish pitch. The curtain hiding us from view of most of the audience was in front of the monitors flashing each number from ten to one. Each was followed by either an album cover, or an action shot or close-up of a band member. The cheers were loudest for me and Jericho. As our quirky front man and the face of the band, I had a huge following, especially on social media. Jericho was Mr. Sex Appeal, and he knew it. Played it to his advantage. Wore it comfortably, like a favorite sweatshirt. I swung from enjoying the limelight to wanting to disappear for a while, depending on the day of the week. But I kept my reticence hidden. I couldn't sell the band if I was invisible. And when I was on, I could work a room, or an interview, like nobody's business, and even enjoy it, to a degree. Only it took a lot of energy and focus to pull it off.

The number four flashed across the screen.

Rafe drummed on my shoulders. "You ready, buddy?" He had to shout to be heard above the thunder bellowing on the other side of the curtain.

I nodded.

Three. A shot of Jericho playing behind his head.

Two. The cover from the album that launched us into the spotlight.

One. Me, doing my signature gymnastics pass across the stage. It was a great black and white shot of me doing a back tuck, with the light shining from behind me. The concertgoers lost it. Just Short of Chaos's logo flashed, and Rafe ran out to take his place on the stage, locating his bass and swinging the strap over his neck. Dex followed him, climbing the ramp to his drum stand. Jericho and I brought up the rear, waving our arms and smiling at the audience.

The noise swelled so it was almost a force, pushing against us. We broke into our latest hit, "Burn Through You," which had held the number one spot on the charts for the past eight weeks. It was a real crowd pleaser about a guy in a hot relationship that started at a beach bonfire. I carried the burning theme throughout the song until the last verse where the guy was holding the pictures the couple took in one of those hokey photo booths and putting a match to them. It satisfied our fans' inner pyromaniacs.

About halfway through the piece, I thought about what was coming next. I always gave a shout out to the town we were in. But I realized I had a small problem. I couldn't remember what town we were in. All of the stadiums looked the same. I couldn't see the various local advertisements spattered around the place as most of what lay beyond the first ten rows was in utter blackness.

Shit. Shit. Shit. We were in St. Louis last night...or was it Detroit? No. It was St. Louis because one of After Midnight's band member's girlfriends, who was from Germany, thought the Gateway

Arch was a sign for a gigantic McDonald's. But was Detroit our next stop or Kansas City?

Desperate, I searched in front of me for a clue. Two guys chest pumped, spilling beer everywhere. One brushed at his shirt, spotted with his splattered drink, and I zeroed in on the Royals logo on it. I quickly scanned the area and spotted two more Royals shirts and a Chiefs jersey. Thank God for sports.

I ran down the short runway extending into the mass of people smashed up against the stage, shaking hands and accepting people's phones so I could take a selfie with them. Then I took one where I got the two of us and the throng of writhing music lovers in the background. I learned the biggest way to make lifelong devotees was to include them in the concert in some way. Plus that picture became a free advertisement. They'd upload it to Facebook or Instagram, or any of a number of different places, and perhaps tag me, giving me a second opportunity to interact with them. And it wasn't strictly a self-serving gesture. I really did value our followers and was grateful they shared my love for the music I created. I finished the song back-to-back with Rafe, who was wailing out the concluding guitar lick.

"Well, how the hell are you Kansas City?" I was answered by a roar. "Seems After Midnight and Colton Remkus got you pretty fired up, huh? Let's hear it for them one more time." I waited while they applauded their appreciation. "Well, how about we continue your outstanding concert experience with a little rock of our own. I think you guys might know this one."

All it took was one note. One note and they were going nuts. Of course, many of them would have downloaded our set list from Setlist.fm, or found it some other way, but the opening chords of "Running Out On Love" were easily recognizable. It was a song off our first big album. I'd sung it in an average of fifty shows a tour, for four years now, not to mention the music award show performances, practices, video takes...I sang it more than the number of times I recited the Pledge Allegiance times the number of times I sang "The Star-Spangled Banner." And, like singing "Happy Birthday," I didn't have to put much thought into it. So, like most nights, I began to assess the audience.

Directly in front of me, bouncing to the beat, was a cute girl with brown, curly hair. She was a possibility. She was with a blonde. Girls' night. Perfect. But, I wasn't settling on the first girl I saw. Al awaited my signal. When I found tonight's flavor, Al would wade through the crowd and extend an invitation to meet me after the show to the chosen woman. The dude was amazing at reading facial cues and always seemed to know exactly who I had in mind. Not only that, but he would do the same for Rafe and Jericho. Dex didn't have the luxury of curating his finds. He would have to choose from whoever made it backstage. But, so far, he seemed rather disinterested in hooking up after shows. We wondered, at first, if maybe he was gay. Not that it was a problem. Several of the guys on our crew were gay. However, when groupies actually searched him out, Dex seemed interested enough. He was very discreet with whatever happened after that. Maybe he'd become more open with us as the tour went on.

I continued my surveillance. Two guys were in each other's faces, girls clinging to their elbows in an attempt to keep them from coming to blows. Could be an interesting distraction. A blonde to their right caught my attention. She wore a skintight tank, accenting her...assets. Her midriff was bare, and her bellybutton pierced. I couldn't see the rest of her getup, but I guessed it was equally trashy. As I watched, she slowly ran her tongue around her lips. An easy score, but, in all honesty, it bored me. She pulled her top down to reveal a tat of our logo on her right breast. Impressive. She went the extra mile. I flashed her a grin.

Al was taking it all in, and started moving in her direction, but I looked him in the eye and gave my head a slight shake. Al nodded and returned to his spot in front of the stage, crossing his beefy arms, his observation flitting from one band member to the next, very serious about his role as solicitor of sex.

I went back to the brunette who I first noticed, but this time her blonde friend was facing me. Our gazes met and she smiled wider. It wasn't a come-hither smile, more like a friendly greeting. She didn't seem interested in coming on to me at all. Her girlfriend must be the fan, and the blonde was here for her. Fine. I could respect that. But she seemed to know all the lyrics. Curious. I focused on her. She wore a red top tied behind her neck. The material crossed between her breasts, but didn't reveal anything. Only hinted at her shapeliness. Not your usual concert attire.

The third song ended and we slid into another. I continued to scan the crowd, evaluating. Blondes, brunettes, redheads. Big boobs, bigger boobs, freakishly ginormous boobs. Why did everyone have boobs these days? Black leather, low-cut concert T's, cheetah print, the standards. I located the usual ring of shirtless guys bouncing off each other's chests and knocking women who weren't paying attention over, causing their boyfriends to join in the fray. Idiots. But time and again I came back to the pretty blonde in front of the stage. I'd put money on her being tipsy, and her friend was definitely wasted, swaying on her heels like a pier on pylons during hurricane season. The blonde caught her elbows several times and righted her, laughing and rolling her eyes at her friend's antics. A pair of guys behind them were watching the two with interest, speaking into each other's ears and nodding. I could tell they had bad intentions, which normally didn't bother me that much, but for some reason pricked at me tonight.

I was getting hot. Under the lights, and dancing my ass off, it was like a hundred and twenty degrees. By the end of the night I would be shirtless, kind of my thing, but I needed to leave the jacket on for the next song, at least. It had a Frank Sinatra flavor to it, and I needed to look my most debonair on that one to woo my female fans, though they didn't need wooing. I sang it in a deep baritone the women found sexy, a stark contrast to my more common falsetto singing. I had one of the widest ranges in the industry, and I liked to play with it.

I moved to stage left, singing to a group of four African American women who appeared to be having the time of their lives. A little older than my usual fans, but they seemed like a fun bunch. The song wrapped up and the throwback tune began. I swayed to the retro music accompanying me. I could move, but only to my music. If I was dragged out onto the dance floor to something else I was the nerdiest, most white, most uncomfortable guy out there. I loved dancing to my tunes. It was so freeing. It was so freeing being Zane Sanders, rock star, and not Zane Alexander Salvetti, excruciatingly introverted geek. The persona I created, the image I fashioned over time, took over, and I could be smooth, confident, and in control. It never failed to amaze me.

When I swung back to center stage, I caught The Girl staring at me, as I was staring at her. I don't know when she became The Girl, but she was. And she wasn't even The Girl of the Night, which was even more curious. Only The Girl. Our gazes locked, which seemed to embolden me, and I was suddenly singing to her, and to her only, as I sauntered across the stage deliberately. I was aware, in a peripheral way, of The Girl's friend's jaw dropping open and her elbowing my target. I could read the lips easily. "He's singing to you," followed by a squeal. I couldn't hear one, but I was certain one came from her. My Girl—she was *My* Girl now?—ignored her friend and continued to peer into my eyes, the corners of her mouth quivering slightly, her face bright.

I'm not sure at what point on my stroll across the stage things changed, but they did. The closer I got to her, the more everything was altered, becoming surreal. It started off as casual, fun, flirty—just another night, another stage, another girl. But it was like on those sci-fi shows, I came in range of her tractor beam and I couldn't resist the pull. And nothing felt the same as it was minutes before. Everything seemed to have more weight now, more importance, and I was filled with an odd energy. It was like I'd been asleep for years and awoken in a new and wonderful world.

I came to the lyric, "Don't you want me to love you tonight?" and for the first time, I wasn't simply singing the words, I was expressing them. My heart thundered, like the beat of Dex's drums, and it was as if everything faded away for a second. The fans, the security, my band members, everything became blurry, with Her the only thing in focus. The music became a smear of sound, except for my vocal. "Don't you want me to love you tonight?" It was like I was watching myself, with no control over what I did. Closer and closer I came to her. Then, in slow motion, like in a dream, I watched myself extend my hand to her.

Her brow wrinkled, and she glanced at her friend, but the friend had a goofy star struck expression on her face and wasn't paying any attention to Her. I flipped my headset mic to the side and grinned at her, her discomfort making me steadier in some way. "Come on."

She peered about her, fingers splayed on her chest. "Who? Me?" she mouthed.

I laughed. "Well, I'm not talking to those two assholes eying you for the past fifteen minutes. Come on."

She beamed at me, her mouth sliding wider and she tilted her head. "Really?"

I frowned, and instead of answering her I wrapped my fingers around her forearm. She clutched my wrist as I plucked her from the crowd. Her boots scrambled up the stage wall, and I almost dropped her on her ass, but together we managed to get her on stage.

Uhh. Now what?

I threw a look over my shoulder. Jericho kept playing, but watched me with an amused smile. Rafe's eyes were wide, and he shifted his gaze to Jericho, who simply shrugged. I was still holding The Girl's hand.

Okay. That has to stop.

"What's your name?"

She leaned closer. "What?"

"Your name. What's your name?"

"Oh. Grace." Even with her clumsy climb onto the stage, it suited her.

Again, a wave of energy...confidence?...hit me and I bent over her hand, not breaking eye contact, and kissed it. *"Enchanté."*

Where the hell did that come from? That must be some damn strong whiskey Rafe gave me.

She looked at her friend and giggled.

"Everybody, meet Grace." The crowd roared and some people waved at her. "Should we put her to the test? Make sure her momma named her correctly?"

Grace moaned, but her smile didn't dim. "Oh, no."

I walked us backward to get some room. The chorus played, so I sang as I moved then slid to the right, putting Grace at the end of our arms' lengths. Smiling at her, and actually having fun for once, I raised my eyebrows. "Let's see whacha got."

Slowly, she lifted her opposite arm out to the side, bending her wrist elegantly.

I chuckled. *Challenge accepted.*

I gave her a slight tug and she spun smoothly in to me, until she was wrapped in my arms, her ass against my thigh. I grinned. "Holy shit!" Applause exploded around us.

She laughed, her eyes sparkling in the stage lights.

She's enjoying this as much as I am.

The realization brought with it a surge of power, and further bolstered my confidence. I brought my left hand down to clasp her free hand near her hip and swayed with her as I crooned out the familiar lyrics of the song, I now remembered, was appropriately titled "Dance Into My Heart." Maybe, subconsciously, that was why I pulled her on stage. It didn't matter why I did it, it was simply—I just decided—a brilliant move.

She leaned into me, but it didn't feel like a come-on. It felt...oddly natural. I smelled beer. One of those assholes had spilled on her. But above that I caught her fragrance, light and floral, no hint of seduction.

Interesting.

Despite that fact, it seduced all the same, and I instinctively gathered her nearer, swiveling my head toward her to breathe her in. It should be uncomfortable touching her so intimately in front of a crowd of thousands, but, magic was in the air or something, because I felt only pleasure, and arousal.

And I needed to tamp that down before I really embarrassed the both of us, so I again faced forward, but I couldn't help but bring my cheek next to hers at the same time. I was grateful the lights hadn't made me sweaty yet, although my temperature was definitely rising. She didn't flinch, or turn away. In fact, I felt her sigh and, if I could trust my peripheral vision, her lashes drooped and her lids became heavy. She twisted slightly when I straightened and started the big dramatic finish, and tilted her head to look at me. I drew out the final line—"Until you dance again into my heart."—while staring deeply into her eyes. She released my left hand and languidly brought her arm up, trailing the back of her fingers along the side of my face. I wasn't sure if she moved closer, or I did, but we were a breath away from each other. She was watching my lips and I fought an almost overwhelming urge to kiss her. Although I could get away with a lot as a rock star, it was still always best to let the fan make the first move. The song ended, but we didn't change positions.

The clapping startled us, like an unexplained noise in the middle of the night. I actually jumped then raised my head. Blinking, I took in the cheers, whistles, and applause offered from the throng beyond the footlights then twisted to observe my band members' reactions. Rafe was beating his hands together, Jericho's fingers were in his mouth, coaxing out a shrill whistle, and even Dex the Detached was on his feet, banging his sticks together so hard they were liable to break. My brain was slow to come around.

All part of the show.

It didn't matter I was more turned on than I ever had been in my entire life. I released her and took a step back.

"Let's hear it for Grace."

CHAPTER TWO

Grace

The applause broke the spell and he let go of me and stepped away. For a moment I was alarmed and confused.

What the hell am I doing up here?

Then, when I turned and a whole auditorium was in front of me, it filled me with panic.

What the hell am I doing up here!

Payton, the reason for my being at the concert in the first place, looked like she was going to explode when I finally spotted her. My friend was screaming and bouncing like springs were attached to her feet and she was pretending the floor was molten lava. I laughed, took a little bow, and started moving across the stage.

"Wait!" Despite the deafening roar rising from the floor, I heard him. I faced him, and he grabbed my hand again. "We're not done with you yet." He tugged on me with a grin. "Anyone can dance to a slow song. Let's see what you can bring if we take the beat up a little." He signaled to the band and they readied their instruments.

"I'm really not..." I glanced back at Payton. She fell off her heels again and the guys behind her helped to support her by the elbows.

Should I be concerned about that?

I frowned. Even though we were the same age, I couldn't seem to abandon my mothering instincts towards Payton. She was the life of the party, but sometimes the life of the party had to be watched over so she didn't get herself killed.

I looked at Zane. "I think I need to sit this one out." I was speaking mostly to myself, as I was sure he couldn't hear me above all the noise, but my shaking head did the talking for me.

He leaned away, taking my hand in both of his now. I read his lips. "Come on." His smile was inviting. Tantalizing. Perfect white teeth and beautiful full lips that were all I could seem to focus on. Was I really turning down Zane Freaking Sanders?

My God he was even hotter in person. The last time I saw him on YouTube—which I admit I visited frequently at night after my brother went to bed—he appeared almost scrawny. But I could tell he was solid when I rocked against his chest. With any luck he'd do his usual thing and strip down to his amazing leather pants. His green eyes were even more smoldery in person—was that even a word?—and that hair. What I wouldn't give to run my fingers through those dark, thick locks, waving around in pompadourish style...man.

"Come on. Come on."

Great. The mic was on now and I could actually hear the pleading in his sexy voice.

"I don't think I should," I murmured again, forgetting my voice wasn't amplified by a mic.

He appealed to the audience. "What do you say, guys? Do we want to see more of Grace's moves?"

They responded affirmatively. I looked at all the smiling faces. Some were nodding and appeared to say, "Go on." A few of the girls seemed pissed. I imagined they would have loved to trade places with me. I swung my head back and the way he was staring at me with those laser beam eyes of his melted my reluctance away. I let him pull me to center stage and the volume of the mob rose even higher.

"You play dirty," I said when we were close again.

He wriggled his brows. "I know."

But the song the band was playing happened to be my favorite song, "Night of Awakening." It was a breakup song, but playfully and cleverly written, with a fun Latin flare I loved. It was that song I had to play at full volume in my car, singing until my throat was sore, but I was happy. It wasn't one of the band's bigger hits—much to my bewilderment—but I found it impossible to listen to it and be still. And on stage? On stage it was even better. Dex's drums—of course I knew all their names—were beating in my bloodstream. Rafe's bass and Jericho's guitar battled, swirling around me like children playing tag. My adrenaline rose, taking control.

"I freaking love this song!" I couldn't help but say.

He blinked. "You do?" Was the multiplatinum star surprised by a compliment? "Uhh...good."

I jabbed a finger into his chest with a faux frown, although my smile threatened to split the corners of my mouth. "You're lucky it's good, because you made me dance to it."

He captured my hand in both of his, pressing it over his heart as he sang the first line. "I lived in the dark, safe but alone. 'Til you came along, warmed me down to the bone." He sang conversationally, like he wrote the song for me. I shimmied, moving my body loosely but sensually, calling on my wicked Zumba skills to get me through the song. He seemed to like it, if the light in his eyes and spreading grin were any indication. Touching my hip, he stretched his opposite arm out. My fingertips naturally fell to his side, gliding over the smooth leather encompassing him, and I clasped his extended hand. He took a step forward and I took a step back, our shoulders rolling with the music. I watched his face and somehow knew, without looking, what he was going to do next.

Were it any other song, I would be scared shitless. I was the girl whose heart raced any time I sat at a table with strangers and we were told to go around in a circle and introduce ourselves. In my head I would keep repeating my name, afraid I'd freak out and draw a blank when it was my turn because the focus was on me. On a regular day, dancing was a struggle. Payton or Lexi, or both, would drag me out on the dance floor. Yeah. The dance floor. Surrounded by tables of people watching the participants shaking their stuff. Uncomfortable was not a strong enough word. Personal Hell was more like it. But I'd do it. Because I loved my goofy friends, who can both, of course, dance better than I can. I would move a little, or a lot, depending on how much I was drinking and how much I loved the song.

But stand in front of a crowd of twenty thousand plus? No way. Yet here I was. Zane Sanders must have some sort of magic and/or potent brainwashing skills.

The music faded with the first chorus and left only his voice. His wonderful, silky, sexy voice. His mouth caressed the words with such care I was carried away with the sound of them.

The tempo increased again and he released my hip to separate us and create room so he could watch me move.

"Are you a professional dancer?" he shouted.

"I guess I am tonight," I responded with a grin, twirling and looking at him over my shoulder as I did.

If I thought much about it, I'd be halting and awkward. But, what the heck. It was my moment in the sun and I was going to relax and enjoy it, even if it killed me. My twelve dollar beer must be doing its job. My feet moved rapidly with the tempo and I tossed my hair, really getting into the song now, and singing along with him. He mimicked my movements effortlessly. I playfully put my fingers on his shoulder, dancing forward and making him step back to the rhythm. Applying pressure, I advanced again, backing him up a couple more feet. Then, with a grin, I spun and danced away. He came after me and grabbed my arm, twirling me under it in a commanding way. We continued left and right across the stage, like we acted out a little samba tug-of-war. I was amazed by the way our feet moved in synchronicity, like it was a well-practiced, choreographed dance and not two people who didn't even know each other having a little fun.

I felt wild and free and...happy. I was usually so uptight, worried about finances, about my brother, about the tiny flower shop I owned. But tonight, for the first time in a long time, I left that all behind, stepped out onto a stage and into a stranger's arms and I was loving it.

ZANE

I was having a blast. I had no idea such a live wire lay under the surface when I lifted her from the crowd. The girl was amazing. Her footwork was phenomenal. And the way she shimmied those hips? God, help me. I'd have thought she had some Latino blood in her if it weren't for her fair complexion and blonde hair. I was so distracted by her, I didn't realize she moved me halfway across the stage. Assessing my position, I did a little hop to the side and landed on the curved ramp leading to Dex's elevated drum stand. Undaunted, she continued her onslaught, a hand on the front of one shoulder, shaking her ass and continuing to force me to retreat.

"Are you a professional dancer?"

She shook her head then tilted it and grinned at me. "I guess I am tonight."

I smiled wider. I liked her. Really liked her. She was fun, and unusually comfortable with me. Most of our fans were either awestruck babblers when around me, or super aggressive, like they were asserting their own importance. Few people treated me like an equal, or acted like she was at the moment, quietly challenging me. The spotlight followed us along the ramp, but eventually we'd run out of real estate, as Dex's drums covered most of the top. But I was inspired with a solution. I leaped off the side of the ramp, onto the stage. Grace looked confused for an instant, maybe even hurt I abandoned her, but when I reached up for her, that wonderful smile of hers returned and she waited to see what I would do. Which is kind of what

I was doing, too. This was all so spontaneous, I didn't know where each second would lead. I took her hand, walked her to a lower point on the ramp, then wrapped my arms around her legs, lifting her from the metal walkway and allowing her to slowly slide down my body until her feet touched the ground. She had to kind of grab onto my shoulders for support at first, but as she was lowered, she automatically clasped my neck. I didn't release her, if anything, my muscles tightened, daring her to try to escape. But she didn't seem interested in escaping. Her gaze wandered over my face then landed on my eyes and stuck. She was playing with my hair, something almost all of the women I was with did. The difference being, it generally annoyed me when others did it, but the way she did it was freaking glorious, and I never wanted it to stop. Again I wondered what it would be like to kiss her, and actually bent my head in, but, damn it, I needed to sing the lyrics for some reason, although what that reason was, at the moment, escaped me.

When the last note ended, I had an idea that was either brilliant or disastrous, but I didn't make it this far by not taking chances. I tapped my headpiece. "Stay here," I told her, but I held onto her to guarantee she didn't leave, and walked toward Jericho and Rafe. "Change in plans. We're playing 'Don't Fade Away.'"

They looked at each other. "But Shayna's not here," Rafe pointed out.

Shayna accompanied me on this song, and her mournful vocals were really what made it work, so we usually only did it when she joined us on tour. I scrutinized Grace. "I know." I'd heard her voice when she was close and I knew she could carry the part.

"What's going on?" Grace asked hesitantly as I led her back out to center stage.

From behind me I heard Rafe ask, "So, what do we do?"

Jericho didn't hesitate. "Play 'Don't Fade Away.' He'll sing it either way and we don't want to look stupid, so we play it."

Thatta boy. You know me well.

"Oh, no," Grace said firmly, catching on to my intentions. "Dancing is one thing, but singing is an entirely different thing."

I ignored her. "Rafe. Play the acoustic."

"All right," he said begrudgingly. I owed them some apologies later for switching the set. But that was later. Usually I played the acoustic on this song, but I didn't want the added pressure at the moment.

I signaled to a stagehand. "I need a floor mic." They always had one ready in case my headset went out. The guy ran off.

"I-I don't know the words."

This hadn't occur to me, but one peek at her face and I knew it wasn't a problem. "You're a bad liar, Grace."

I took her shoulders and realized she was shaking. An unfamiliar emotion stirred within me. Guilt. Zane Sanders never felt bad about anything, never had time for regret. But it never occurred to me she might be truly frightened up here. I never was, and she didn't appear to be either—before I decided she should sing with me. It was strange I even wanted her to do it, but a desire to share myself with her hit me, and singing together could be very intimate. "Grace, look at me." I don't know why I said it, because she already was staring at me, but she quit fidgeting and seemed to focus in on me more. I kept my voice low and steady. "You can do this. I heard you earlier. Look at me and I'll get your through it."

She gave her head a slight nod. I considered giving her a way out, but decided against it. Mostly because the music was starting.

"Okay. So we all know Grace can dance, right?" Loud applause followed. "Let's see if she can...sing." The laughter and cheers were about evenly matched.

Grace took a deep breath. "Oh, man."

She was giving it a go. I began the first verse. Grace sort of appeared as if she might puke.

That would be a waste of a ten dollar beer, or whatever the hell she was drinking earlier.

She was still standing awkwardly to the side, as straight and rigid as a brick wall.

She'll never be able to sing like that.

I took her hands as I sang into my head mic and they swooped in with a mic stand. I stepped behind and embraced her, laying my cheek against hers again. Her body relaxed little by little. Extending my arm in front of us, I acted like I was showing her something when I sang the line, "A world's out there waiting for me. But I'm still here with you, down on my knees." I made a fist with the last.

It was a song I had written after my mother's death. For many years it had been only the two of us. I never knew my father, and my mom never talked about him. But when I turned sixteen, she met and married a man with two young daughters, eight and twelve at the time. They were sweet girls and I loved them like crazy. It was my stepfather I could do without. We lost my mother to cancer four years to the day after the wedding.

It was always a struggle to get through this song, and the only reason I could was because I wouldn't want to make Shayna uncomfortable by breaking down. I walked backward, leading Grace to the mic stand that was now ready for us. I raised my head mic and continued singing into the one provided. She started trembling again as we approached the chorus, the part where Shayna usually joined in. I did my best to reassure her with my eyes and squeezed her hands. My heart skipped a beat when she was late coming in, but I was blown away by her when she did let her voice come out.

I blinked, my eyes widening. I had known her voice was good when she was singing earlier, but had no idea it was this good. "Holy shit."

The audience laughed at my reaction and roared its approval. She looked at me and seemed as surprised as I, and I caught a wisp of a smile, although her gaze was still darting around. I turned to catch my bandmates' impressions with raised brows. Jericho and Rafe were shaking their heads and laughing. Dex actually came out of his seat and missed a beat before hastily picking up the song again. He whooped.

She was good. She was more than good. Arguably better than Shayna. With a little voice training, she would be incredible. And our voices melded well together. And why wouldn't they? Everything else was magical since she hit the stage, so why not this, too? I wanted to hug her, but it was hard to sing when someone was squeezing the hell out of you, and I wanted to listen to her more. She was still standing too far away from the mic, so I urged her closer.

We finished the chorus and she took the next verse, which was Shayna's, continuing to get stronger with each note. I wanted to sing my best with her so I calmed my head that was exploding with a gazillion thoughts, and concentrated on the emotion. It was emotion that brought songs to life and to perfection. But as I did, I was hit again, as I always was, by my grief over losing my mom. The pain was specific. I knew how its particular flavor tasted. It was like when I saw a bruise on my body and pressed on it and the unique pain of that injury reminded me of how I acquired it. This pain had the same way of bringing me back to its origin. Tasting her death again. I never felt so alone and lost and still struggled with it on a daily basis.

I looked into her eyes and watched her face change. I must have revealed too much because tears threatened to slide over her lashes, as they did with mine. The joy I sensed earlier morphed into concern for me. Our eyes said so much for us, there was no need for words. But the emotion made the song infinitely stronger, made it capable of moving people, of reaching in them and wrapping around their hurts and heartaches. I had to sing it this way. It deserved to be sung this way.

When we finished the last note, hanging on to it as long as we could, I drew her in. The second she was in my arms, with the music not there to hold me up anymore, I about lost it. I clutched her and tried to draw strength from her comfort. I never sang that song so close to the edge. It was dangerous to do that. But in a way it felt good. Felt right, to pay tribute to my mom like that and sing for her.

"It's all right," Grace whispered in my ear, squeezing me tighter.

We had been holding each other for far too long and I needed to pull it together. I returned my focus to her and found my strength, easing away.

"Damn!" I shouted. "The girl can sing, can't she?"

She ducked her head, color rising in her cheeks, and nodded moving away.

No. Not yet.

She dropped my hand, but I wouldn't let go of hers. "Wait. We're not finished with you." I turned to face the crowd, needing their help again to keep her on the stage. "Y'all notice how she keeps trying to escape the stage for some reason?"

They laughed, aware of how uncomfortable it must feel to be yanked out of a crowd and thrust into the spotlight.

I couldn't hear her but could read her lips and attitude. "What now?"

I had to think of a reason for keeping her from leaving. Looking back at the band to buy a little time, I stumbled on it. "That, well, that was kind of a mellow way to end things between us, don't you think?" I tilted my head. "We can't end on a sad note."

She walked over to the microphone, using it for herself for the first time, cocking a hip. "He made me dance. Made me sing. What the hell else is he going to make me do?"

I checked the audience's reaction. They were eating this up. This would definitely be a concert they'd remember for a long time. I laughed. "Just one more dance. That's all I'm asking for. I have something in mind."

She peered out over the mass of people in front of us. "Well, those words scare the shit out of me." I must have misread her at first. Clearly she was comfortable in front of a crowd. She stared at me for a long moment, then lifted a finger. "One. Just one." This was followed by cheers and whistles. She stepped back from the mic, but continued saying, "One," and shaking her finger at me.

I flipped my headphone mic down, grinning. "I have something that'll challenge you."

She moved in range of the sound system. "Now he tells me."

I looked at the guys and made a motion like I was playing the keyboards, hoping they would catch on. They stared blankly for a minute, then Rafe nodded, and turned to shout to the others, who also nodded and readied themselves. We only had one song that started with keyboards. Rafe put his guitar in its stand and shifted over to rattle the keys.

"Oh, shit," she said. "I think I know what you have in mind." She put a hand on her forehead. Rafe began playing. "Yep."

It was a piece called "Coming Home" and the beginning sounded like a music box. Then the vocals and drums kicked in with a driving beat. In was kind of an unusual composition, but I was kind of an unusual guy, so it worked for me, but the shift in tempo made it difficult to dance to.

Grace studied me out of the corners of her eyes and her lips twitched. I knew she had concocted something. Taking a deep breath to compose herself, she curled her arms in front of her like a ballerina and pirouetted to me, stopping within feet before the crash of the drums. Then, with a wicked smile, she changed to a more bump and grind style, circling me, her fingertips grazing over my blazer between the shoulder blades as she passed behind me. Once in front, she grabbed my tie, pulling herself against me.

Oh, yeah.

She had my engine revving at an obnoxious speed, and I loved it. Realizing with her in front of me, the audience couldn't see what I was doing, I got an idea. Taking her hand, I guided it to my blazer button. Her head jerked up to look me in the eye. She knew what I wanted all right. I lifted my chin slightly, daring her with only that small movement. And boy did she take the dare. A smile spread from cheek to cheek. Unbuttoning my jacket, she ran her fingers along my chest, down to the top of my leather pants. My thoughts flashed to hot scenes of us in bed together, and I had to refocus to remember the lyrics I had written and performed for years. Taking a hold of the side of my blazer, she rolled out to her left, pulling it so I could shrug out of it. Orbiting again, she took the fabric from one shoulder, but didn't satisfy me by taking it completely off at first. Instead she maneuvered until we were back to back and gyrated against me, leaning in and gliding her hands along the outsides of my legs as she first lowered herself then came up. Her head was turned to the side, driving me crazy with the near proximity of her lips. I had only to roll slightly to claim them.

Remembering the audience I fanned myself in an exaggerated fashion, although I wasn't exaggerating about my heat level. She laughed then rolled away from me, causing me to fall a little with the loss of the weight of her body pressed to mine. She peeled the jacket off and gazed out over the writhing mass of music lovers with an "oh, my, what did I do?" expression. Hunching her shoulders and putting her fingertips on her chin, she opened her mouth in a wide, tempting circle. She took a few big steps away, pointing her toes, then whirled and strode across the stage, the jacket hung over her shoulder.

Background vocals were forgotten as the rest of the boys on stage were shouting and cheering her on. I chased her and grabbed her by the shoulders, spinning her to me. I snatched the blazer from her and squinted at her in what I hoped was a menacing fashion.

It must have worked because she said, "Uh-oh." She covered her mouth again, but her eyes were flashing with amusement in the stage lights.

I realized the lyrics I was about to sing were highly inappropriate, and thus maybe not the right choice at this particular moment, but they also worked perfectly with what we were doing. I stroked her cheek, belting out, "She was an angel in my head..." I strolled around her and draped the jacket over her shoulders, leaning in to add, "But a devil in my bed." I pivoted to face the fans. They shouted my next words with me, "And Lord, I guess I was an unrepentant sinner." Continuing my circuitous route, I ended standing before her, my hands on her hips. "Because every time she is near, I hear this screaming in my ear...." With the next, the crowd response was even louder, "And God I'd give my soul if I could just be in her." But while the fans had gotten louder, I put my mouth to her ear and sang the words in a low murmur. My intent was to turn her on, but I was the one who had to brace myself to keep from licking her earlobe.

Must not engage.

My inner voice sounded like one of those Dalek robots from Dr. Who. I laughed at my own weakness and odd sense of humor. But I was rewarded when her breathing picked up. I wasn't the only one feeling the chemistry. When I pulled back, though, a sliver of fear haunted her eyes. I scared her. I went with my instincts, as I'd been doing all night, my thinking too muddled by her presence. I took her chin, tilted her head so she had to look at me, and tried to give her a bolstering smile, throwing in a wink for good measure. For a moment, I wasn't sure if I made things better or worse. Like when she lied to me, and I knew it with one glance, her face gave away her emotions. At least to a degree. She was no longer frightened, but she wasn't smiling either. She looked...disappointed? Sad? I knit my brows, searching her for an answer. Women could be so hard to understand for a guy. Where to go next? I had to salvage this somehow.

While I thought, I absentmindedly skimmed my thumb along her jaw. She dropped her gaze, so I no longer had a chance at reading her. We came to a guitar riff without vocals and I switched my mic off.

"Did I...do something wrong? I'm sorry if I was being too forward. I...." I had no idea what I would say next, but luckily she saved me the trouble.

"No. I'm good."

I doubted the truth in that, but she did seem to relax a little. I almost forgot to click my mic on for the next verse, which made her laugh—and made my blunder totally worth it. I resolved not to whisper provocative comments in her ear for the rest of the evening, if possible.

Soon I seemed to woo her back into a more playful mood and she began messing with my tie, eventually sliding it off and wrapping it around her neck, leaving the ends to dangle in the front like a more masculine version of a boa. She took hold of a shirt button and peeked at the audience. They cheered her on. Peering at me she bit her bottom lip for a second before unbuttoning the first one. She worked her way down, and when it was finally open, slipped her hands under the fabric and along my chest. Her touch was driving me crazy. I took a step away and ripped my shirt off, tossing it on the stage and grabbing her. She laughed and we swayed for a moment.

But the song was coming to a close and I didn't know what to do next. I didn't want to let her go, but I couldn't keep the poor girl up on the stage the whole time either. After the last verse was sung, the piece slowed again to the music box tinkling of the beginning. The juxtaposition in the musical styles was supposed to mirror the meaning in the song, which, when I was feeling pretentious, I would describe as the duality of the human soul. The fight of good and evil inside all of us. If I were to be truly honest, though, it was more about my conflicting feelings for my sex addiction at the time and my religious upbringing.

We needed a big finish, so, taking her idea of mimicking the ballerina spinning inside a music box, I attempted to sweep her around the stage in elegant fashion. The song ended with a single line sung as the last notes of the music faded. I stopped twirling her and bent her into a dip. Slowly. Sensually. She seemed to anticipate it. Again, I was struck by the way she seemed to read me, know me. The way she intuitively knew what my next move was. But odder still, I seemed to be able to do the same with her. I knew when the song was ending, she was getting ready for me to dip her. How? Did I feel a ripple in her muscle where I touched her? Or did I see it in her eyes as they rolled back and closed? I bent over her and we held the position for a beat after the music faded. We were peering into each other's eyes, knowing the magic was about to end. Her gaze flickered over me. The kiss was a natural extension of the dip, I told myself. But it was much more than that. I may have initiated it, but her hands sought my face immediately, taking it to another level. The lights went down, and we didn't stop. Couldn't stop.

"Umm...I hate to interrupt." Rafe's voice was like a fly's incessant buzzing as it tries to get out of a closed window. "But...we do have a show going on here...."

I tore my lips away from hers and lifted her to fully vertical. She still had her fingers on my cheeks. "Grace..." I breathed out.

Her gaze shifted from one of my eyes to the other. "Shit." Hers filled with tears and she fought to disengage herself from my embrace. When she did, she fell off balance a little, stumbling away from me. The first act she had performed without grace. She was still staring at me with her mouth open. Was she crying? I needed to say something. "Oh, shit." She sobbed once, then turned and ran away, running past the stagehand, who simply moved aside as she charged toward him.

"Grace, wait!" I finally got out, but it was too late. "Stop her!" I barked at the guy, but the dumbshit didn't react. Desperate, I searched for Al. He was already halfway across the stage, booking it at a sharp clip just short of a run, but she had a lead on him. When he was within hearing distance, I shouted. "Stop her and make her come back. Or, if you can't, get her number or find out where she lives."

Al nodded curtly and hustled out a side door.

The audience roared. They seemed to think it was all part of an act.

I stood confused for a moment. The fact I was giving a concert chimed in my head.

I have to give a concert.

But I felt like my heart was ripped out and fled with Grace.

Rafe tried to pick up his slack. "Well...that was...something. Let's hear it again for Grace." I lifted my gaze to his, but couldn't find my voice. "Umm...our next song was written in a pool hall, after we...well, had a few." Rafe knew my routine. Knew it as well as I did. He bought me enough time to compose myself.

I got through the rest of the concert somehow. Solely by routine. I doubted anyone even was aware of my bewildered state. I stuffed it down until I wasn't even aware of it anymore and finished. On the way off stage, though, I looked in the direction that Al left the auditorium, searching for the big man. He wasn't there. Maybe he was talking to her. Maybe she was backstage.

The guys were even more hyped than usual. Jericho was following me off stage and clamped his hands on my shoulders. "That was incredible." We bunched up in the area where we downed the shots before the show, which seemed like eons ago.

"Yeah, man," Rafe seconded. "When the hell did you find time to put all that together without us knowing?"

I was pinching my lips together, sorting through what happened and was only aware of their conversation in a vague sort of way. But when everybody waited for my answer, the quiet jarred me. "Huh? All what?"

Rafe crossed his arms. "Come on. You know what I'm talking about. The dancing."

"Yeah," Jericho mimicked Rafe's pose. "Who's the girl? And, more importantly, is she available?"

Dex grinned. "Yeah. No shit."

They were all staring at me, waiting for an answer. "I have no idea who she is."

That's the problem.

They glanced at each other. Dex chuckled. "Come on, man. Are you trying to tell us that wasn't choreographed and practiced?"

Rafe rolled his eyes. "Yeah. Right."

I looked from one to the other. "That's exactly what I'm trying to tell you."

Again, they peered at each other. Jericho shrugged. Rafe took over the questioning, swatting my arms. "He wants to keep her for himself."

"I can't blame him," Dex commented.

I took a step forward. "I swear, man. I never saw that girl before tonight."

Jericho studied me then lifted his shoulders with a laugh, shaking his head. "Yeah, I don't know."

Rafe wasn't about to let it go. "Oh, come *on*."

"I'm not shitting you."

Rafe stared at Dex, his mouth hanging open. Jericho sat his ass on a crate, still shaking his head, then scratching his chin as he studied me.

Dex shifted his weight. "So..." His gaze swung to Rafe.

"I don't know, man." Rafe threw up his hands and grabbed a towel to mop his neck.

Dex was working his jaw. All three of them wore amused smiles. "So, what? Did she call you over or something?" He looked back at the guys, but they were watching me.

"No. It all just sort of...happened."

Dex tugged on his earlobe and nodded. "Uh-huh."

I scanned the group again, trying to explain something I myself didn't understand. "I just...I don't know. I saw her in the audience and..." I stared off.

Jericho jumped to his feet. "And what?"

They all drew in closer. "I don't know." I rubbed my chin. "I guess I asked her to join me on stage."

"Mmm." Dex raised his brows.

"To dance?" Jericho continued.

I raised my arms to the side, palms out. "No. To tell you the truth, I don't know why I asked her." I observed them, then tried again. "And I didn't have a fucking clue what to do with her when I got her up there."

Dex looked at Rafe out of the corner of his eye. "Could have fooled me." This was the most the drummer had ever talked since joining the group.

"It sure the hell seemed like you knew what to do with her. We practically had to hose you guys down."

Jericho interrupted. "So, let's review." He held up a finger and stared at me. "You don't know her."

"No."

"Never saw the girl before."

"That's right."

He huffed. "Oh, come on. That kiss says differently."

"Yeah. That was hot," Dex added.

"You have no idea." I zoned out for a moment, recalling the feel of her lips on mine. I rubbed my mouth.

Rafe chuckled. "Well that silenced him."

"You don't kiss girls like that," Jericho insisted.

"I don't kiss girls like what?"

"Dude. It was almost like you cared about her." They all nodded.

"I do care about her. Wait. I care about her?" Great, I was babbling now.

"Kissing a random girl you snatch from the audience?" Dex jerked his head to the right. "Jericho, maybe but—"

Jericho turned to him. "Shut the hell up."

Rafe jumped in. "What? You know it's true." They all laughed.

Jericho was the horniest of us all. In fact, we had a running joke about a time when he had three girls in his bed. Two were doing each other for his entertainment while the third was going down on him.

Afterward, Rafe ribbed him. "What? Can't you handle four?"

And Jericho responded seriously, "Not in a bed that size. And besides, you can only pay attention to so much at a time. Four is too much."

Ever since then it was, "How many donut holes do you want? Four?"

"No. Four's too much, right, Jericho?"

"Yeah," I joked. "At least I only pulled one girl from the audience."

They all stared at me for a second then Rafe took charge. "Don't fucking change the subject."

I exhaled. "I don't know what you want me to tell you."

"Okay. Fine. We'll go with..." he flapped his hands in the air "...you don't know her." He paced, which was hard to do in the tight confines. And roadies were now here and there, breaking down the set and acting like they weren't interested in the goings-on. "So...she's a professional dancer then who—"

"She's not a dancer."

They all stared at me.

"I asked her."

Jericho slapped his leg. "Oh, come *on*. You're telling us the samba cha-cha-cha shit you were doing to 'Night Of Awakening' was completely spontaneous."

"Y-yes."

"Oh, my God." Dex spun around and mumbled something to himself. Rafe pivoted away, then back again. Jericho hung his head, shaking it.

"Dude." Rafe took a deep breath. "No way could you two just...do...what you did without practice." He smacked me again, only this time it hurt.

"Ouch." I rubbed my arm.

"You...you...you can't even dance." They chuckled and grunted at that.

Dex, turned, raising a hand. "True."

I was becoming frustrated. "I know. All right? I can't dance worth shit. Usually. But she...just...."

Dex grinned. "God, she was hot."

Jericho sighed. "That tight little ass...."

Rafe grinned. "Good God, yeah. She—"

"Could you not—" My voice came out a little stronger than I intended. "We probably shouldn't talk about her like that." I regretted it the moment I said it.

They all looked at each other. Jericho was the first to burst out. "Why the hell not?"

"Yeah?" the other two added.

"Because..." I started to move around them. "You know, I don't need to deal with—" As one, they moved over to block my path.

"No," Rafe said sternly. "You don't get to run away with your little secrets. I played acoustic for you, man. You need—"

Al came running from the side of the set, winded.

I rushed over to him. "Did you find her?"

"No. I tried to, but...."

I swallowed the crushing feeling pounding at my heart. "No. That's okay. Thanks for trying." I kept my head low so no one could see my face. "I'm going to take a shower."

"We're not done here," Rafe called, but I waved him off. One more word and I was liable to snap and slaughter everyone backstage.

CHAPTER THREE

Grace

The lip-smacking coming from the back seat was making me nauseous as I sat behind the wheel of my car. I glanced over at the other guy. The guy who hoped to get down my pants but who was unequivocally shut down from the get-go. He was pissed and disappointed, possibly hurt. But it wasn't that I was judging him. I couldn't do those kinds of things without feeling something for the person I was doing it with. And he gave me nothing to make me feel for him. Right now he was acting like he was staring out the window, but I saw him adjusting the side mirror so he could at least watch the action in the back. So nice of Payton to invite both of them back to my car. Not.

Ugh.

"Payton. It's time to go."

The fairly unattractive guy with a shaved head in the back cleared his throat. "Maybe you guys could go for a little walk."

The gentleman on my right nodded and reached for his door handle. I put a hand on his leg, which was all the action he was getting tonight from me. Tonight or ever. I looked at him. "No need. We're not going anywhere. Payton?" I raised my gaze to the rearview mirror. Payton was pouting.

"Why can't I ever have any fun? You always—"

I rolled my eyes and pounded on the steering wheel. "Hyacinth!" It was stupid but it was the word we used to say, "You're being a moron and you'll get us both killed, so listen to me." It was a lot more concise.

"Not Hyacinth," she whined.

"Hyacinth, dammit!" I snapped.

"Isn't she that Indian princess who did John Smith?" the guy next to me spouted, sealing my opinion he was a complete idiot.

"Okay. Geesh. Hyacinth. Hyacinth." Payton opened her car door and her "date" grabbed her arm. My anxiety climbed. I hated these situations.

"Ouch."

"Uhh. Sorry. Where are you going?" He leaned up, spitting at me through gritted teeth. "Take a walk, Blondie."

Again the bozo at my side cracked his door. I grabbed his arm. "We're not leaving."

"Well if you're not letting me do her...." Faster than I thought possible, the guy in the back seat had one hand in my bra, the other around my neck.

I opened my door, jerked away from him, and wrenched the back door open. "Get out." Normally, I would be frightened of the hulking, bald dude in the back, but it had been quite a day/night. My emotions were raw. He didn't move. I stomped my foot. "Get out of my fucking car."

He put his hands in the air and slid out. "Okay. Okay. Shit." He tweaked my chin as he passed by me. "You need to get laid." I slapped his hand away. "Ouch. You're a little tiger. Maybe I picked the wrong girl to screw." He started to come around the door at me and I took advantage of positioning, steering the door into his crotch. He grabbed his balls, grimacing.

What a baby. I only nudged him.

"Come on, Keith," he growled. Then he raised his gaze to mine. "You're hot. Are you sure—" He again moved in my direction.

"Are you kidding me?" I huffed. "Am I not making myself clear?" Beyond his shoulder I noticed a couple, probably in their forties. He was holding the door for her to get in the car, but they were both watching me. When I took my focus off Backseat Guy to peer their way, he jumped, grabbing my wrist. I gasped.

"Hey! Hey!" the guy yelled from across the lot, rushing toward them. "What's going on there?"

Baldy threw a glance over his shoulder. "Damn." He stepped up to me, squeezing my wrist, his jaw tight. "Your loss, baby." He pulled back his leather vest to display a leather holster with a wicked looking knife in it. "I would have been gentle." My heart clutched. He grinned with tobacco-stained teeth and spit to the side. I jumped at the movement, and he laughed. The older gentleman was approaching. Baldy shoved me, knocking me into my car door. The edge hit me down the center of my back, and I winced.

The older guy behind Baldy had a hand on my trunk and was sort of bent over, panting. "You...okay?"

Baldy jeered. "She's fine, Gramps. Everybody's fine. Only having a little fun." He walked away, yelling without turning. "See ya around, Grace."

A stab of fear shook me. He knew my name.

The man who came to our rescue brightened. "Hey. You're the Grace who was on stage, aren't you?" He didn't wait for an answer. "You have a helluva voice."

I switched my attention to him, while still watching over his shoulder to make sure Tweedle Dee and Tweedle Dummer were actually leaving. "Thank you." I gave him a smile. "And thank you for coming over. Most people would look the other way."

He waved it off. "Oh," he glanced over his shoulder, "I could see those guys were up to no good." He stared at my wrist, which I was rubbing. "Are you sure you're okay?"

I examined it. The creep's fingermarks were still visible, and little white spots where he dug his dirty nails in. "Nothing a tetanus shot won't cure."

He grinned. "You're funny." He checked on the lady who was with him. "Well, I better get back to my wife." Twisting to face me again, he studied me. "Are you sure you're okay to drive? We'd be happy to give you a ride."

His offer coincided with the sick splash of Payton's puke hitting the asphalt on the other side of the car, followed by a moan.

Great.

He stared at Payton.

"We're fine. But thank you again for your concern."

He backed away, his gaze still on Payton. "If you're sure."

"We're sure. Thank you."

"All right. Take care." He wrinkled his nose. The odor of the hurl must have wafted to him on the light breeze. He turned and jogged away, making a slight gagging noise.

I eyed Payton over the roof.

"I don't feel so good."

No shit.

I glanced in the back seat. Leaning in to scoop a Cheetos bag from the floor mat, I noticed a condom pack on the back seat. "Eww." Pinching it between two fingers I dropped it in the Cheetos bag, swung the door shut, and walked around the back of the car.

"Holy shit, Payton." The diameter of the splatter was far bigger than I expected. The smell was making my stomach roll. Standing on the far side of the vomit puddle, I looked up. "Do you think you can make it home?"

Payton bobbed her head and slid into the front, as the door was left open.

I stretched to close the back door, careful not to get anything on my boots. I circled the car, got in, and handed the bag to my friend. "Just in case."

Payton nodded, her eyes closed and head hanging weakly. A wave of sympathy hit me. I put my hand on Payton's shoulder, then noticed some puke in her hair and withdrew it. "Are you sure you're okay?"

"Yes. Thanks, Grace. I'm sorry I was such a dumbshit." And that was pretty much the last I heard from Payton for the entire two and a half hour drive back to Jefferson City.

Which was actually fine with me. I wanted to sit and absorb what happened. Did I really go on stage with, dance with, sing with, and kiss Zane Sanders? It was every woman's fantasy. And he was even better in person.

Images flashed through my mind. The moment I took his shirt off and ran my hands over his gleaming pecs, unbelievably hard, yet as smooth as marble. And his tattoos...I normally wasn't into them, but Zane's were so him, they summed up the whole package. A tribal band wrapped around his huge bicep, accenting the definition of his muscles there. The little tattoo on his forearm that read, "If lost, return to library." I only wished I'd gotten a firsthand look at the one on his back that I'd seen on the cover of "Rolling Stone" magazine. The picture had drawn me to it dozens of times, to stare at the detail, which was phenomenal. It was a bat, the body between his shoulder blades, the wings across the shoulders. Whoever did his tattoos was gifted.

Then I relived the moment he lifted me off the ramp and let me slide down his luscious, amazing body. It had almost seemed like he wanted to kiss me then. Perhaps the most captivating image, his eyes, just his eyes, when he was singing "Don't Fade Away," the unshed tears making the green glow even more intensely. But then there was that cocky little smirk of his when he led my hands to the buttons of his blazer, inviting me in, ever closer. And of course, the dip. The way it felt to have his strong arm supporting me. The expanse of skin, tapering down to those leather pants of his, the black suiting the mystery of what lay beneath it. Even now it had my pulse racing.

It was interesting...I didn't imagine him to be so fun. I always sensed a...heaviness in him I didn't see when we danced together. At the same time, I never understood the depths of his pain until I stared into his fathomless eyes when he sang "Don't Fade Away," the song about his mother's death. In the moment, it made my heart cry out to him.

As I thought about it driving home, it made my heart cry out for my parents, who I lost when I was eighteen. I understood his pain because I shared it. I was glad Payton stayed sleeping. I allowed the tears to slide down my cheeks and let myself return to that horrible time, a time I usually forbade myself to go back to.

But before I lost it altogether, endangering my life and Payton's, I had to rein it in. I thought about the kiss to distract myself, and it was quite a distraction. The way he looked at me before he lowered his lips to mine...it was easy to imagine what it would be like to be kissed by someone who really cared for you. For him it was a moment forgotten. In fact, I was sure he was doing a lot more than kissing some lucky woman right now. But what I felt when he kissed me was unforgettable. It was an overwhelming feeling...a feeling of being alive, really alive, maybe for the first time ever. An exquisite, gripping pain and fear. The moment contained an unexplainable depth and an irresistible, electric draw to him I couldn't fight. Surely simple lust. But something I never felt before with any other man. Odd....

I ran a finger over my lips once, softly, closing my eyes for an instant. My body reacted even now. Only lust. Pounding, soul-searing lust. No wonder the man was so successful. If he could make a complete stranger feel that way.... Again I imagined what it must feel like to be loved by him. The words and music he wrote, I always knew he was one of those people who really felt things—love, loss, passion—at a cellular level. But to see it etched on his face, feel the pain and passion, and imagine the love, it was amazing.

Like I imagined Zane did, I always knew I was different. As a girl, it isolated me. The other kids didn't understand why the beauty of a sunset would make me cry. They didn't get how someone could become so absorbed in books, to a point they lost track of time and circumstances. My sensitivity would occasionally, briefly endear me to someone when I sympathized with them when someone hurt their feelings on the playground. But when their group welcomed them back, the memory of my kindness evaporated like a Popsicle left out on the stoop on a warm summer's day. It wasn't long before they were ridiculing me again. Those times hurt the worst. When I hoped maybe I could connect with someone then they turned their back on me.

It was this imagined connection I sensed I had with him. But like my childhood fantasies, it was unreal. Simply the product of my desire to belong to someone else. Be part of them. Even a hint of a bond like that couldn't exist with Zane Sanders. We knew *nothing* about each other. The things I read into his music, into his actions, were more a creation of my flights of fancy, of the particular circumstances of my childhood and the way I was. I was projecting that onto him. I knew nothing about him. Maybe he promoted that image of himself, but was it real? I had no way of knowing. Still....

I blinked. Was that my exit sign I passed a second ago? I peered into the dark ahead. Surely we weren't home already. I glanced at the clock on the dash.

Talk about being lost in your imagination.

The exit sign confirmed it. I turned on my blinker. Within ten minutes I was pulling up in front of our five-story building. It was on the historical registry, built in the early 1830s, and used as an infirmary during the Civil War. Rumor had it the apartment directly across the hall from me was where they performed surgery and holes were drilled in the floor to allow the blood to drain through. Amputated limbs were thrown out the window, collecting in a pile. I didn't know if it was true or not because the couple who lived there never spoke to anyone in the building, nor did they seem to have guests. Despite the place's interesting background, the historical society didn't do a lot for the upkeep of the place, but I still loved it. It had a charm about it and it was only four blocks from my flower shop. I was pleased to find a parking spot right in the front at the late hour we were returning. I peeked at Jamie's window. I couldn't help but be disappointed, even though I knew it was way past his bedtime.

"Payton." I touched my friend's arm.

She shook her head and opened her eyes. "Home already?"

I laughed. "It seemed plenty long to me."

Payton yawned. "I guess time flies when you're pass-out drunk."

"You said it, not me. Are you feeling all right?"

Payton paused as if evaluating her status. "Yeah. I think I'm fine. Just need to get a good night's sleep."

"Okay. If you're sure."

"I'm sure, babe. I know you want to check on Jamie."

We exited the vehicle. "Got me," I confessed. I nodded toward the building as I closed the door. "But his light's out."

"Oh, shoot. Well, tomorrow then."

We walked side-by-side. Payton lived on the fourth floor and Lexi had the "penthouse."

Payton scratched her temple. "Was Hyacinth called?"

"Yes. Multiple times, actually."

"Hmm. I thought so." She stopped abruptly. "Hey. We never really talked about that kiss."

I shrugged, heat building in my face. Continuing walking, I avoided eye contact. "Not much to talk about."

Payton ran ahead and walked backwards in front of me. "Oh, like you play tonsil hockey with a multi-platinum—or whatever—rock star every day."

That tickled me. "No. Only Tuesdays and Saturdays. Luckily it's Saturday. Uhh. You may want to turn around before you fall."

Payton's heels hit the steps leading to the door. She put her hands on my shoulders. "Come on. Give. What was it like? Because it looked super hot."

I was happy for the semi-darkness—a light post wasn't too far away—because I was certain my cheeks were red as they burned and sweat was rising on my skin. I smiled, trying to blow it off. "I don't kiss and tell." I tried to skirt Payton, but she moved with me, keeping me blocked.

"Since when."

I had to laugh at that.

"Come on. Dish. Was he good?"

All kinds of good.

I exhaled. "Okay, fine. I guess you could say he was."

"You guess?"

"Payton...?" My friend wouldn't budge. "Hyacinth."

"What? What danger am I putting us in?"

In her moment of confusion, I managed to get around her. "You're going to be in danger if you don't leave me alone." I opened the heavy glass entry door and held it. Payton frowned, passing over the threshold. "By the way, you have puke in your hair."

She lifted the ends to examine them. "Eww." I passed her and climbed the steps to my door on the third floor. "Wait. Wait. Wait." Payton ran up behind me. "At least tell me why you ran away."

I turned to her. "Ran away? I didn't run away."

Payton narrowed her eyes, studying me. "That's what it looked like."

"Well, I didn't run away. We were finished, is all."

"He didn't seem finished. In fact, he appeared to want to mount you there on the stage."

I slapped her arm. "Don't be crude."

"I'm just sayin'..."

"Payton. It's late. Can we talk about this tomorrow?" *But hopefully you'll forget about it.*

"I guess." She rounded the newel post but paused with one foot on the bottom step. "But I'm not forgetting about it."

"Good night," I said in a sing-songy voice.

"Good night." Payton mimicked my tone, climbing the stairs. "Sweet dreams. Don't get the sheets too sweaty with thoughts of your rock star boyfriend."

I leaned on the newel post cap, stretching to hiss up the stairs, aware, even if Payton wasn't, that people were sleeping. "I don't have a rock star boyfriend."

Payton yawned and waved an arm.

I sighed. "She's never going to forget this." Shaking my head I unlocked the door to my apartment. The room was dark, but the glow from the TV lit my friend, Holly's face. She was stretched out on the couch with a throw blanket over her, a pillow tucked under her arm.

"Hey," Holly whispered, reaching for the remote. "How was it?" She switched the screen off.

"Uhh." I set my keys on the end table. "It was good. Thank you so much for watching him." Holly was one of the few people I trusted to stay with Jamie. She was good with him, the experience she got working with people with disabilities was invaluable.

"Oh, no problem. He was a sweetheart. And it was only a three ice cream sandwich night."

"Three?"

"Well, he—"

"You know what? Never mind. If I can harm my body with alcohol, he can harm his with sugar. It's only fair. Besides, I know, despite what you said, it isn't easy. You do whatever you have to do."

Holly folded the blanket and draped it over the back of the couch.

"Has he been asleep long?"

My friend picked up the pillow, searching for something. "I don't know, what time is it?"

I looked at the phone in my hand. "Twenty five after one."

"Oh, there it is." She found her phone under a magazine on the coffee table. "Uhh...." She exhaled. "Probably for like an hour and a half then. Maybe a little more."

"Mmm." *He'll be a bear tomorrow. Good thing it's my day off.* I walked Holly to the door.

"Were you able to get very close to Zane or Rafe?"

Very close to Zane. Too close. What was I thinking? "Uhh, yeah. Payton wormed her way into the front row. Like usual." I opened the door. "I can't thank you enough for watching Jamie. I really needed the break."

Holly tapped my cheek. "I could tell."

"Oh, no. Was I crabby?"

"No. No." She took my hands. "It's just...everybody needs a break every now and again, Grace. You should do it more often."

I hung my head. "Yeah. I know. You're right." I looked back down the hallway to his room, even though he wasn't there. "It'd probably be good for both of us."

Holly raised her eyebrows. "It would do wonders for your sex life."

I laughed. "Oh, God forbid." I scrunched my nose and put a finger to my lips. "Now what is that again?"

Holly chuckled.

"I'm so sorry to keep you this late."

Holly paused with her foot on a step. "It's not a problem. Really." She nodded up the stairs. "Russ would keep me awake with his snoring anyway."

I crossed my arms and leaned against the doorframe. "And I need a sex life?"

"Oh, honey. We manage." She grinned. "Good night. Sleep well."

"Thanks." I turned and walked back into my apartment, closing and locking the door. I sashayed over to the front window.

Sex life? Who needs one?

I was perfectly happy with things the way they were. Instead of pulling the drape shut, I stared out the window.

But, my God. That kiss.

I was never kissed by a man like that. Like they were interested in my getting pleasure out of it as well as taking it themselves. It was never that way with Brad. Even before things got messy with him. The thought sent a shiver up my spine. I stepped back and yanked the curtain closed. I bent to switch out the light on the end table, and coasted by the coffee table by the light shining in from the alley behind the place. I didn't have a curtain on the kitchen window as I was in and out it a lot. On the fire escape I could take a break from Jamie without being too far.

I wandered into the kitchen. Running my hand along the kitchen table as I passed it to stare out the window at the building across the way from mine, without really seeing it.

That kiss was hot. Fantastically, incredibly hot. He was hot.

I giggled.

I kissed Zane Sanders. Sure, I ran away like a little baby afterward, but it was no baby kissing him back.

Then I thought about Payton's question. Why? Why did I take off like that?

I don't even really know. I felt panicked, and took off.

I made it back to the car and bawled. Again, unclear what the reason was for that. But it did make me feel better, so who cared why I did it? I swiveled on my heel and made my way to Jamie's door, having to turn the hall light on to see. I opened it as quietly as possible. It squeaked, but he didn't move. Light from the window, whether streetlight or moonlight, illuminated his face. He always looked so peaceful and angelic when he slept. I tiptoed across the carpet to his bed. With a feather light touch I pushed the hair back across his forehead. He was smiling.

Are you having good dreams, buddy?

This was my life, here. There wasn't any more room in my heart for any other man. I crossed my arms and stared at him. He was snoring a little, his mouth hanging open. My love for my brother filled me with warmth. He was all that was right in the world. I squatted, lacing my fingers together on the mattress and resting my chin on top. I watched him sleep. When my legs cramped, I sat on the floor, resting my hands in my lap, lulled by his even breathing. After a bit, I curled up on my side, tucking my hands under my face. I listened for a while, but since I couldn't see him from that angle I flopped on my back and stared at the ceiling. When I noticed my breathing getting rhythmic, I shook and rose, going to the door. I closed the door behind me, but stopped with it cracked and peered in at him. I must have fallen asleep, because he was on his side now. I eased the door shut and slid my phone out of my back pocket.

Three-thirty. I did fall asleep.

I went to my room and sat on the bed to tug off my boots. Standing again, I peeled of my jeans, leaving them in a puddle on the floor. I didn't bother to remove my top, simply pulled the sheets down and slipped in bed. I was asleep in minutes.

"Gracie! Gracie!"

I opened my eyes. A body was jumping on my bed. I flipped over.

"You're home!" he screamed.

Oh, Lord. What time is it?

I didn't check my phone, instead, doing things the old-fashioned way, I read the numbers on my clock radio. Nine o'clock? He let me sleep till nine?

"Jamie. Shh. People are sleeping. Come here."

Taking one more high bounce he plopped on the bed. I drew him into my side.

"Were you good last night?"

He looked at me with his frank, open stare. His glasses were so smudged I couldn't imagine he could see my face, even as close as we were. "Uh-huh," he said solemnly.

I squeezed him. "I knew you would be."

He flew up into a sitting position. "Can we have pancakes?" It's Sunday."

It was my day off, and he knew the routine. Sundays were for pancakes. "I don't know. Aunt Holly said you had *three* ice cream sandwiches last night."

He grinned. "Four."

"Four!" I gave him a playful shove. "You little piggie. Maybe we should have scrambled eggs today."

"No. Pancakes. It's Sunday."

Did I really want to argue with him today? I smiled. "Okay. But you can only have two trillion of them."

"No. Five trillion." He picked up my St. Louis Blues cap from the other side of the bed and put it on his head.

I tugged on the bill. "We'll see. Now, hop on down and go get the pancake bowl out and the mix and I'll be right there."

"Okay." He bounced on his butt to the end of the bed and scrambled away. I watched him with a smile on my face as he ran to the door.

"Jamie?"

He turned.

"I love you, buddy."

He ran back and gave me a sloppy kiss on the cheek. "I love you, Gracie." He took off. "Five trillion pancakes. Five trillion pancakes," he sang.

How could anyone be anything but happy with him in the room? I threw the covers back and got out of bed. Other than the wrinkles Jamie created when bouncing, it hardly looked slept in. I pulled the sheets and comforter into place, smoothed out errant creases, and found some clothes to wear.

I could hear Jamie rummaging about as I walked along the hall. When I entered the kitchen, he swung around with the carton of eggs and one flew out and landed on the floor with a *splat*.

Jamie froze staring at the mess. "Uh-oh."

Knowing if I didn't act fast a major meltdown would take place, I swooped into the kitchen and grabbed a paper towel from the roll on the counter.

"Uh-oh," Jamie repeated, his voice getting more panicked.

"No big deal, bud."

"I broke it." Tears were already pooling behind his lashes.

I hated myself for this. Brad always made him—and me, for that matter—feel bad for even the slightest mistake. It wasn't until the day he struck Jamie for the first time—knocking him to the floor—that I left. Tears were forming in my eyes, too. I spoke over the lump in my throat. "Hey. Want to see a magic trick?"

"Magic?"

I got on my knees and waved a hand over the broken egg shell and sticky mess spreading out from it. "Now you see it." I worked up a smile and looked at him, placing the paper towel on top of it. "Now—" I scrunched everything into my fist, "—you don't." Sweeping it away with flair I added. *"Voila."*

He gasped. "You know magic?" He knew perfectly well I was holding the egg, but it was one of our special jokes.

I winked at him then scanned the table. "You got the mix and bowl out. Good job."

He trotted over to the kitchen table and put the carton of eggs next to the bowl, then pulled a chair out, scraping it against the floor. I almost said something, but decided, coming on the heels of the whole egg incident, it might be best to let it slide. I stood and gathered the ingredients, glancing at him. He had a fork fisted in one hand and a knife in the other, their ends poised on the table. "Oh, I see you got your fork and knife, too. Good thinking."

I made the batter and warmed the skillet. "How would you like to go fishing today?"

"Really?" he jumped out of his chair and tore out of the kitchen. "I'll get my stuff," he yelled over his shoulder.

I chuckled. "Not so interested in five trillion pancakes now."

He ducked back into the kitchen, opened a cabinet, and grabbed out a plastic bottle of syrup. He slammed it on the table and ran out without saying a word.

I tilted my head, whisking the eggs. "I stand corrected."

It was a glorious day, but the park was fairly empty.

I guess most people are at church right now.

I had tried church with Jamie. I shuddered at the thought now. Some sacrifices had to be made in these situations. I would occasionally ask my daytime sitter, Lexi, to stay late so I could catch a service, during Holy Week especially.

Birds were singing in the trees, enjoying the summer sunshine. Their happy chatter made me smile. It was pretty here. The pond was at the center of the park, with walking paths and a smooth rolling hill sloping up to the street above. Recessed as it was, people using the park felt like they were in the middle of a forest meadow, not blocks away from the capital building. A slight breeze was blowing and on the other side of the lake a little boy and his dad were playing with a motorized sailboat. Jamie was fascinated by it, and I was, too, actually. I was squatting beside him, gesturing to the pair across the water.

"See that little box the boy's holding?"

Jamie nodded solemnly.

"That's how he steers the boat. Like I steer the car."

Jamie inhaled deeply. "Neat." The tip of his neglected rod was underwater.

"Hold the rod up, buddy." I rose. "Good."

"Grace?"

I whipped my head around. I heard that voice in my nightmares.

"Brad." I could hardly get the word out. I backed away, spreading my arms wide, not even wanting him to see Jamie. "How did you find me?"

He took a big step forward, his fingers in his front pockets, thumbs out. "Not that hard, Gracie when you're whoring yourself all over the Internet with some rock star."

"You— Someone...?" I couldn't think clearly. My gaze darted everywhere. Why weren't people close?

He moved nearer. "I see you haven't learned to speak any better." He sucked air in through his teeth. "But it sure looked like you learned how to *kiss* a whole lot better."

I retreated more, bumping into Jamie. I actually forgot how scary my ex was. We moved to Jefferson City four years ago and I got lulled into complacency.

My focus landed on a squad car pulling to the curb on the street above the park. "The p-police are right there."

He spoke quietly, but with a lethal edge to his voice, still coming closer. "Aww," he cast a glance in their direction then closed the gap between us, "they're not worrying about our nice little family." He slid the back of his hand down my face, his steel gray eyes twinkling with malice. It was like I was mesmerized by them. Frozen in place. He took a step back and ran his gaze over me. "You look good, honey." I wasn't afraid for myself, he'd done his worst to me. But I was terrified of him hurting Jamie.

"Grace?" I heard a splash then Jamie gripped my arm. The sound of his voice gave me the incentive to fight back.

I raised my chin. "You get away from us."

"Grace?" Jamie was getting frantic. This was a nightmare. One of my nightmares come to life. I checked for the policemen but they had left their cruiser and crossed the street. I had missed my opportunity.

Brad lunged and grabbed my arms. He sneered. "That would sound a whole lot tougher, Grace, if your lip wasn't trembling." Now he was staring at my lips. "Fuck. I bet that rocker guy really enjoyed that kiss you gave him."

Jamie tried to get around me and I searched for him with my hand, struggling to keep him back.

"Leave her alone."

I finally got a hold of Jamie and pushed him back behind me. "It's okay, Jamie."

Brad grinned at me. He knew me. Knew my weakness. "Hey, Jamie," he said slowly. "You remember me, don't you?"

"Don't touch him," I shrieked. I closed my eyes for a moment. I needed to keep my cool for Jamie.

"Oh, I'm not interested in touching him." He jerked me to him. "I'm more interested in touching you. All over."

"Stop!" I shoved him, trying to break his hold.

He laughed, leering at me and squeezing my arms mercilessly. "You know that don't work, Gracie. And it usually makes me madder."

"Stop!" I screamed, a sob choking my voice. I jerked and got my arm partially free, the one I was shielding Jamie with. I brought my hand up between us and tried to push against his chest. He laughed harder.

"Leave her alone!" Jamie shoved Brad's side, knocking him off balance a little.

"What the fuck?" He took his attention from me and raised his arm to Jamie.

I took advantage of the distraction and wrestled my arm free and before he could do anything to Jamie I slapped Brad as hard as I could. His head jerked to the side, his hair, which he usually combed back, fell into his eyes. He spit then turned to me, shaking stray strands out of his face. "You'll pay for that."

Male voices came from the street above and we all froze. The policemen were involved in an animated conversation, walking our way. Brad released me and gave me a shove. I stumbled backward and fell on my butt.

He spit at me, but missed. "I'm not done."

Propping myself on my elbows, I watched Brad jog away between flowering red buds.

"Jamie! Jamie!" I sprang to my feet and looked him over. "Are you all right?"

"Yes. I'm all right. You're the one who fell on her butt."

I clutched him to my chest and kissed his hair as I fought back the tears that seemed to come out of nowhere. Lifting my head, I scanned the area again. The policemen were still talking, getting into their car. Brad was a speck in the distance.

"Jamie, Jamie, let's go." I gathered our things, my hands shaking.

"But you said we could fish."

"Jamie, we have to go," I barked. I had the bait box and the rod. Was there anything else?

"You shouldn't yell at me." He sounded like he was about to cry.

Struck with remorse, I fell to my knees in front of him, taking his arms. "Oh, no, buddy. I—" I took a breath. "I'm sorry. You're right. But...I don't feel good. We have to go home."

"Okay," he said doubtfully.

I rose. "Come on." Walking in the opposite direction from which Brad left, I moved as quickly as I could, throwing fearful glances over my shoulder. I had to make sure Brad wasn't following us back to our place.

"Does your stomach hurt?"

For a second, I didn't understand why he was asking me that. "Oh, yeah. My stomach hurts." It wasn't really a lie.

"Was it because Brad pushed you?"

I looked at him. He remembers Brad? That was four years ago. Or did he overhear me use his name? Despite Jamie's diminished mental capacities, he was often sharp, even seeing and understanding things other people without his difficulties missed. The doctor told me it was to be expected. The brain was a complex machine. And, as my bad sleep attested to, Brad was a hard person to forget.

CHAPTER FOUR

Zane

Al stormed into the snack room where the band was gathered waiting until it was time to go on. "I found her."

I was leaning back, my chair on two legs. I let the front drop with a bang. "What? Where?"

Dex frowned. "Were we missing somebody?"

Rafe was on his laptop. "You're still searching for her?"

"Were," Al said with a grin. "I found her."

"How?" Jericho and I said together.

Al waved an iPad. "Through the magic of the Internet."

He slammed it on the table in front of me, looking smug.

"Someone uploaded this to YouTube?"

"Oh. The girl. Grace." Dex finally caught on. He and Jericho hovered behind me, peering over my shoulder.

"Sixty-four somebodies. They have single songs, parts of songs...some even recorded the whole time she was on stage."

"Make that sixty-five. Someone loaded another one a few seconds ago."

Jericho abandoned the small screen and circled the table to watch the video on Rafe's laptop. "Hey, this is pretty good footage."

"What part are you watching?" Rafe asked, not looking away from the screen.

I stirred. "Uhh, when we sang 'Don't Fade Away.'"

"We've got 'Duality.'"

"No way." Dex joined the other two. "Let me see." He chuckled. "Man, that girl could dance."

My heart was racing. I gave up hope of ever finding her again. I wanted to see her, if only to apologize for...whatever I did wrong. "Where's 'Duality'?"

Jericho lifted his head. "Third one down. The one titled 'Grace in Action.'" A few seconds later, he pointed at the screen. "Here comes the kiss."

"Holy shit! It's even hotter close-up," Rafe commented over Jericho's whistle.

Jericho grinned at me. "I need a cigarette."

"Hell, I need a cold shower." Dex bent back over Rafe's shoulder. "Show it again."

"Shit. You'd think you guys were a bunch of sex-starved teenagers rather than guys who are getting laid every night."

"Uh-oh," Jericho quipped. "Someone's getting crabby."

"Shut up," I growled. Seeing her again, even like this, was filling me with need. Besides, "The Kiss" was about to take place. It was weird watching myself kiss someone.

Rafe peered over his laptop. "Look at his face. He's watching 'The Kiss.'"

"Shut up."

He wouldn't let it go. "He is, isn't he?" Dex raced around the table, but Al was already bobbing his head yes.

"Man, she's got a nice ass."

I bit my tongue.

If he doesn't stop talking about her like that, I'm gonna fucking bash his brains in.

I focused in on what happened after the kiss, to see if it provided any answers to why she ran off, but it clarified nothing.

From across the table came the hiss of whispering followed by someone clearing their throat. I glanced over. Rafe and Jericho were smiling.

"Umm...Dex?" Rafe leaned back in his chair. "Take it from a seasoned band member—see that vein throbbing in Zane's neck? Well, if you don't stop talking about her like that, he's gonna bash your skull in."

I turned slowly to eye Dex.

"Oh, yeah?" His gaze darted to Jericho and Rafe. They nodded. He turned to me. "Uhh...sorry. I didn't understand."

"There's nothing to understand," I said evenly. "We should just maybe clean up our language around here."

Jericho and Rafe busted out. "Well, that ain't gonna happen."

Dex chuckled nervously. I swung to Al.

"So, we have the video. How does that tell us where she is exactly?"

"Oh. It doesn't." He grinned. "But the comments do."

I turned to peer at the screen. The first few comments were lewd suggestions that had my jaw tightening again, but the third was from Al Connors asking if anyone knew who Grace was. Jericho and Rafe must have been reading, too, because Jericho asked, "So your last name is Connors?"

"Yep. That's me."

I scrolled down. "How many of these videos did you comment on?"

"All sixty-four of them. The only one I didn't comment on is the one that just came up."

"Two," Jericho commented. "We're at sixty-six. And check out those views. Good God."

Rafe twisted his head to stare at Dex, who had crept back to their side of the table. "Unless those are all Dex here."

Dex held his hands in the air, looking at me. "They aren't man. I swear." He knocked Rafe's arm and said under his breath. "Shut up. You wanna get my ass kicked?"

I narrowed my gaze then returned my attention to the screen. "There are hundreds of comments here. Which video had the information on her?"

"Oh," Al bent closer to his iPad. "It's number thirteen. Title's 'The Kiss.'"

"I wish everyone would quit calling it that. It was only a kiss," I muttered.

"Dude, if it was only a kiss, you wouldn't be sitting here watching it," Rafe pointed out. The other two chuckled.

I frowned. "Don't you guys have somewhere to go?"

"I don't," Rafe turned to the others. "Do you guys?"

"Nah. I'm completely open right now," Jericho said with a grin.

"Me, too," Dex added.

"You're all enjoying this, aren't you?"

"Yep." Again Rafe looked to the bandmates behind him.

Jericho crossed his arms. "I'm finding it very entertaining."

They glanced at Dex. He was bending close to the screen, watching the video again. He jumped. "Huh? Oh." He threw up his hands. "I plead the fifth, man."

"You're a pack of assholes, you know that?"

My screen made a whirring noise and went blank. "What the hell? What happened?"

"Oh, shit. Battery must be dead."

"Rafe, can I see yours?"

"What? You want to borrow this asshole's laptop?"

I reached and slid the computer over. "Knock it off and let me see this." There were a few more rumbles of laugher from the others, but I tuned them out, finding the video in question and scrolling through the comments.

"Good thing break begins tomorrow so you can go make your—" Rafe made air quotes. "—'apology.'"

"Yeah." Jericho elbowed Dex. "But make sure someone's filming it for Dex here."

I picked up a half Oreo and zinged it at him, catching him on the arm. "Ouch! Touchy, touchy."

"Can't you guys go find something to do?"

Rafe pushed away from the table. "Come on, guys. Let's leave him alone and go get the shots ready." They filed out, Jericho making kissing noises as he passed. I knew they were only having fun teasing me but, one, I didn't like being the center of attention and two, I was uncomfortable with how much I did want to see Grace. It was so unlike me.

"Jefferson City, here I come," I said in a low voice, clicking on another video.

I wandered into Flowers by Grace wearing a black leather jacket, ball cap, and shades. Bells jingled over the door.

My heart stopped when she looked over. "I'll be right with you, sir." Then she gave me that wonderful smile.

I cleared my throat, speaking in a low register. "No problem."

Pretending to examine a display, I gazed beyond it at her as she helped a customer. Guy seemed to fawn over her. And who could blame him? She looked good. She was wearing a black sundress with big pink and red roses on it. It had wide straps and a collar and buttoned in the front. Her hair was in a high ponytail. They moved my way, so I shifted to keep the display between us. I got a better view of the guy. He was probably all of seventeen.

I snorted.

Probably using his paper route money to pay for whatever it is he's buying.

"Well, I sure appreciate your help. I know my mom will love them."

She was working the register, not paying attention to the guy. "I'm glad I could be of service."

The kid wasn't taking his eyes off her. I grabbed the first bouquet of flowers I could find and walked up behind him. She gave him the total and he got money out. Peeking over his shoulder, I saw the kid had a condom pack in with his bills. He handed her some money. "I'll probably be in next week, too. It's her birthday."

Yeah. Sure it is. I'd put money on those being for some girl and he's not telling Grace so she thinks he's available. Like she gives a fuck.

I not so subtly set my flowers on the counter, crowding the kid. Grace gave the kid his change, glancing in my direction. I dropped my head. "You have a nice week, Jimmy."

"Sure thing, Grace."

Get your ass out of here, kid. The adults need to talk.

I turned and watched until he was out the door.

"I'm so sorry for your wait, sir. I see you found what you needed?"

I spun back slowly, taking my glasses off. "Yeah. I sure did." I took pleasure in the way she jumped. I was pissed at her for all the hell I went through in the last several days when I was thinking about her nonstop.

"Wh-what are you doing here?"

I sneered. "Buying flowers. And they damned well aren't for my mother. They're for a woman."

"Oh, okay." Her gaze darted around, looking at anything but me. "Oh, I should ring you up, that's what I should do," she muttered to herself.

I intended it to be a stab at her, but the tears in her eyes, and the way her hands were shaking made my heart sting. I lowered my head to gather myself. Suddenly unsure of my purpose. I thought about the sleepless nights I had lain in bed, fantasizing about her and thinking about the stricken expression on her face when I kissed her, and thinking about how that kiss made me feel.

"Umm...that's sixteen forty-three...sixteen thirty-four. I'm sorry. I mixed the...." She let her voice trail off. I noticed about three-quarters of the inside of her right arm was scarred. So she wasn't perfect after all. But it didn't matter.

I reached into my pocket for my wallet and gave her a twenty. I had to think of something to say to her. She fumbled giving me the change and our hands touched for a second. She whipped hers back as if burnt. "Uhh...sorry about that," she tried to say lightly. "Uhh...would you like a bag for those so they don't drip?"

I exhaled, stuffing the money in my coat pocket. "Yeah. Give me a damned bag." The transaction was almost over. I needed to say something.

"Okay," she returned stiffly, taking the bouquet off the counter to put it in some clear plastic sleeve. She sniffed. "Can I do anything else for you?"

I stared at her wondering why she evoked such strong feelings in me. "No. There's clearly nothing else you can do for me." I turned to leave, but stopped and whirled back. "Yes, you can do something for me. You can tell me why the hell you ran out on me?"

She blinked rapidly. "What?"

I was acting like a lunatic, but the anger was seething out of me, oozing from every pore. "Why did you run out on me, Grace? Or is that what you do whenever a guy kisses you?" I was practically shouting at her.

She looked around at the handful of customers in the place. "C-could you please lower your voice?"

My anger was like a runaway train now. "What?" I swung my arm out to the side, indicating the rest of the shop. "You don't want them to know you kissed me or something? Well, it's too late for that. It's all over the Internet."

She glanced at the customers again, who were obviously watching us, although they were acting like they weren't. "Please, Zane. I...."

"You what, Grace? Why was it you left me standing there like an idiot?" I moved my hand in a circle. "Come on. Tell us all. We're dying to know."

Her mouth hung open, trembling for a second, then she snapped it shut. "You know what?" She slapped the flowers down on the counter and marched around to stand in front of me. "I don't know what your deal is. So some girl leaves on you? I'm sure you could have substituted with a dozen more."

"Yeah," I bit off. "I could have, but I didn't. Because I was confused about why you would come on to me then—"

"Come on to you? You were the one who pulled me out of the audience." She was shrieking and a tear crept over her lashes. "I didn't...ask to be on stage. I didn't come to that concert to meet anybody. I was—"

"Well, that low-cut blouse said different." I don't know why I said it. Her shirt wasn't low-cut. But part of me wanted to hurt her for making me hurt for lack of her.

She pressed her lips together, her eyes turning cold. "I have work to do." She pivoted to walk away.

"Don't act like you didn't fucking feel it, too!"

She spun slowly on one heel. "Get out of my store."

"You can't just walk away from me." Of course she could. What was wrong with me?

She stomped her foot—which was damned cute—her hands fisted. "Get out. Get out of here." She brought her fingers to her temples. "Just *get out*!" Her voice pitched into another octave.

This wasn't what I wanted. But I didn't know what it was I wanted to begin with. I wanted to see her, that's all. Well, I saw her all right. And like an idiot I spewed out a lot of hateful things without her ever giving me reason to. "Grace, I'm sorry." I said it so quietly, she probably didn't hear.

She raised her gaze slowly, blinking tears left and right. "Get out," she said distinctly. Some of the customers were gathering behind her.

"I...I'm...." I couldn't think beyond the headache pounding in my cranium. I turned, and left, the bells jangling harshly as I rushed out.

I spent the next several hours on a bench in a nearby park, berating myself.

What the hell is wrong with me? She didn't deserve that. I came here to apologize, not go off on her.

I had to ask for her forgiveness, and I had to do it right this time. But not in front of a store full of people. I looked up her closing time. I had three hours to kill. I went to a drug store and got some ibuprofen and downed four with warm soda that had been sitting in the car all day. As I was wandering back up the street, my hands jammed in my pockets, rehearsing what I was going to say, she stepped out onto the sidewalk half a block away. I checked my phone. It wasn't even quite seven yet.

Well, she's probably had one hell of a day, thanks to me, and is closing early.

She locked the door, not looking around, and walked at a brisk pace in the opposite direction. I started to follow and someone moved out of the recess created by the door to a store. The tall, skinny man smashed out a cigarette and trailed after Grace.

Shit. Someone else was waiting to talk to her, too. My fucking luck.

I pulled out my keys, intending to leave and come back the next day, but I noticed the guy didn't call out to her. She twisted to look back, perhaps hearing the guy's footsteps, and he ducked into a doorway. He waited then stuck his head out, and seeing she continued walking, he hastened to follow her.

He's stalking her.

I pocketed my keys and, keeping in the storefront shadows, kept pace behind him. Grace didn't seem to be hunting for a car, and after a couple of blocks, she turned to climb the stairs into a building.

"Grace?" the guy called out and she whirled about. I ducked behind a tree so she wouldn't see me. When I peeked around the corner the two of them were on the top step by the door. The guy had his hand buried in her hair and they were going at it.

Without thinking, I stepped out from my cover. "What the hell, Grace?" The guy spun, still holding Grace's hair and I jogged the final few steps to the bottom of her stairs. "Who the hell are you?"

"What the hell do you mean? I'm her boyfriend. Who the hell are you?"

Grace tried to say something, but it was drowned out by testosterone.

"I'm the guy she kissed last Saturday."

He squinted at me, then took his hand from Grace's hair and faced me. "You're Zane Sanders?"

The question threw me for a second. "Yeah."

He trotted down the stairs and stuck his hand out. "Well, I'll be damned. Zane Sanders. I love your music."

I shook with him, though leery. "Uhh...thanks." I glanced at Grace.

The guy put his arm over my shoulder, grinning ear to ear and turned back to the door. "So, you know my Grace."

I looked from the guy to Grace and back again.

"You are both crazy!" she screamed at us. "You are my ex-boyfriend, Brad. We ended things four years ago. *Ex*-boyfriend. And, so help me God, if you ever touch me again you will draw back a nub. And if I see you lurking anywhere near me, I'll get a restraining order. And *you*. I would have thought you said enough earlier. Both of you, leave me alone." She whipped around and ran into the building.

When the door closed behind her, the quiet was a stark contrast to her shouted words. We stood for a second, stunned, then the Brad guy said, "Wow. She's mad at you. What did you do?"

I stared at him balefully then ran up the stairs.

"Nice meeting you," he called after me.

I shook my head, pulling the door open. *Guy's freaking tripping.*

I could hear her keys rattling above, so I bolted to catch her before she went in, but when she saw me, she quickly yanked them out and scrambled inside. I took the final flight in two big leaps and put my foot in the door before she could close it. Hearing a male voice behind her, I lost it and pushed my way into the room. Then all hell broke loose.

This kid was squealing at the top of his lungs. Some woman stared at me from the couch. And Grace was on her knees in front of the kid trying to calm him down. "Jamie. It's okay. Jamie, please." She wheeled on me, tears in her eyes again. "Get out. Why don't you just leave me alone?"

What could I do? I backed out the door and closed it behind me. Ever since I'd met this girl I was in like an alternate universe or something. I didn't know what to say or do, and always chose the wrong way to approach both. I was toast. I couldn't take it anymore. With my back to her door, I slid to the floor and put my head in my hands.

What the fuck, Zane? What did you just do?

The kid was still screaming, but I could hear Grace's voice over it.

"Take the fire escape. You don't want to have to deal with that...mess, out there." Then she was shushing the kid. "Hey, buddy. It's okay. No one will hurt you. I'll make sure of it."

The kid's crying cut through me. He sounded so pathetic. I did that to him.

Oh, my God, Grace. I don't know why I keep being such an asshole to you. I need to control my damn emotions. I'm not eighteen anymore, screaming in self-preservation. I'm supposed to be an adult.

And I thought I got myself together. But like everything else in my life, I fucked that up, too. The sleeping giant that was my rage and insecurity was awake. I turned to put my ear to the door. I could hear her.

"Sh-sh-sh. It's okay, honey. I won't let anyone hurt us. Just relax. Lay on my chest. It's okay. Everything is all right...."

His sobbing quieted some, and her voice got steadily softer as she soothed him. I don't know how long it went on like that. It seemed like hours. But her voice was lulling me, too. Like some siren I heard it calling to me, reaching a place deep inside of me and comforting me.

If I gave a damn about this girl, I would leave. She deserved so much better.

CHAPTER FIVE

Grace

After a horrid night's sleep, I almost didn't answer the phone when it rang at eight a.m.

"Uhh...Gracie? Whatcha doin'?"

Payton. I had to smile. "Making pancakes. What else would I be doing? You'd think the kid would get sick of them at some point."

"Uhh...yeah. You might want to come out into the hall."

I stopped stirring. "Oh, God. Why?" In my head I saw horrible pictures of Brad wreaking destruction on the building and its tenants.

"'Cause a rock star's asleep on your doorstep."

"What?" I rounded the kitchen corner and stared at the door as if I could see right through it.

"Zane Freaking Sanders is asleep out in the hall and he even looks hot unconscious. How does he do that? Anyway. I'm kind of afraid someone will step on him or trip over him if they round the corner too fast. And his neck has to be God-awful stiff."

"Okay. Thanks."

He slept out in the hall? Could my life get any more bizarre?

Jamie was in my bed watching cartoons, so that would buy me a little time to deal with Zane.

When did dealing with a rock star become part of my life?

Again, I had to laugh. Because sometimes that was all I could do to keep from crying. I'd had enough emotional turmoil lately. Seeing Brad in the park after four years. Out of the blue. Having him show up at my place, grab me by the hair and force a kiss on me. Followed shortly by Zane and Brad having a pissing match, Zane following me in, barging into my place, and scaring the shit out of Jamie. And Lexi and me. Oh, wait. I forgot the lovely scene at the store where Zane called me a slut in front of my customers. That had to be counted in there, too.

I am so glad I'm single.

Even as I thought it, I knew it was a lie. I was horribly lonely. I mean, I had lots of friends. Great friends. But...I needed someone in my bed to hold me when I didn't think I could take anymore. I needed someone in my bed who could help me to figure things out, like how would I make rent? How would I get Jamie to school today if Lexi was sick? How would I keep from crying when every last nerve was frazzled? I needed someone in my bed to...well, I needed someone in my bed. I needed to feel loved and cared for. And hot, sweaty sex wouldn't hurt either.

Staring at the door, I took a deep breath. I would face this like I faced everything, straight on. Stiffening my chin, I marched across the carpet to the door. I went to draw the lock back then realized I had never locked the door. With Brad practically threatening to rape me outside, and a raving lunatic of a rock star apparently inside. I frowned and yanked the door open, and he fell right between my legs with a thump. His head hit the ground pretty solidly. Payton and I gasped. My first instinct was to help him and make sure he was okay, but the shock of a man flopping through my door first thing in the morning had my brain kind of whirring.

He groaned, blinked, and opened those wildly green eyes of his. He grimaced and seemed to try to focus on me while rubbing his hair. "Grace. Hi," he said as if this all was a normal part of the day.

"I'll let you guys be alone then." Payton exaggeratedly tiptoed down the stairs.

I went with blunt. "What are you doing here?"

He scrambled to his feet then teetered. "Mmm." His hand went to the back of his head again.

I took a step forward. "Are you hurt? Is it bleeding?"

He dropped his hand. "No. No. I'm fine." He stared at me. "Can I say you look very nice this morning in your robe?"

I totally forgot what I was wearing. I pulled it closed more. "No, you may not."

"Fair enough." He seemed to struggle to find words.

Funny. He was throwing them around easily enough yesterday.

"You slept out here in the hall?"

"Uhh..." He inspected the area. "Yeah. I guess so."

Did he hit his head that hard?

"Grace, I'm so, so sorry for the things I said and did yesterday. So sorry. I can't even tell you how bad I feel. I was a complete and utter jackass."

No argument there.

"And I have no excuse for it. No explanation even, other than...I haven't been able to stop thinking about you." He dropped on his knees, his hands folded in front of him. "Please, Grace, say you'll forgive me."

So, okay. My heart melted. I know it was stupid...but my heart didn't always listen to what my mind was screaming at it. Brad was proof of that. Knowing Payton was outside and one of my neighbors could literally trip over us at any second, or worse yet, Jamie might see him, I tried to think of a solution. "Zane. Please get up."

Obediently, he jumped to his feet, watching my response to his every word like it was a lifeline and he was a drowning man.

"We can't talk out here. Come in." I waved him in, and he brightened, following me. "We can't let Jamie see you," I whispered. "He'd freak out." I hurried him into the kitchen, opened the window, and stepped out onto the fire escape. I folded my arms around myself. The morning breeze was chilly, and I didn't have much on. I turned and he was standing there, in front of the window. "No." I took him by the shoulders and moved him to the other side of the window, pressing him against the brick wall. The brick and the fire escape had been added to the old building at some point. Touching him was a mistake. His chest was huge and strong, and...it was not a good idea. "Zane...what are you doing here? How did you find me? How does everyone keep finding me?"

"Uhh...there might be a few videos of us on YouTube?" He winced.

I exhaled, spun, and crossed to the opposite side of the landing, gripping the railing and rocking from heel to toe. "Great." I put a hand on my head, closing my eyes.

He came up behind me and took my shoulders. "Grace..."

God, he felt so good. I truly wanted to fall into his embrace. To press him against the wall and kiss the hell out of him. But that wasn't going to happen. He needed to leave. I twirled in his arms, like we were dancing again. And weren't we? "Zane. You have to go."

"What? You won't let me explain?"

"Grace?"

"Shit. It's Jamie." I pushed Zane back against the wall again. "Coming, bud." My voice was shaky. I needed to get a grip before Jamie caught on. "You stay here," I hissed. "Do not, under any circumstance, let Jamie see you." I slipped back through the window, which they had thankfully widened during renovations. Jamie came into the kitchen about two seconds after my feet hit the floor. "They're not quite ready. You get the syrup, Syrup." It was our little joke. He asked for a nickname at one point and all I could think of was that it should be sweet because he was such a sweetie, and...maybe the syrup bottle was out, which it was much of the time, and that's where I got my inspiration. So I called him Syrup, and it stuck. Of course it is sticky.

I exhaled, gave the batter another stir, and turned on the burner. We hadn't talked about Zane barging in last night yet, and I hoped he wouldn't bring it up. Luckily his mind was totally filled with pancakes. He came to get a fork and knife and stopped on the way back to the table to hug my waist. This was why his name was Syrup. I ruffled his hair. "Aww. Thank you, bud. Only a few more minutes." I smiled at him and he looked at me with twinkling eyes. If pancakes made him happy, I'd make them every day for an eternity. "Let's see. We have the syrup, a fork, a knife...what else do we need?"

"Pancakes!" he shouted.

I laughed. "Well yes. But anything else?" I tried to teach him to be as self-sufficient as possible. My biggest nightmare was what would become of him if something happened to me. He wrinkled his nose. "What will I put the pancake on when it's finished?" I flipped it. "Your hand?"

He lifted his hands with a grin.

"No, silly. That would maybe hurt because it would be hot. Not to mention it would be very messy. What else could we put it on?"

He held up a finger. "A plate." He scurried to get one.

"Exactly. Good job." I poured him a glass of milk, took the plate, and brought it back to him with my first batch. "Miss Lexi should be here in a little while. What do you think you'll do today?"

He was shoving in pancakes so I didn't expect him to answer at first. "Go fishing."

"No. Remember? Miss Lexi doesn't like worms."

He nodded.

I almost said I'd take him after I got back from work, but I didn't want to promise anything I might not be able to deliver. And he would remember I promised, for sure. I flipped my next batch and came over to the table. "I'm sure Miss Lexi will find something fun." He nodded. "Hey, dude. Smaller bites. We don't want you to choke." He choked once when he stuffed an entire piece of spice cake in his mouth. Scared the shit out of me. I returned to my work, wondering if Zane left. That would be a relief. And a disappointment, damn it.

"Gracie?"

"Hmm?" I brought some more pancakes over.

"Is Brad going to come back again?"

God, I hope not. "No, bud. I think he's gone. He doesn't live here, remember? He's in Montgomery City."

"But what if he moved here?"

A chill ran up my spine. I didn't think of that. He was psycho enough to do it. I squatted beside Jamie and put a hand on his leg. "I don't think he did, bud. And even if he did, I'd make him go away."

"What about that other man?"

Shit.

I knew if Zane was out there he could hear every word we were saying. "Who? Zane? He's one of my friends."

"He didn't seem like a friend."

"He was upset. Like you get if I don't make you five trillion pancakes every morning. Right?"

He nodded and dug in again.

I thought about Zane outside. If he was still there, he was probably hungry. I tried to subtly slide a few pancakes on a plate for him. When I turned around, Jamie was behind me, holding up an empty plate. I raised my brows. "More?"

He nodded in an exaggerated fashion. He eyed Zane's plate. "Are you having pancakes today?"

"Uhh...yeah."

"No yogurt?"

"Not today. I felt like it was more of a pancake day. Is that all right?"

"Sure. I'll share," he said lightly, focused on the pancakes I was about to set on his plate.

When he finished, I told him to watch cartoons until I came to get him. He ran off happily. I grabbed a fork and knife from the drawer, poured syrup on Zane's pancakes and stepped outside, half expecting him to be gone.

"Oh, my God. You're an angel. Those smelled so good." He dug in right away, but commented between bites. "Your son seems to really like pancakes."

"Son? Oh, no. That's my little brother."

"Oh?" He frowned. "Quite an age difference, isn't there?"

I crossed my arms, watching him eat. I was tempted to tell him to eat smaller bites, too. "Sixteen years. He probably seems a lot younger than he is. He has certain challenges." I always found it hard to explain Jamie's issues. Hell, the doctors weren't even sure what caused it, other than saying my mom was forty-one when she had him and her eggs were probably expired by that point.

"Oh." He continued eating, his brow furrowed. "So, umm...he's visiting then or...?"

"No. He lives with me. My parents died when he was two. I pretty much raised him."

He swallowed hard. "Wow. That's—wow." He tapped his fork on his plate. "That must be hard."

I shrugged. "It has its moments." I felt uncomfortable talking about myself. "So, listen. You didn't come here to get the Grace Clayton Prescott bio." I sighed. "Why did you come?"

He stared at his plate for a moment then set it on one of the steps going up. "I want to apologize for...causing a scene in your shop. I was completely out of line. And what I said later...." He stepped forward, tentatively grasping my biceps. "Grace, I didn't mean any of it, I swear. Sometimes my mouth...." He released me. "I don't even know what to say. I was totally out of control, acting like a crazy person." He took a step back. "I don't know, maybe I shouldn't have even come." He ran a hand over his face. "I don't know."

"Why did you come? Before all the craziness, what was your reason for coming to Jeff City?"

He looked at me. "I had to see you."

I think his confession shocked us both. I stepped toward him. "Why, Zane?"

He glanced away and back. "I had to know if you—" He stopped, taking a breath. "After we kissed, why did you leave?"

I wasn't expecting that. I lowered myself onto a stair. He moved his plate, and sat beside me. I played with the edge of my robe, trying to make myself understood. "To be honest, I don't know. I...I was scared."

"Of me?"

"No. Of...the way I felt when I was with you." I looked away. "God, this is embarrassing."

He lightly took my chin and turned me back to him. "No," he said quietly, gliding his thumb across my bottom lip. I was surprised to see he was teary. "I felt it, too." His gaze roamed over my face. "Grace, I've thought about kissing you since that first time on stage. I fantasized about kissing you softly and gently like this...." He bent in, brushing his lips over mine, before kissing me tenderly, teasing me, drawing me into him. I never was kissed like that, so full of...something. I could feel his need. And my own urgent need for him. He separated from me, but stayed close. "And I fantasized about kissing you hard and dirty like this." He trailed his fingers down my throat and applied more pressure with his mouth. His tongue was wicked, stirring me, bringing me to life.

This is crazy.

I pulled back, my palm on his cheek. I lay my forehead on his for a second, squeezing my eyes shut. "Oh, God. No." I wanted him, but I was deluding myself. I got to my feet, covering my face. He rose, too.

"Grace...."

"This'll never work." I screamed. Then, realizing Jamie might hear us, I lowered my voice. "Can't you see that?"

His hands were in my hair again. "No." He looked at one of my eyes then the next. "All I see is you."

I shoved away from him. "Stop! Stop. This...it's impossible."

"Why do you say that?"

"Why do I say it?" I stared. "Where should I start?" I moved away from him, because I had to. I couldn't think when I was near him. "You're a rock star. I'm a glorified flower girl."

"So, because I'm a rock star you're not going to give me a chance?"

He was getting mad. Good. That was what I needed. "No. I can't do this right now. I have to take care of Jamie."

"Let me come in," he pleaded. "I'm good with kids."

"He isn't your normal kid. He—"

He waved a hand. "I know that. I can see—"

"No, you can't," I shouted. I took a shuddering breath. "I made a mistake once."

"What? That guy from last night? He was the mistake?"

"Yes."

"Well, who the hell is he? What's his problem?"

"He...he was the superintendent of my building. I...I didn't have money to pay the rent. He offered to...let me move in with him."

"Shit." He put a hand on his chin for a second then studied me. "It was a mistake. I get it. He hurt you. But I won't do that."

"How can I know that? We don't even know each other. I...I can't make the same mistake again. Not when Jamie is involved."

He pressed his lips together.

Good. Get mad. Say hateful things to me again, to hurt me, so I won't fall any more deeply in love with you.

"So you're going to live your life alone because you made one mistake."

"I'm not alone. I have Jamie."

He exhaled sharply, looking down. His jaw was tight. It was like I could see the anger rise.

"So, because you slept with some loser you're not going to give me a chance."

I stuck my chin out, my own ire rising. "You can't judge me. You don't know what I went through. I—"

"So you traded in your virginity to pay the rent, but I'm the one who ends up paying for it in the long run."

Even though it was what I wanted him to say to me, it hurt so bad it took my breath away. I could tell he regretted saying it the moment it left his mouth. But it was too late. It was said.

"Get out."

"Grace, wait. Fuck!" He looked up to the sky with his hands on his hips.

I pointed to the steps. "Get out and don't come back. Don't wait around on this fire escape because I won't let you in. Just—" I was losing it. "Go." I turned away and crossed my arms.

He stood for a couple more seconds, then bolted down the stairs. I closed my eyes. Every bang of boot against metal pulled out a sob. When he reached the bottom, he didn't bother with the ladder. His boots hit the gravel with a *slap* when he landed, and he was gone.

I was fine before I met him. He made me realize how much I was missing. Emphasized the hole in my life. I wanted to fall apart. I wanted to lie in my bed and cry for days. But I had Jamie to take care of, and I needed to leave for work. I probably didn't even have time for a shower. I brushed angrily at my tears.

Fuck Zane Sanders.

CHAPTER SIX

Z*ane*

I sat in my car staring straight ahead. I'd started the ignition over five times but didn't move from my parking space. Somewhere in the back of my mind I knew I had to return the rental Trans Am eventually. I considered going home to see my little sisters, but didn't think I could handle my stepfather. He was worse now than when I was growing up. I'm not sure why he hated me so much, but since I was hating myself so much at the moment, that might be a lethal combination.

I don't know why I said what I did other than the fact that I was so frustrated. Maybe I was turning into a prima donna, spoiled rock star. It was like ever since I met Grace I was on full throttle. And the really strange thing was, I couldn't even explain why. She was right. We didn't know each other. We shared a couple dances. A kiss. Maybe twenty minutes. Was it lust? I mean, everyone said "The Kiss" was so hot. That's lust, right? But...it wasn't only that. Sure, I was physically attracted to her. But I had been with actresses and models and all kinds of gorgeous women...but none of them were her.

It was so stupid. What was it about her? What was it about her that was driving me stark raving mad? I felt the last year, since Devin's death, I grew so much. Outbursts like the ones I had the last several days, I thought they were a thing of the past. That I was gaining some maturity, calming down. Becoming a more acceptable member of society. What a bunch of bullshit. I was the same old fucked up me I'd always been.

I had a really strong desire to drink until I blacked out. Until I forgot about her. But I guess that is one thing I learned. Drinking doesn't solve things. It numbs them, buries them, but it can never solve things, and the actions of the past several days clearly demonstrated I had some things to solve.

What was I doing sitting in my car? I had blown things with Grace; there was no reason to stay in this Podunk town any longer. But where to go? I could just drive. Think and drive, until I couldn't think and drive anymore. Lord knew I had enough money I could stop somewhere. But the idea of spending the night by myself, in a room full of all the creature comforts when nothing could comfort me—that was even more depressing than sitting in my rental car outside of—I glanced over—Phil's Bar and Grill. Great. Alcohol was only feet away.

I wouldn't compound this wrong by adding more to it. Then, of course, my mind kept going back to her. To the way her face looked when I spewed out my vicious words on her like acid. Here she was, some girl raising her little, disabled brother by herself since the age of eighteen.

And there it was, at least in part. That was the thing I liked about her. She was strong, in a good way. Not a throw-my-weight-around way. Compassionate. Undaunted. The idea of me raising my little sisters when I was eighteen? Hell, I was a mess. My mom newly remarried. My stepdad was a bastard, always making me feel like trash. But Grace—that's how her name suited her, she handled things with grace, whereas I handled them like a gorilla with sticks of dynamite.

I groaned, lying back and staring at the car's ceiling. "Why are you such a fuck up, Zane?" My words rang through the empty car unanswered. "Shit." I rolled my head, peering out the window at Phil's. Then I lifted it. I was pretty sure that was the spot where that loser was hanging out last night, waiting to stalk her. I thought about her words. *If you ever touch me again...restraining order*. Those words repeated themselves in a loop for a moment. She didn't want to kiss him, he forced himself on her. His hand—holy fuck, he was pulling her hair to try to control her, not caressing it. "Oh, my God," I groaned, laying my forehead on the steering wheel. And then I go an accuse her of— I rolled my head back and forth on the wheel, wanting it to hurt. The motion caused me to accidentally honk the horn and I quickly looked around to see if anyone heard it.

I sat forward. Grace was walking down the street. She had on another pretty dress. This time a purple one with white flowers with a matching purple sweater buttoning at her throat, where I was tempted to kiss her. "Shit." I slouched until I was almost below the dash, but I could still watch her. Her head was bent, as she seemed focused on her thoughts. I doubt she would see me if I was in full view. If that horn blast didn't alert her to my presence, nothing would. She went into her shop.

Now what.

A thought struck me. If I was out here watching her, could he be, too? I scanned all of the cars parked on the street, then the doorways. I wanted to check the alleys but was afraid she might see me. I decided to wait and watch until she left work and make sure she got home okay. It was the least I could do after making her so miserable. But what then? It wasn't like I could stick around every day and stake out her place, although I had nowhere I needed to be for a couple of weeks....

At about two forty-five I saw that friend of hers from the concert walking up the street. Did everyone walk in this town? I got a few stares from somebody waiting for a bus and was surprised a cop hadn't knocked on my window yet. But maybe one was watching me watching her. The friend went into Grace's shop. And what about that? She owned her own shop. Pretty impressive.

"Whoa." I sank lower again. They were coming out. But instead of walking away from me, to her house, they were coming towards me. "Oh, fuck. Oh, fuck. Oh, fuck." They stopped right beside my door. If Grace looked down, I was a dead man, but she didn't. They went into Phil's. I exhaled. Close one. I checked my phone again. Kind of a late lunch. I was starving. Two little pancakes does not a full rock star make. But I considered myself unworthy of sustenance and I wasn't about to leave until she was safely home.

So I waited.

And waited.

Five o'clock rolled around. I think my stomach was eating its own lining. My neck was killing me. I wasn't sure if it was from sleeping in her doorway last night, or from slouching in the car. At the moment I was curled on my side facing the grill to relieve my ass a little bit. How long of a break was she going to take?

It got dark. I'm pretty sure one guy saw me, but he kept walking. People didn't care about each other anymore. About seven-thirty it dawned on me there might be a back door to the place. Man, I would be hacked if I spent the day watching a door for no reason. I decided to go in. If for nothing else than a sandwich and cold beer.

"Oh." Unfolding myself from the car became a monumental undertaking, and I discovered my feet were asleep and almost went to my knees, catching myself on a bike rack. Quite a few people had gone in, so I was pretty sure I could blend in and not be noticed by her if she was still around. I lost my ball cap somewhere along the way, but luckily I had a spare. I had no desire to be recognized at this point. I held the door for a couple, then followed them in.

The place was hopping and loud. It was also dark and it took several minutes for my eyes to adapt. My ears were assaulted by country music. Someone needed to take out the guy at the juke box. I strolled up to the bar and subtly scanned the area.

"What can I get you?" the bartender asked, but I spotted her.

"Uhh. I'm good for now. Thanks."

She and her friend were out on the dance floor. She no longer had her sweater on, and the cocktail in her hand was obviously not her first. More laughing and drinking was going on than dancing. And the moves she was using at the moment were nothing like the ones she used on stage with me. Of course, she hadn't been nearly this inebriated. As usual, a pair of guys was watching them. It didn't look like they were leaving anytime soon so I grabbed a stool near the door and ordered a beer and burger. I don't know if it was because I was starving, but the burger was outstanding. I woofed it down and considered ordering another. I checked on them. One of the guys had positioned himself behind Grace. I sat straighter, stretching my already sore neck to see around some people who blocked my view. Of course, since he was right behind her and she was dancing like a maniac she bumped into him. He twisted and said something to her, and the next thing I knew, they were dancing together.

Wow. Smooth move, Exlax.

"Another beer?"

"Huh? No." The bartender turned to walk away. "Hey, can I get my tab?"

"Sure. Be back in a sec."

I absentmindedly pulled some bills out and laid them on the bar. The little shimmy Grace was doing was quickly evolving into a lap dance, and his hands were getting a little too friendly for my liking. I threaded through the crowd. Now his arms were all the way around her from the back. It appeared as if he was trying to say something in her ear, but she was flailing about so much that seemed like a dangerous enterprise. His tall friend, boasting a cowboy hat, was all over Grace's friend, reaching from behind to touch her stomach. This wasn't good.

"Grace."

She stared at me with unfocused eyes. I shot her dance partner a dirty look.

"What are you doing here?"

"Ya know, I'm really not sure. That's a good question. Let's explore it on a walk to your place. I think it's time to go." I touched her elbow and she drew back.

"No," she said like a three-year-old. "I'm having fun."

"Yeah. A little too much fun. I think we should go."

"You can't tell me what to do."

I hoped for an easy extrication because the longer this took, the more prepared these guys would be to kick my ass, and possibly recruit some help.

I took her elbow again. "Grace. Come on." She shook it off.

"I don't think she wants to go with you, pal," her dance partner said, straightening.

"Don't talk to him like that," Grace said in my defense.

I sneered at the guy. I turned sideways to the door and extended my arms, hoping maybe she'd cooperate if she didn't feel like she was forced. "Let's go, Grace."

"I don't want to go anywhere with you."

"See," the guy said with a sneer of his own.

I stepped closer to her and lowered my voice. "You don't have to go with me, but please go. I don't think these guys are looking out for you."

The redneck stepped forward. "I am, too. Aren't I, sugar?" He was holding her hips and trying to gyrate in time with her.

Grace flipped her hair. "Yeah." Then she did a little hip dip that may have been sexy, *may* have been sexy, if she hadn't fallen off her heels. "Ouch." She stumbled and I seized my opportunity.

Careful to keep her dress in place, I bent and grabbed her around her legs. "Up we go." I hefted her over my shoulder. I started to leave but saw the guy in the cowboy hat getting cozy with her friend again. "You." I snatched her hand and dragged her along with us. "You're coming, too."

"Okay," she said brightly.

Meanwhile, Grace was beating on my back and hollering for me to let her go. By chance I saw her sweater on the back of a chair and plucked it off. "Did you have a purse?" I tried to remember if she had one when she came in.

"No."

"Okay." I wondered how she was supposed to buy drinks without a purse. Her friend collected a cell phone from the table. Next to it a fishbowl sat with ice in it and two straws sticking out at odd angles. "Did you guys drink that?"

She looked. "Oh, yeah. Two of them."

"*Two?*"

She nodded proudly. I hoped for their sake Phil served watered down drinks. I took her hand again, and she came willingly.

"Hey," some guy said as we were passing. "Aren't you that Grace from that concert on YouTube?"

Grace lifted her head and answered in a bubbly way. "Yes. That's me."

I rolled my eyes and forged through the crowd, which, thankfully, parted for us. I breathed a sigh of relief when we hit the pavement. All-in-all, I thought that went about as good as it could go. Grace was still now. I let go of her friend so I could shift Grace's weight. Her friend continued to walk beside me. The silence felt uncomfortable.

"So, I'm Zane. You are...?"

"Payton."

"Nice to meet you, Payton."

"Thanks." She kicked a rock ahead of us. "You weren't very nice to Grace this morning."

I grimaced. "She told you that, huh?"

"Yes. That's why she wanted to get drunk."

Knowing I had hurt her bad enough she needed to escape in alcohol for the evening pierced me. "Damn it." I muttered under my breath.

Payton walked out in front of me and spun to face me, holding a hand out like a cop. "I'm not sure I should let you take her."

I chuckled. "All I'm doing is taking her home. I swear."

"Okay." She walked beside me again. I got the feeling she was a real hoot. "I think she's had too much to drink."

"I agree with that summation."

"To tell you the truth, I was a little worried about getting her out of there myself." She turned to look at me. "It's usually her yelling Hyacinth, not me."

"O...kay."

She smiled. "She takes care of me."

"Yeah." I stopped to adjust again. "I get the feeling she takes care of a lot of people."

She nodded. "She does. She does. She's the best," she gushed.

"Mmm." I looked ahead. How many blocks was it to her house?

"Is she heavy?"

"Not really. Just awkward."

"Ahh." We walked on in silence for a bit. "Why were you so mean to her?"

Ouch. Out of the mouths of babes and drunks. I exhaled. "I don't know, Payton. I really don't. I wish I did."

"You made her cry."

I stopped, closing my eyes. "I know. I was a real asshole."

"Yes, you were."

I frowned. "Do you always say what's on your mind?"

"Most of the time."

"Mmm." I continued walking. I shook my head. The conversation was both amusing and painful.

Payton turned around, walking backward, which I considered quite an accomplishment in her state. "You were right about those guys. They were losers."

"Well, I'm glad to hear we're in agreement."

"You're not a loser, Zane."

That cheered me. "Thanks."

"You're a jerk."

I laughed. She was a piece of work. "Well, I can't exactly argue the point because you're right. I am a jerk. And an asshole. And a whole lot worse."

"Ooh. What's worse than an asshole?"

I turned to observe her. "A Zane."

She held a finger up. "Ahh. I see."

I was getting winded. "How much farther is it?"

"A block and a half."

"Okay. Can we stop for a sec?" I redistributed the weight on my shoulder again. "Could you hold the sweater?" It kept slipping.

"Sure." She folded it over her arms.

I twisted a little. "Is she breathing?"

Payton bent, rotating her head so she could look in Grace's face. "Grace? Are you breathing?" No answer came. "I think she's breathing."

Not exactly reassuring.

"So, what do you know about that Brad?"

"Brad?"

Oh, shit. She didn't tell her best friend about it? Maybe they're not that tight.

Well, if Grace didn't reveal it, I sure the hell wouldn't. "Yeah," I diverted, "wasn't that the name of one of those guys you were dancing with?"

"I don't think so. They said their names were Wes and Michael." She took a sharp breath in. "But maybe they were *lying.*" She said dramatically. I was really starting to like her. I wondered if she and Rafe would make a good fit.

"Do you have a boyfriend, Payton?"

She burst out laughing and then stopped abruptly. "No."

"Oh." I shrugged my free shoulder. "You probably just haven't found the right guy yet."

"Maybe." She snorted. "But I found a lot of the wrong guys."

I looked up. "We're there, aren't we? Thank God." I was breathing heavily. "Now the steps."

"Do you want me to help?"

"Well, I thought about switching her to my arms, but I'm afraid I'll drop her. If you could get the door...."

She climbed ahead of us and held it. Once in, she snuck past us. "I have a key."

"Oh, good. I was wondering about that." I checked my path. Three flights. I could do this. "Here we go," I said under my breath.

When I struggled to the third floor, Payton had the door open. The lady from the night before was on the couch. "Oh, wow. Is she okay?"

Payton answered. "She's fine. Had a few too many fishbowls."

The lady raised her brows. "That'll do it. Jamie went to bed about an hour ago. He was exhausted from..." she glanced at me, "last night." She studied me before shifting her gaze to Payton. "Uhh...should I stay?"

"No, we're good, Holly. I can try to find her purse and pay you...."

"Don't worry about it. I'll catch her later." She gave me another doubtful once-over. "Good night."

I huffed. "Payton. Bedroom?"

"At the end of the hall."

The door was cracked when I got there, so I shoved it open with my foot, hoping I didn't wake her little brother. Now, to get her on the bed.... I clumsily bent over and got her rear on the bed and Payton helped me lay her back. Then we needed to spin her. She moved her head from one side to the other on her pillow, her face scrunched up. "Oh, I don't feel good."

Payton and I exchanged wide-eyed looks. "Shit." She ran around to get on the other side and we helped Grace to the bathroom. Payton got the lid open in the nick of time.

"Oh, God," Grace cried.

Payton lifted her head. "I've got this."

"Are you sure?" She seemed a little green herself.

Grace lurched forward again, and Payton put one hand on her back and waved me off with the other. I went out to the living room. My arms felt like taffy that was stretched too far, and my neck and back were harmonizing in the key of pain. I didn't want to leave until I was sure everyone was okay. I plopped onto the couch and stretched out to alleviate my back. I groaned. I was beat. Physically, emotionally, spiritually beat. I twisted my head. My ball cap sat on the table. I must have left it in the hall. For some reason knowing she brought it in, and didn't light it on fire, made me feel good. I grabbed it and held it on my stomach, tipping the one I was wearing forward to block the light from the lamp on the end table behind me. I yawned. At least I'd be here if that Brad guy showed.

Poor Grace. It was my fault. She wouldn't need to go out and get ripped if I stayed away. Maybe I should leave now before I did any more damage.

I'd wait to make sure Payton didn't need any help, then I'd do what she asked me to do ever since I got here. Leave her alone.

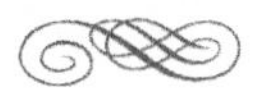

GRACE

When I opened my eyes, I wished I hadn't. The light was blinding, and my head was screaming for mercy it wouldn't receive. But there was Jamie to take care of, so I would have to drag my butt out of bed. I felt guilty I wouldn't give him my best today. Sitting on the side of the bed, working up the energy to stand, I turned to look back toward the window. Hangover aside, the light seemed too bright for this early in the morning. I squinted at the clock.

Shit. Jamie must be starving.

I stood a little too quickly and discovered I had a string of mystery injuries. My ankle hurt and appeared to be a little swollen. My forehead was tender to the touch for some reason, and it seemed like I'd hyperextended, or somehow strained, a muscle in my right armpit area. That one hurt the most. I shuffled out of the bedroom rolling that shoulder and trying to work out the pain, but wincing with each rotation. A faint odor of burnt food permeated my nostrils, which didn't help my nausea. Alarmed that Jamie might have tried to cook for himself, I hobbled faster, using the wall as counterbalance for my hurt leg, all the while telling myself Holly just burnt some popcorn last night. As I got closer, voices drifted down the hall from the kitchen, and I stopped. My lips quirked. So either Holly or Payton had spent the night and made breakfast for Jamie. Must be Payton if the food was burnt. The idea tickled me. Either way, I really owed somebody. Getting up at whatever insane hour Jamie did would have made this day murderous.

The smile faded from my face when I heard his voice.

"What do you mean catfish aren't purple?"

"They're gray," Jamie stated matter-of-factly.

I crept forward and peeked in. Zane's and Jamie's chairs were close together as they worked on the same, full spread coloring book page. Jamie had Zane's black ball cap perched on his head while Zane sported a blue one.

"But we don't have a gray crayon."

Jamie explained patiently. "You use the black one, but do it lightly."

We had the same conversation about the lack of a gray crayon a few days ago.

"Well...maybe this catfish is like a punk rock catfish who dyes his scales to be different from the other fish."

Jamie shook his head with a grin. "Oh, Zaner."

Zane chuckled and tugged on the bill of his cap.

"Gracie!" Jamie hopped down and came to hug my waist.

Zane pushed back so quickly he almost toppled the chair. "Oh, hi." He glanced around and popped to his feet to take some syrup laden plates to the sink. "I...uh...thought you'd sleep longer." He rinsed them off.

"Zaner made pancakes but they were terrible."

I rubbed Jamie's back. "Oh?" I couldn't help but be amused.

Zane twisted with a broad smile, clicking his tongue. "Come on, they weren't that bad." He leaned against the counter.

Jamie peered at me and shook his head, sticking his tongue out.

Zane looked at me sheepishly, drying his hands with a towel. "Okay. They were pretty bad." Still holding the towel, he pointed at Jamie. "But the second batch was decent, weren't they, buddy?"

He shrugged. "They weren't as good as Gracie's."

Zane clutched at his heart. "Ouch."

I grinned. "Mine are pretty good."

"Oh, I see how this is going to be. You all are using that whole brother/sister thing to gang up on me." He turned back to open the dishwasher and put the plates in. "He wanted five trillion, but settled for one hundred bajillion."

"Sounds about right."

"Gracie, come see what Zaner did to the clownfish."

Zane shrugged. "I'm Zaner now, Gracie." He seemed proud of it.

I checked out the coloring page. Zane put a red nose on the clownfish and a polka-dotted hat. I laughed. "Very nice."

Zane nudged Jamie. "See? She likes it." Zane looked at me, his mouth open in a smile, but slowly his face fell. He lowered his head. "We-e-ell I guess I should probably get going."

"No-o-o!" Jamie ran over and clutched Zane's waist like he had mine.

Zane fell off-balance and grabbed the counter, letting out an exclamation of surprise and delight.

Jamie peered up at him and Zane brushed his hair back. "Do you have to?"

"Well, buddy...." He considered me. "I probably should."

I pursed my lips, wrinkling my brow.

He dropped his gaze to Jamie, resting his hand on Jamie's head. "You'll be good for your sister, right?"

Jamie nodded, but turned his cheek to rest it against Zane, squeezing him tighter. Zane's expression softened and he bent over Jamie, giving him an awkward hug back. Then he took Jamie's shoulders and squatted. "I had fun this morning. I'll have to remember, catfish, gray, clownfish orange and purple, right?"

"Orange and white."

"Oh, yeah. Orange and white. Got it." He encircled Jamie with his arms and laid his cheek on Jamie's hair for a second before straightening.

Jamie hung his head then took the ball cap off, looked at it, and gave it to Zane. "Here's your hat."

Zane smiled sadly, took it, and put it right back on Jamie. "You keep it."

"But it's yours."

He tugged on the bill again. "It'll make me happy to know you have it." He moved forward, not making eye contact at first. "Bye, Grace. Thanks—" He glanced to the side and took a deep breath. "Thanks for everything," he said sincerely, his gaze roaming over my face. He dropped his chin and quickly moved past me into the living room.

I couldn't speak. My heart was in my throat. His hand was on the doorknob. "Zane!" I screamed.

He swung around with an expression of alarm.

"Don't—" Forgetting about my ankle I took a step forward and almost went down. Faster than I would have thought possible he was at my side, supporting me.

"The ankle?"

"Mmm." It throbbed. I gritted my teeth. "Yeah."

"I was afraid of that. You twisted it pretty good on the dance floor."

Wait. He was at Phil's?

The pain in my ankle suddenly seemed the least of my worries. "Fire escape."

Jamie rolled his eyes and went back to coloring. "Uh-oh."

Zane looked at Jamie. "What? What does that mean?"

"Payton says it means she's in trouble when Gracie says that."

Zane blanched. "Oh."

I grabbed on to the kitchen chair, then transferred to the table, and to a chair again on my way to the window.

"Are you sure you should—"

"Yes."

Zane sucked in a breath. "O-o-okay."

"Good luck," Jamie said resuming his coloring.

Zane tried to help me on my other side. "Thanks." He moved in front of me. "Let me go out first and then I can maybe help you on the other side."

Rather than climbing through, like I usually did, I sat on the sill and swung my legs out, and Zane pulled me to my feet.

"Do you want to sit on the stair?"

"Probably should."

He helped me to get settled then sat beside me.

I hesitated. "Uhh. This is kind of embarrassing."

He waited with a quizzical look on his face.

"You... were at Phil's last night...." I tried to make it a statement rather than a question, but he saw right through it.

His lips lifted in the corners. "You don't remember."

"I remember some of it," I said defensively.

He laughed.

"A fishbowl was involved...."

"Two fishbowls." He combed through his gorgeous hair.

"*Two* fishbowls?"

He nodded. "You know, they give you those things with multiple straws so you can share them." He peered up at me, raising an eyebrow and wearing that shit-eating grin of his.

I could feel the tug of a smile on my lips. "We shared."

He jumped on that right away. "You shared two. That's one apiece. Plus you were drinking something else on the dance floor...and a couple of glasses were on the table, too."

"Ooh. No wonder I feel like shit." I tried to recall the rest, but it only came in snatches. "Was there some...inappropriate dancing on my part?"

He stared straight ahead enjoying this far more than he should. "I guess that would be a matter of opinion. But yes, there was some dancing and that's how you hurt your ankle. Let me see that." He assessed it. "We might need to wrap it. Do you have any Ace bandages?"

"Probably, but we'll get to that later. If my ankle was that messed up, how did I get home?"

"Well," he squinted ahead, "to be honest, I didn't know how bad your ankle was, but...uhh...."

That didn't sound good. "Tell me."

"No. It's not something you did, it's something I did. And I was kind of hoping to leave on a high note."

I waited. I learned through Jamie that if I waited long enough, people felt uncomfortable with silence and they eventually talked, telling me what I needed to know.

He sat back, resting his arms on the stair behind us. "I probably shouldn't have done this. But I didn't see any other way in the moment."

"Yes...?"

He sighed and looked to the side. "Well, I decided—someone who has no right to make decisions for someone else when I'm such a fuckup myself...." He sat forward, obviously agitated by whatever he was about to admit. "I decided it was time for you to go home. These guys were lurking around, and I didn't like the way they were acting with you and Payton, and...when you wouldn't leave on your own—" he got to his feet, turning to face me, "—I slung you over my shoulder and took you on out of there." He raised his gaze right away to catch my reaction.

My mouth hung open. "You just...picked me up, and slung me over your shoulder and carried me out like a sack of potatoes?"

He grimaced, looking in through the window at Jamie. Then he squatted in front of me. "But those guys were— I don't know. I was worried. And...maybe a little jealous, too. I shouldn't have done it."

It came flooding back. I was dancing, his hands were on me, I wasn't listening....

"Wait. I remember now. It was a definite Hyacinth incident."

His face clouded. "What the hell does that mean? Payton said that last night. Hyacinth, fire escape...it's like I need a translator. You guys have your own language." He sat back on his tush, knees bent, hands hanging loosely between his legs.

"Sometimes in a Hyacinth situation you have to take drastic measures." I knew that only too well through my experiences with

Payton. "Hyacinth is a code word we use—*predominately I* use—to tell the other person they are getting out of control. Believe me, if I could have put Payton on my shoulder and carried her out of some places, I would have."

He exhaled, closing his eyes. "I'm so glad you understand."

"So then you put me in your car—"

"That may have been the logical thing to do, but I wasn't sure I could transfer you safely, and at that point you were still a flight risk, so I carried you home."

I blinked. "All the way from Phil's?" That was like, four blocks.

"Yeah. I mean, I don't want to make me out to be some kind of he-man. It was difficult for me. But carting anything that distance would be," he hastily added.

"I imagine. So you brought me home, put me in bed...."

"Then you got sick."

"Oh. I remember that." I poked my forehead where it was sore. "That's why my head hurts. I kept hitting it on the toilet seat lid when I, you know, got sick."

"Really?" He leaned forward, lifting my hair to examine it. "It looks a little puffy, but I don't think it's bruised." He stilled, his mouth hanging open a little, and his gaze wandered over my face. He abruptly stood. "So, anyway. Now you know the whole sordid story. You didn't do anything awful, so...no worries." He gestured toward the window. "Anyway, I should go."

"Do you have a show tonight?"

"No. We're on a two-week hiatus."

"Then where are you going?"

"Uhh...I'm not sure to be honest. I'll figure it out. Can I help you back inside?"

I took his hand. "Wait, please. I have a few more questions."

He studied our hands then gave mine a squeeze and withdrew his. He turned his back, walked over to the railing, spread his arms out wide and leaned on it. "Okay. Shoot."

I wanted to see his face, but I was afraid to trust my ankle yet. "Why were you there last night? I thought you left."

He spun around slowly and peered at me. Leaning back on the rail he let out a breath. "Like I am now, I wasn't sure where to go. And I was a little concerned about that Brad guy." He pushed away from the railing. "I was afraid he might try to come back here so I wanted to, you know, make sure you got home safe." He glanced to the side, stuffing his hands in his pockets. "That's all."

He's so cute. He slept in my hall. Carried me home. Wanted to keep me safe from Brad...and two guys who may or may not have been a threat. Tried to make pancakes for Jamie and colored with him—

"I'd like to say one thing more, if I could."

I nodded.

He took a few steps closer. "Although I made these words seem hollow and meaningless with my behavior yesterday, I am speaking them from my heart. I wish I could take back the hurt I caused you. You are an incredible woman and you so deserve to be loved and treated like one by someone a whole lot better than me, and—though it kills me to say it—I hope that man finds you and brings you great happiness. Thank you for letting me get to know you and Jamie." He nodded toward the window. "He's a great kid, and I'll always remember my time here." He took a deep breath. "I'm done." He looked toward the window. "Should I tell Jamie goodbye, or would it be better to—"

"Please stay." My voice cracked, and I couldn't say anything else.

He stared at me for a long moment then twisted and walked over to the other railing, the one opposite the window. Grasping the top rail he bent over it, wringing it with his hands like he was revving a motorbike. After a few seconds, he straightened and covered his mouth with his fingers then spun to face me. "I can't do that." He swallowed. "I can't do that to you. It would be wrong. As much as I don't want to, I'll make that mistake again." He threw his arm out to the side. "I'll say something ugly and vile and completely untrue, and I'll hurt you. You don't know how much I wish I could do better or how much it pains me to say this." He stared at his feet. "Funny thing is, this must mean I love you an awful lot because this is the first unselfish thing I've ever done in my life." And without another word, he rushed down the stairs. I pulled myself up by the banister.

"Wait, Zane."

He didn't stop.

"Zane, wait. Please don't make me chase after you on an injured ankle."

His feet slowed little by little until he came to a stop. He stood gripping the rails on either side, not looking at me. He breathed and half-chuckled. "You know you're ruining my grand exit." He gazed out over the parking lot. "No. You were right the first time. It won't work." He started moving again and I hobbled over to the stairs, putting my weight on the railing.

"Please, Zane. I listened to you. Now, damn you, listen to me." My heart was breaking.

He stopped. He was at the landing where he'd either have to jump or take the ladder to the ground. Both hands on his hips, his head lowered, he said. "You don't play fair."

"I know."

"It won't work."

"Are you too afraid to even give it a try?" I was pricking his pride, but I was desperate.

He peered at me through the hole in the center. "That's not fair."

"I know. I—" For an instant I forgot about my ankle and tried to step down so I could be closer to him. The pain caused me to lose my balance and fall against the opposite railing then on my ass.

"Grace!" He shot up the stairs. Grabbing me in a full-out panic he asked, "Are you okay?"

"Yes, yes. I'm fine." I leaned against the side of the stairs. His legs were split, one on the step below me, the other lower. We were both breathing hard.

"Shit." He ran a hand over his face. "I thought you were going to do a header." He swiveled to sit hard on the steps, panting. "I was never so scared in my life."

Folding his arms, he put them on top of his knees and laid his head on them. I scootched closer, spreading my knees to put him between them.

He straightened then leaned into me and reached back to touch me.

"Don't leave."

"Gracie?"

"Oh, shit. Not now." He must have heard all the racket.

Zane patted my leg. "It's okay. Go to him."

"No. You'll leave if I do."

He put his head in his hands, not denying it.

"Give me a couple of minutes, bud," I called out. I tried to listen to see if he went away, but didn't hear any movement. He didn't say anything though. "Can you come up here on my level so we can talk?"

He begrudgingly complied, but didn't look at me. I touched his chin to turn him to me and was surprised when his eyes were teary. "Zane." I searched him. "Don't you believe in yourself?"

He still wouldn't make eye contact with me. "No."

I lifted his chin. "Then believe in this." I kissed him, nibbling on his bottom lip, then coaxing his mouth open. He brought his hand to the back of my neck and kissed me back, taking it deeper before pulling away. He moved his palm to my cheek.

"It's a mistake."

"Then let's make it together."

He dropped his head and shook it. "It doesn't make sense. You know that, right? You said it wouldn't work, I hurt you, and now you're saying I should stay."

"I never claimed to be logical." I hoped to make him smile. "Come on. Let's give it a try. If it doesn't work, it doesn't work. I'm not as fragile as you think I am. I can take more shit than the average person."

He at least chuckled at that. "True." I waited for his answer. He lifted his face. "You're a hard person to say no to."

I moved in closer. "Then you probably shouldn't even try." I kissed him.

He checked to see if Jamie could see us, then leaned in, speaking quietly.

"Mmm." He pulled back a fraction. "If we're doing this, we're doing it right." He took my hands. "Will you go out on a date with me tonight?"

"A date?"

"Yeah. I heard people do that."

"Oh, um, well..." I looked at our hands. "Here's the thing...I've used Holly a lot lately. Last night, the night of the concert, the week before the concert my cousin got married in Fulton and she spent the night.... I'm afraid to overuse her."

"Oh." His face fell then he brightened. "What about Payton?"

I frowned. "I thought you met her last night."

"I did."

"Zane, I wouldn't leave Jamie alone in a room with Payton, let alone leave the premises. The last, and only, time I tried, I came home and Jamie was smoking, drinking, and was entertaining a prostitute in his bedroom." I smiled. "She's a great friend, but when I get someone to stay with Jamie, I usually try to get someone more mature than him."

"Oh. I can see that." He rubbed his chin. "Hey, I have an idea. It's really short notice, and she may already have plans, but I can try to get my stepsister Whitney."

"Oh. That's sweet of you but...Jamie can be difficult."

He seemed excited. "No. That's not a problem. She's involved in this thing at school. It's called the Panda Project...or Pumpkin Project or something. But she's done it for a couple of years, working with special needs kids to put on a play. And she volunteers for the Special Olympics—she's great with kids."

"But...where does she live?"

"Stanton. It's only an hour and a half from here. I'll get her a room here so she doesn't have to drive back late."

I really wanted to. It would be so much fun. I smiled. "Go ahead and call her and see if she's available."

CHAPTER SEVEN

Zane

She answered on the third ring. "Zane! Are you in town?"

"Hey, my beautiful little sister. How are you?"

I could hear the smile in her voice. "What do you want?"

"What makes you think I want anything? Okay, I do. I have a humongous favor to ask."

"What's up?"

"How do you feel about a little road trip tonight?"

"To meet you? I'm all over it."

"Even if it entails a little...babysitting?"

"Is there something you want to tell me? Last time I checked, I didn't have any nieces or nephews."

I grinned. She had really come into her own since starting high school. More mature. More confident. "So, there's this girl...."

"No way. Wait. Is it that girl from the video? The one you got all hot and sweaty with?"

I frowned. Maybe too mature. "I was not sweaty."

"But you were hot, weren't you?"

"I'm choosing to ignore that. Yes, it's Grace." I glanced in the window. She was on the couch next to Jamie. We'd wrapped her ankle, and she'd changed. "She has a brother who has...some challenges. But he's a real sweetheart. You'll love him."

"Sounds like it's right up my alley. When would you need me?"

I grimaced. "This evening?"

"Oh." She paused. "What's it, a little under four hours to Kansas City?"

"Oh. We're not in Kansas City. Jefferson City. It's less than two."

"What time would you be back? I don't want to drive back terribly late."

"I'll get you a room, if you can stay. And this is totally a paid gig."

"No. No. You are already way too generous."

"No. I'd insist."

"Let me do something for you one time, Zane."

"Whit. You know I like taking care of you and Tatum."

"I know you do. But one time, let me have the pleasure of doing something for you."

"We can work that out later. Can you do it?"

"Absolutely. I still have to shower, but I could be there around noon."

I exhaled. "You're the best, Whitney. I really owe you. It's a lot to ask."

"I didn't have anything going on anyway. And Tatum is at that band competition all weekend, so it's only me and him. Believe me, an opportunity to get out of the house is a godsend. You could ask me to come and hoe potatoes and I'd jump at the opportunity."

It made me feel bad for leaving them behind, but they wanted to finish up school in Stanton. Tatum had stayed for Whitney and attended the local community college when she probably could have gone to any school in the country, she was that bright. Now she studied aerospace engineering at St. Louis University and drove over an hour each way so she could be home with Whitney. The two were tight. "Well, I won't make you hoe potatoes and I'll take you out to lunch when you get here."

"Cool. I can't wait to see you."

"You know, I miss you guys an awful lot. If it weren't for him, I'd visit a lot more. But I know things are worse for you when we get into it, so—"

"I completely understand. I can't wait to graduate and get out of this house."

Another stab of guilt speared through me. "You know, you could still—"

"No. We talked about it. I want to finish at St. Clair. I lived with him seventeen years, what's one more? Now let me get off the phone and get on the road. Ooh. I can't wait to meet her. How did you guys meet?"

"At the concert."

"No, I mean before that."

"We didn't meet until that night."

"You learned those dances in one day?"

"No. I didn't know her until I pulled her on stage."

"And you kissed her like that?"

"Uhh...yeah. It was like an instant attraction or something."

"I'd've slapped your face."

"Gee. Thanks."

"You'd think you got enough action with groupies."

"Uhh. Could we change the subject?"

"Now I really can't wait to meet her. How old's her brother?"

"Uhh...I'm not quite sure...maybe...Grace said there was a sixteen-year age difference. She's about my age, I think...so...somewhere between eight and seventeen."

"Wow. That really narrows it down. It doesn't matter. I'll find out when I get there. I'll text when I'm on the way."

"You really are the best."

"Save it for my yearbook. See you soon."

I peered through the window again and Grace was turned toward me. I gave her a thumb's up and she looked as excited as I was.

I hadn't dated since I was in my teens. I hoped it was like riding a bicycle.

Whitney met me at the hotel, a nice place called The Capitol Plaza in the downtown area. It was one of those big convention center hotels with a wide open atrium, circled by rooms on seven or eight floors. It boasted fountains, chandeliers, plush carpet, and two glass elevators, but the rooms weren't anything special. Then again, it wasn't New York or Chicago. When did I become a snob?

It was great to see Whitney. Grace recommended a pizza place near the capital called Arris', claiming it was "the best pizza in Jeff City." It wasn't far from her place, in a nondescript building with a nondescript interior. I was starting to wonder if it was only adequate pizza and all the other places in town sucked, but it was actually pretty good. I held all pizza joints up to the measure of a little place in St. Louis called Imo's, and while this didn't beat it, it was closer than most.

We went back to the hotel and both took naps then I got dressed in what I hoped was passable attire. Grace insisted on no fancy meal. Since Brad, she had a rule about letting men pay for her. I needed to work on that. If I didn't fuck this up and got a chance to, that is. So apparently we were going to an Irish pub called Paddy Malone's. I chose a blue button-down shirt, brownish gold tie and brown suspenders with dark jeans. I also brought along a fedora, to keep me semi-incognito, although the fedora at times made me more recognizable.

When Whitney and I arrived at Grace's and she opened the door, I was stunned speechless for a second. It's not that her outfit was particularly spectacular, but she was spectacular. And the outfit wasn't the usual Grace fare. She wore dark, ripped skinny jeans, a white tank and a short, tan, suede-like jacket with a wide collar, zippers on the sleeves, and a belt. Short boots completed the outfit and she somehow added some soft curl to her hair and had on more makeup than usual. I stood with my mouth open and she ran her gaze over me, smiling and turning to my stepsister and extending her hand. "Hi. You must be Whitney. I'm Grace."

"Oh, yeah. Sorry," I mumbled, shaking my head.

Jamie poked out from behind her. "And this is Jamie." She laughed.

"Hey, Jamie. My name is Whitney. Nice to meet you."

"Wanna watch Big Fish Man?"

"Sure."

He grabbed her hand and pulled her into the room.

"Whoa," Grace said to me, without moving from the doorway. "She must be the Jamie-Whisperer. He never takes to someone that quickly." As she stood lost in amazement, I stepped up to her and said in her ear, "You look very nice."

She grabbed my suspenders and coaxed me to her. "And you are *très debonair.*" She gave me a quick peck, since Jamie and Whitney were occupied, but I knew the way Whitney was smiling after it she caught it. I tried to wait patiently while Grace gave Whitney the babysitting lowdown. Her number, Jamie's bedtime, what he could eat....

When I finally got her out the door, she seemed apprehensive. "She'll take good care of him, and if she has any problems, she'll give us a call."

"Yeah. Yeah." Her voice was tight. I rubbed her arms.

"We don't have to do this if you don't want to."

"No. I want to," she said with more confidence. "Your sister seems very sweet and mature. I just...worry about him. I know I shouldn't but—"

I raised her hand to my lips. "It's understandable. If at any point you feel uncomfortable, we can turn around and come back home."

"No. It's fine." She gave me a small smile.

"Good. Because I'm pretty excited about tonight."

"So am I."

Paddy Malone's showed more promise than the pizza place from the outside. It was a quaint brick building that appeared to have chimneys on both ends and sported red doors. The inside was nothing fancy, but it had a homey feel, much better than about ninety-five percent of the dives we played at when Just Short of Chaos started out. We decided to sit at the bar, at least at first.

"Oh, will you look at that," Grace said pointing to a chalkboard. "It's karaoke night."

"Huh," I glanced at her out of the corner of my eye. "I think I've been had."

"Oh, you don't like karaoke? I thought you would, because of your music. But maybe you're tired of it. I should have thought about—"

I put a finger on her mouth. "It'll be fun. I was only teasing you because you seemed like you were trying to act like you didn't know."

"Because we could do something else. Like...."

"No. I want to perform for you. Here, and later I will give you a *private* performance."

"Ooh. I like the sound of that." She kissed me and the bartender showed up at the same time.

"Oh. Bad timing."

"No," Grace said.

"Yes."

"Stop." She elbowed me and the bartender chuckled.

"What can I get you kids? Grace, I assume a Magner's."

"Oh, yes. By all means."

"You don't have fishbowls do you?" I grinned at Grace.

"Not here but at—"

"Phil's," I finished, smiling at my beautiful date sweetly. "I'll take a Guinness."

He stepped to the tap to fill our order. "Come here often, do you? He knew your order."

The corners of her mouth twitched. "Oh, from time-to-time."

He brought Grace's cider. "I'm letting the first layer settle," he said to me.

"Good man. You know how to pour one right."

"Oh, of course." He cocked his head. "Do I know you from somewhere?"

Here we go. I didn't want this to be an issue tonight. "I don't think so," I responded casually. "I'm from out of town."

"Yeah. You look like someone famous. I can't put my finger on it."

"I get that a lot."

"It'll come to me. Enjoy your drinks. You guys eating?"

"Yeah." Grace answered. "But we'll probably grab a table for that."

I was about halfway through my Arthur Guinness when he startled me by snapping his fingers. "I have it. I have it." My heart dropped. "That Dr. Who guy."

I almost spat out my drink. I wiped my mouth. "David Tenant?"

"Yeah. That's the guy."

"That's one I never got before." I didn't look at Grace, because I knew she was ready to lose it. "Could be the suspenders."

"Yeah. Could be."

When he walked off, priding himself in figuring out I resembled David Tennant, I whirled around. "David Tennant?"

"What? That's a compliment. David Tennant's cute."

"Yeah, but..." it had to be said "I'm cuter."

She turned straight on to the bar. "Ehh."

I grabbed her and pulled her in, while she wriggled and laughed. "You think he's cuter than me?"

"Yes."

Wow.

She leaned in to whisper in my ear. "But you're way hotter than he is."

Her lips that close to my ear gave me a shiver of desire. "I think I can live with that. *Who the hell* is texting me?" I dug my phone out. "I've gotten like twelve texts in the last fifteen minutes. Ahh. It's Whitney."

Grace's eyes widened and she actually came off her stool as if ready to dash out the door. "Why? What's wrong?"

"Calm down. She wanted to tell me she likes you."

"Oh. Well. That's sweet." She tried to peek at my screen. "She must have said more than that if you were getting so many notifications."

"Yes. She said you were even more beautiful in person—she's seen the video, too—and she could tell you had triple the I.Q. of any of the other girls she's seen me with. And you're not slutty." I continued to read. "Then she ends it by telling me to not mess this one up. Gee, thanks for the vote of confidence, sis." I could feel the bartender looking at me. I leaned forward. "Is he watching me again?"

"Yep." She giggled. "This is even better than I imagined it would be."

The guy stepped over. "Or maybe that Jonas kid."

"Nick Jonas?"

"Yes." He frowned. "Sort of."

"I do get that one a lot."

"Or even a young Elvis Presley." He nodded and started to walk off then stopped. "And a little like that guy from Just Short of Chaos."

I couldn't help myself. "The lead singer?"

"No. The good looking kid. The guitarist. Rafe Something."

"Raphael Santiago?" Grace prompted. Surprisingly composed. She squinted at me. "I can see that."

He stroked his chin, walking slowly away. "No. That's not it either. Hmm."

Grace was cracking up.

"I don't favor Rafe in the slightest. Well, maybe the dark hair, but that's where it ends."

She was fanning herself and catching her breath.

I took her hand. "Come on. Let's get a table before he figures it out."

She stopped laughing long enough to get out. "No. By the stage so I can have a front row seat."

"Okay." I pulled out her seat for her and leaned in to tell her, "But if I'm doing it, you're doing it, too."

She rolled her shoulder a little. "Okay. But we pick each other's songs."

"Ooh. I like that." I took my chair. "But not country. I don't know those songs."

"No. I'll pick something you'll know."

I rubbed my hands together. "This could be fun." I wanted to pick something challenging, so I could really hear her voice.

An hour later, after we'd eaten, they called her to the microphone. People clapped for her right away. The lyrics were on the screen, so they must've like my song choice, "Rolling in the Deep," by Adele. As expected, she belted it out like a pro. She even had stage presence, the little tart. And with the jeans and jacket on, she looked the part of an entertainer. She brought down the house. I rose to pull her chair out again and kissed her on the cheek. "Well done."

She was beaming. "Thanks."

Before I could even sit, they called my name, or rather, the name we gave them. "Zack? Do we have a Zack?"

I headed for the stage, staring at the screen to see what she chose. 'Ahh-yeah." I cast my eye on her. "I can do this one."

She grinned. "Let's see it, Zack."

The lyrics for "Lovin', Touchin', Squeezin'" by Journey appeared on the screen, but I didn't need them. I asked the DJ how far I could walk with the mic.

"Just stay in the room. And not too close to the speakers or you'll get feedback."

"Got it."

The music started, and I was excited.

We need to do a cover of this.

With the first line about the girl making the singer weak, I began slow, deliberate steps down the short staircase in front of the elevated stage, focusing on Grace the whole time. When I reached Grace, I got on both knees and held her hand. The crowd ate it up, as I knew they would. I was high on the song. It was just so fun to sing. I stood. I think Grace thought she was off the hook, but I grabbed a chair from a neighboring table and pulled it next to her, spinning it around backwards so I could straddle it, singing with my elbows on the top, staring at her.

She was glancing at the others watching us. I knew she was both uncomfortable and loving it at the same time. Realizing my hat was a hindrance, I plucked it from my head, and plopped it onto Grace's. She looked adorable.

I got to my feet, took her hand, and led her to the bar. People were on their feet cheering. They always went in for theatrics, and I was the guy to give it to them. During a break in the singing, I asked a guy at the corner of the bar if we could take his seat for a moment. He was more than happy to give it to us. I patted it for Grace. I realized my timing would be wrong for what I was planning if I didn't hustle. I sang, still gazing at her, but taking giant, hopping steps backward. A chair was in the way, but instead of seeing it as an obstacle, I saw it as an opportunity. I whirled, climbed the chair, and put my foot on the top, tipping it and riding it to the ground. The guys and I had spent hours perfecting that one day when we were bored waiting for our time on stage. I'd only hoped the chair was sturdy enough, or my grand feat would wind up making me seem like an idiot. But I did it as quickly as I could to limit the stress on the chair's joints, and it worked beautifully.

The place went wild, but I needed to keep moving. Luckily, the pub had big, heavy, scarred tables, because I used another chair as a step stool to an empty table shoved into a corner near the dance floor.

I did a number of moves I learned from studying Elvis clips, combining rubber legs, with a hip slide, then right into the classic windmill where I swept my arm in huge circles, and coordinated it with twisting my knee in. Synchronizing my movements to the length of the song without practice turned out to be difficult, and I realized the song was much shorter than I'd anticipated, so I couldn't waste a second. I jumped from the table and basically ran to the end of the bar opposite Grace. I hopped, again using an empty stool tucked in to the bar rail to make getting on top easier. I eyed customers lining my path and they all caught on pretty quickly, scrambling to move their drinks and paraphernalia out of my way. The bartender was into it, too, and removed one of those tray things that held garnishes and some other stuff. Ha. The timing was perfect.

My path was clear, the piano built to a crescendo, before the verse where the cheating girl gets her comeuppance, and I began my version of a fifties style stroll along the length of the bar, turning sideways to Grace and doing a lazy spin step to face the other direction, stepped, rocking my hips into another spin, all while animatedly smiling at her. Her eyes shown with delight and her smile threatened to burst her cheeks. I made it to her, then spun and ran back to where I started. About two-thirds of the way there I hit a wet spot and skid, but somehow managed to stay on top.

Big finish time. I ran toward her and dropped to my knees for the last fourth of my track, sliding to her. I was a beat or two off at the end, but nothing that wouldn't be overlooked considering what I accomplished up to that point. I jumped down next to Grace, took her hand, holding it high and brought her back to her seat before returning to the stage. People were cheering and patting me on the back and shouting out compliments. I laughed. I was so lucky to even come close to pulling that off without trying it all first, but, I didn't get to the top by playing it safe. I even surprised myself at times.

I returned the mic to the DJ and he slapped my back. "That was awesome, man!"

"Thanks." I worked myself into a good sweat and I was still breathing pretty hard.

As I headed to Grace in a more normal fashion, the DJ yelled into the mic. "So who wants to follow that?" He waited for a response. "No one? Really?" He laughed. "I think I'll take a break." He was about to turn the system down, but added. "Now that's something I won't soon forget."

As I waded through people to Grace I heard a female voice say, "That's Zane Sanders!"

Someone responded. "No it's not. Why would Zane Sanders be in Jefferson City?"

One reason, and one reason only. The woman I was with tonight.

More voices chimed in. "I don't know, man. It really looks like him. And who else could dance like that?"

I had known losing the hat would come with a price. I bent in to Grace when I reached her. "Hey. I think I was spotted. Mind if we get out of here?" I dropped a couple of hundreds on the table and put my arm around Grace, ready to protect her if the crowd should push in. We were able to swim barely ahead of the wave of recognition. By the time we got to the door, Grace clearly was hearing the uproar, too.

"I'm telling you, that's him."

I was relieved when no one followed us out. I guess they were satisfied with their impromptu show and/or not willing to abandon their drinks.

"That was fun."

Grace gushed. "I can't believe you did that."

"Me either." I exhaled. "Do you think it was too much?" I teased.

"Oh, no," she said with an exaggerated head shake. She laughed and slid her hand behind my back, squeezing herself to my side.

"I thought about doing a back flip off the bar for a dismount, but the music had ended and it might be considered a little hot doggy."

"A touch," she said, holding up her thumb and pointer finger inches apart. When we were in the car and heading to her place, I took her hand. "I'd still like to have a drink or two with you before returning to the Capitol Plaza, but if you're too tired, I understand. I know you have to work in the morning."

She smiled at me. "Are you kidding? I couldn't sleep now." She glanced at the console clock. "Besides, it's still early. I'll get Jamie in bed and we can drink on the fire escape. I'd hate to waste this beautiful night.'

"I'm kind of gross. How about this, I'll take Whitney to the hotel, and take a quick shower while you get Jamie tucked into bed. Then I'll come back and we can enjoy the night a little longer."

"Sounds perfect." She was pretty much glowing. Totally worth the risk of breaking my neck and making a fool out of myself. At the next light, she stretched over the console to kiss me.

I'd say this date is going pretty well.

CHAPTER EIGHT

Grace

We were laughing all the way up the stairs to my apartment, still high from our karaoke fun. It was like a crazy scene from a movie acted out in front of me. I still couldn't believe he danced over a chair, on a table, and along the bar. And how he danced? Mind blowing. The way he moved his hips, his pelvis, the sexy expressions on his face.... Now I understood why women screamed for Elvis, because inside every fiber of my being was screaming out yes to Zane for every second of that song.

Yes, I love you. Not the imagined you I thought I knew coming into that concert. Zane Sanders, aka, Zane Salvetti. Born in the Midwest. Platinum record producing singer at the age of nineteen. Sexy frontman for Just Short of Chaos. Then I knew the Wikipedia version of Zane.

Now I knew the whole package. And for me, Zane was perfect in every way. His body, gorgeous hair and strong jaw were definitely arresting. But what made him perfect was the fact that, along with being a sex god, he also bordered on nerd. Along with being accomplished, he was still a child in many ways. Along with the smooth confidence he showed on stage was someone riddled with doubt, someone for whom making it through the day could be a struggle. It was these things that made him breathtakingly, beautifully flawed and human.

I spent enough time with him now to know he was like me, life-challenged. For someone who felt as deeply as he did, an average day could wipe him out. A story of someone dying alone, the beauty of a sunset—no, anyone could be moved by the glory of the sun setting, for Zane and I, and many others like us, the beauty of a leaf could make us cry. Hyper-aware of both the joys and the sorrows of the world, knowing we were different, but struggling to be at peace with those differences, that's what made us who we were. Did some venomous words spew out of his mouth at times? Yes. Did they hurt? Deeply. But he was a man of passion, not logic, thank God. Someone who made big mistakes, but made up for them in a big way.

It wasn't that I was thinking these things when we climbed the stairs, but I was feeling them. Later, in the dark, before I drifted off to sleep, that was when I would puzzle out the way he made me love him. But during, and right after, all I could feel was the sheer joy of the moment.

"And when he said you looked like Rafe."

"I know. Rafe is much taller, and broader in the shoulders than I am. And he's got that beard...our faces aren't even shaped alike...."

"It was great to be the person sort of on the outside of that conversation. To take in his perplexed expression as he sorted through images in his mind to find the one matching yours, and the shock on your face when he hit Just Short of Chaos but thought you reminded him of Rafe...it was almost too good to be true. I wish we had someone filming this entire evening because I never want to forget an instant."

He grabbed me by my hips on the doorstep. "Well I'm ready to create a few more memories for you." He kissed my neck and had me wrapped around his finger. When his mouth met mine it was all pleasure, reaction, and instinct.

Then Whitney opened the door on us. "Oh. Uhh. Sorry. I heard your voices and thought I'd save you the trouble of getting your key out."

"Oh, well, you did." I didn't even really feel embarrassed. I was too full of jubilance, too full of him for anything else.

Jamie sat on the couch with a book open in his lap. Whitney returned to sit beside him as she talked. "Well, you guys are home early. What? Did you get thrown out?"

We stared at each other and tried to suppress our laughter.

Whitney stretched an arm over Jamie's shoulders and moved the book so it was between them, looking from one of us to the other quizzically. "What? You end up dancing on the tables again?"

I turned on him playfully. "You did this before?"

"No."

I frowned.

"No. I swear. I never danced on a table before tonight."

Whitney sat forward and slowly laid the book on the coffee table in front of her without looking. "Wait. You really *did* dance on the tables?"

"A table," he corrected.

I set my purse down and started to shrug out of my jacket, and Zane helped me get it off. "On the table, on the bar...."

"No way. No way!"

I peered at Zane. "Oh-h-h, yes."

"There's probably a YouTube video of it."

I grinned. "Oh, God, I hope so."

She grabbed her phone and searched. Jamie silently took everything in. "Did you guys do some shots first, or what?"

I put a hand over my stomach. "Oh, no. I had enough of those yesterday to last me for quite a while."

Zane put an arm over my shoulder. "It was karaoke night."

She glanced up, her smile spreading. "You karaoked?" She scrolled furiously. "Man. This is great." She gasped. "Here it is!"

I came around and bounced down beside her. "Let me see." She shared her screen and Jamie leaned forward, interested.

Whitney put a hand over her mouth, drawing in a sharp breath. "No way." Under her breath she added, "No bleepin' way."

"Hey, Syrup."

I didn't visually see it because my focus was glued to the screen, but I knew Zane fist-bumped Jamie.

"Zaner," Jamie responded, sounding happier than I heard him in a long time.

Whitney looked up. "When did you learn that chair thing?"

Zane shrugged. "We were goofing around backstage one time."

"Here comes the big finish," I warned her. We hunched closer.

When it was finished she dropped her phone in her lap, covered her face with her hands, and threw herself back on the couch. "I can't believe you did that."

Zane chuckled. "To be honest, I can't believe I did it either."

I beamed at him with pride, and a little lust when he turned his smoldery gaze back to me. "He was phenomenal."

"And Grace was, too. She sang 'Rolling In The Deep.'"

I waved it off. "Oh, please. That was easily forgettable. Not like this." I motioned to her phone. "Let's watch it again."

She enthusiastically grabbed her phone. "Why don't you do this kind of stuff when I'm with you?"

He straightened. "Because I'm setting a good example."

She rolled her eyes. "Uh-huh."

"I want an ice cream sandwich," Jamie interjected.

"I'll get it pal. Those women are crazy."

Jamie hopped to his feet to trail Zane.

"Umm...he's already had two." She winced at me apologetically.

Zane spun and raised his brows. "*Two*?"

She rolled a shoulder. "They're small."

Zane looked to me. I sighed. "Why not?"

"Yes." Zane high-fived Jamie then they turned to go in the kitchen.

"You know, you sound good here, even without professional equipment. You guys should cover this."

"Funny you should say that," he yelled from the kitchen. "I wrote a note to myself to talk to the boys about it."

Whitney laughed, putting her hand over her mouth again. "You almost bit it."

"Yeah," Zane said from the kitchen. "The bar was wet. Hmm...these are small." A few seconds later he called. "Can I have one?"

"Sure." Whitney and I were shoulder to shoulder. "This is where people started recognizing him." It was interesting to see their reaction, because at the time I only had eyes for Zane. "How many are left?" I called out to him.

"Oh...there's still a half a box of them."

"Could you bring me one? Do you want one?" I asked Whitney.

"Sure."

"Bring two, please."

When he came out, licking his lips and handing us our sandwiches, Whitney asked, "What got into you?"

Zane gazed on me tenderly. "I'm not sure."

We shared a look I thought was subtle, but Whitney exclaimed, "Oh, you two are so cute."

Jamie trailed out of the kitchen, appearing sticky, but satisfied, licking his fingers.

Zane put a hand on Jamie's shoulder. "Let's get you cleaned up." They took off down the hall.

Whitney and I simultaneously sank into the couch cushions to enjoy our ice cream sandwiches and chuckled about our similar reactions.

"Jamie is a doll. He told me *all* about fishing."

"Oh, I'm sure he did."

I nudged her. It would seem I had an instant comfortableness with anyone Salvetti, although I wasn't sure if that was her last name. "I think he has a crush on you."

She put a finger on her chin as if considering this. "He might. He only asked me to marry him three times."

I laughed. "Oh, my gosh."

She nudged me back. "I told him I wasn't old enough." She twisted toward me. "Maybe I shouldn't say this but, you guys are really good together. I've never seen Zane this happy."

It made me warm. "He makes me happy, too."

"Are you sure? Because Jamie explained to me all the intricacies of the fire escape and said Zane visited it."

I laughed. That kid. You never knew what would come out of his mouth. And he was so observant. "Oh, that was simply a misunderstanding."

"Well...." She hesitated. "I know Zane can...lose his cool and spout out things he never should say, but he's really a great guy." She cast her gaze down for a moment. "I may be a little biased, because I'm his sister, but...." We smiled. "But really—even before he made it big—Zane was always good to me and Tatum. I mean, you couldn't have a better big brother. He would go to bat for us, and he took a lot of shit to save us from having to. And now, I mean, you'd think most guys would leave and never look back, but he calls us—even when he's on the road—to check in on us. And I know he'd drop everything if we ever needed him."

I squeezed her arm. "Speaking of which, I'm really grateful to you for coming at the last minute, and driving all the way up here. And—"

She patted my leg and stood. "No problem. I didn't have anything going on and the drive was over before I knew it. Do you want me to take your wrapper?"

"Oh, thanks."

Zane reappeared. "He's getting his pajamas on." He rubbed Whitney's hair as she passed then stuck his hands in his pockets.

Because he was so near, I couldn't stand to not touch him, so I stood and went to him. Without precursor I put my hand on his cheek and kissed him.

He drew me into a hug, one side of his mouth turning up. "You really like it when I sing to you, don't you?"

I brought my lips to hover over his. "I *really* do."

He started to take the kiss deeper.

"You guys are too cute."

We broke apart, but left our arms around each other. Jamie ran out in his red flannel jammies and latched onto us.

Zane chuckled. "Don't you look dapper?"

"Do you think those might be too hot, buddy?" I didn't even know where he got them from. They should have been with his winter clothes in a storage container under his bed.

He smiled at us. "Nope."

It was one of those moments my love for him squeezed my heart. He had gotten really sick with pneumonia when I was nineteen. I blamed myself for not getting him the nutrition he needed. Money was tight. The medical bills were what forced me to move in with Brad. I could still remember Jamie lying—so tiny in this huge island of a hospital bed—on a ventilator with tubes running out of him everywhere. I could hardly even find a spot to touch him without being afraid of disconnecting something. I sat for hours brushing back one lock of hair from his pale face. I never felt so alone. Ever since then, every day with this boy with the big heart was precious to me.

"Okay. If you say so."

Zane rubbed my biceps. "I should probably take Whitney back to the hotel. I'll take a quick shower and hurry right back so we can...hang out a little longer."

"Sounds perfect."

"Whitter, you have to leave?" Jamie sounded so sad.

Whitney crouched beside him.

"Man. I didn't get a nickname until I was with him all morning," Zane interjected.

She smacked his leg before saying to Jamie, "I do have to go now. I'm tired, aren't you?"

"No," he said mournfully, staring at the carpet.

Whitney ruffled his hair. "I bet you will be when you climb into bed. I had a great time with you tonight."

He threw his arms around her, almost knocking her back. She wrapped him in a hug, then looked at us with a smile, but wet eyes.

"Hey now. If it's okay with your sister, I'll come back again and visit you."

"You are welcome anytime."

"See. I'll come back, and you can show me the capital building like you talked about earlier."

He brightened. "Really?"

"Yeah. It'll be awesome." She straightened. "It was really nice meeting you, Grace."

I stepped over to give her a quick hug, too. "It was nice meeting, you, hon. And thanks again. Oh. Wait. I didn't pay you yet." I searched for my purse.

"No, I got it."

I found the purse and dug around in it. "No. Remember what I said, no man pays my way."

He took my purse and held it out of reach. "Darling, I was paying my way. To an evening alone with you." He kissed me. "And it was worth every penny."

I frowned. I could tell this would be a problem. He started to move back and I jerked him to me by the suspenders. "We're talking about this when you get back."

Whitney leaned in. "Ooh. I see fire escape time in your future."

Jamie nodded vigorously. "That's the tone she takes."

We all laughed. I straightened Zane's tie. "Hey. My doorbell doesn't work so I'll leave the door unlocked because there's a chance I won't hear a knock."

"Okay." He bent in to whisper in my ear. "I'll hurry back."

When the door closed behind them, I gave a huge sigh.

"You like Zaner."

I looked at him sideways. "I do. You like Whitney."

We turned to head to his bedroom. "She's pretty."

"Yes, she is. And very nice, too."

"*Very* nice."

When we got to his room, his winter clothes box was out and was rummaged through. He purposefully got those pajamas out to impress Whitney.

ZANE

After my shower I changed into different jeans and a thin, soft, black sweater. My eyes were tired so I took my contacts out and put on my glasses, the trendy, nerdy kind. I rushed so I could stop and purchase a few things before returning to her place.

When I got back, I could hear Grace reading a story to Jamie. I was tempted to join them, but decided it might get Jamie wound up again. So, trying to be as quiet as possible, I went into the kitchen, opened a few cabinets to get what I needed, and took the stuff I purchased at the store out on the fire escape. It was a beautiful night and it was less likely Jamie would hear us there. When she came into the kitchen I was ready.

"You're back."

"I am. Is he asleep?"

"If not, I'm sure he will be soon. The only thing keeping him awake was the fact he wanted to talk about Whitney. Did she tell you she was proposed to?" She crossed to the window. I was sitting on the sill. When she got close, she saw it. "What did you do?"

I smiled. "It's been a while since we ate, so I grabbed some stuff. How's the ankle?" I helped her through.

She inhaled. "This is amazing." That was overselling it a bit. I had cheese, crackers, some summer sausage and grapes on a plate. I picked up a candle and flowers, too. It did look nice with the candlelight. "Oh, and the ankle's amazing, too. It hardly even hurts anymore. That wrapping job you did worked miracles."

I helped her to sit on the near side of our "table" then lowered myself across from her, in the corner. "I couldn't find a vase, so I put them in a tumbler. I hope that's okay?"

"They're so pretty." Tears were in her eyes. She'd warned me she was a crier, but a little cheese and crackers hardly seemed a reason to get emotional. Her face was ethereal, set aglow by the candlelight. She was so pretty. "I don't think I own a vase." She didn't own a vase? That Brad guy must not be much of a romantic. "I am hungry."

"Good. Oh, they didn't have Magner's so I got you Angry Orchard? The guy said it was their most popular brand."

"Oh, that's great. I'm not real picky."

I popped the top and handed it to her. "I wasn't sure if you liked wine. Oh, and Whitney did tell me about the multiple proposals. She said she'd send us an invite." I held my bottle out to clink it against hers and took a long pull. "She couldn't stop talking about Jamie, either. Then she called Tatum, our other sister, and alerted her to the YouTube footage. The guys texted, too. Dex saw it and texted the other two and, of course, they needed to rib me. Told me if I broke my neck doing shit like that, they'd be out of work, so knock it off. Although Rafe did say he was glad I was able to put the chair thing to good use." I chuckled. "Those guys are hilarious at times." I took another drink. "Dex, though...I'm not sure he's going to make it in the group."

"Oh?"

"I was thinking...the only way he found that video is he was watching our other video. From the concert." Her brow was furrowed, not seeing the connection. "He's a little too into you for my liking."

She almost choked on her drink and had to wipe her mouth. "What? Dex is?"

"Yeah," I growled. "He and I are going to have a come to Jesus moment."

"Oh, stop."

"Seriously."

"You guys seem pretty close, from what I read in interviews."

It was weird to think she read interviews about me. "Yeah. Especially after Devin's death." I wondered when the pain of that would lessen. I stared off over the parking lot, leaning with one knee bent, my arm resting on it, back against the railings. I'd never forget that night. Finding him. Losing it with Rafe.

Her voice was soft, but it startled me. I guess I lost track for a moment. "That must have been difficult."

Difficult didn't even begin to describe it. "Yeah." My voice came out strained. I took a drink to cover it then tipped my head back, resting it against a rail. "Devin was the closest thing I had to a brother. He, Rafe, and I grew up together. Jericho's Rafe's cousin." I looked at her. "But you probably already knew that."

She nodded with a small smile.

"You would have liked Devin. Everybody did. He never...let life get him down. Happy-go-lucky. The opposite of me, really. I guess we balanced each other out." The one year anniversary of his death was approaching. In some ways it felt like forever ago, in some ways, like yesterday. I glanced at her.

She was leaning forward, arms folded on her knees, staring at the candle.

"Can I ask you a question?"

"Hmm?" She took a deep breath. "Of course."

"You never said how your parents died."

She straightened slowly. "It was a home fire, started by a gas leak from our water heater, somehow. The investigators thought my mom was a secret smoker..."

She stared at the candle again, seeming to get lost for a second.

"You and Jamie weren't home?"

"No. We were there." She kept nodding. It was like each bob was repeating her words over and over again. *We were there. We were there....*

My God.

When I sat shocked and not sure what to say, she continued.

"We were asleep one instant, the next all hell broke loose. Flames were swallowing up my home even as my eyes opened. My dad was screaming at me to get Jamie. He was in a panic. He couldn't find my mom. I'd never seen him frightened before. Ever. He always was so strong, bigger than life. But that night...he seemed small and weak, fragile. That's what scared me the most. Not the fire destroying everything, or the heat and not be able to see through the thick smoke. It made a place so familiar to me a foreign battlefield. But what frightened me to the bone was to see my dad like that...." She shook her head.

"Oh, babe."

She hugged herself. "I got Jamie out, but he kept following me back in. It all happened so quickly. No neighbors showed up to hold him back until later...after...." Her mouth hung open, her gaze fixated on the flame in front of her. It was like she was that little circle when a video is buffering, spinning over and over in the same spot, never getting anywhere.

I lifted my arm. "Come—"

My speaking jarred her awake. Her head snapped up and words spilled out of her mouth. "They said the explosion shook houses blocks away."

I blew out the candle and shoved it, the flowers and food out of the way to create more room for her. She came to my side. I simply held her, not knowing what to say. She didn't cry. Didn't move at all, other than running her hand along the inside of the forearm nearest me. "I tried to get to them. I...I saw them. Heard them scream before the second explosion. I woke in the hospital."

The scar I saw in her shop. It was from when she went back to try to save them. My heart broke for her. I squeezed her as close as I could, kissed her hair, fighting back my own tears. We went from one of the most fun nights of my life to opening old scars, making them bleed fresh.

In the quiet that followed, my own Hell replayed in my mind in broken snatches. Finding Devin on the tour bus, wide-eyed, the needle still stuck in his skin, Rafe passed out on the seat across from him, snoring with his mouth hanging open, slumped against the wall, his arms hanging loosely by his sides. Watching as they pulled the sheet over Devin's face. I lashed out at Rafe, who was already feeling like shit, and I knew a part of me still blamed him, even though, in my head, I knew it wasn't his fault. The pain needed somewhere to go because I couldn't contain it all. It was too deep and immense. No one ever supported me like Devin did. Loved me like a brother. Could make me laugh when I felt like crying. I still missed him to the core. His loss struck me at odd times. A word, a phrase, a drum stick, could take me back to that night. That sucking hole left when someone you love is taken from you, she knew that, too.

The moonlight was strained by the grid design of the metal staircase, trying to reach us, but melting away before it could. She jumped, hearing it before I did. Jamie was crying out. Was he dreaming about the fire, too? My heart raced. She got to her feet. "It's okay.

This happens sometimes. Let me calm him down. It won't take long. I'll be back. You won't leave, right?"

Her eyes were so wild and beautiful. I found my voice. "No." I jerked my chin toward the window. "Go to him. I'll be here when you get back." Didn't she know I would fight anything that tried to pry me away from her?

She left without saying anything else. My head lolled to the side. After a few minutes, I got up and cleaned the fire escape. When she came back, I was putting the leftover food back in the refrigerator. "Are you done? Did you want any more?"

"No, I'm good."

I finished putting it away and closed the door and she came to me. I brushed the hair away from her face then cupped it. "Are you all right?" She nodded. I kissed her. Like kissing away a boo-boo. "I'm sorry you had to go through that." I kissed her again, softly. When I pulled away she stared at me for a moment then stretched to take my lips again.

What started off soft and tender became more heated when she slid her hands under my sweater. Something about the way she kissed me was unlike any other woman's kiss. It was like pressing the igniter on a grill, it filled me with heat and energy, coupled with a sense of urgency, of need. I wanted to swallow her, take her into me, make her mine in every conceivable way. In my head a pulse of go, go, go was fighting with a voice saying no, no, no. Beyond that, there was nothing but pleasurable sensation and a deeper need for this person who was so strong, but alone. Who knew pain like my own, but was a better person for it. Who I sensed may not so much need love and comfort as deserve it. For a moment, or four or five, I pushed all resistance away and sought to immerse myself in her.

Next thing I knew we were slamming our bodies against the refrigerator, my arms braced on either side of her, my mouth feverishly devouring hers. She pushed my sweater higher, and I peeled it off, the refrain of resistance growing louder, the need to possess her parried with the need to protect her. She still had the white tank on, but ditched the jacket and wore a soft denim-like shirt over it. That found its way to the floor with my sweater. I slid my hand behind her back, smashing her to me, the tank pulled to bare her stomach so we could feel the flesh on flesh. My mouth cruised along her neck to her shoulder, teeth digging in a little. God, I wanted to take her. I wanted to take her hard, and I didn't give a fuck where we ended up. On the table, in a chair, or even on the fire escape, with the steel biting into my skin and branding me with grid marks.

But an image of Jamie flashed into my mind, as I was sure it must have been somewhere in the recesses of hers.

Not now.

In a hopeless attempt to rid myself of that prick of responsibility I lifted her and moved her to the counter top. I brought my mouth lower, rolling it along her stomach as she held my head there, arching her back. I was so hard for her it hurt. It was as if I was in prison for ten years, rather than the guy getting a piece of ass pretty much whenever I wanted to.

She moaned softly, and my automatic response was, "Oh, fuck."

My mouth found its way to her nipple, sucking through her tank, this time forcing a verbal response from her. "Oh, my God."

Then it was mouths colliding. She pressed against me, locking her legs around my ass as she slid off the counter, bringing her heat to my hardness. Aware her back would take the pressure of the counter edge I circled her with one arm, placing it between us as I dipped and rose against her writhing body.

"God, yes." Her muscles gripped me tighter, and she threw her head back, offering her throat.

Through the fog of lust in my brain, the idea intruded. Every minute we continued like this was an opportunity for Jamie to find us.

Fuck. Responsibility sucks. And she feels and tastes so good. I pressed against her harder and faster.

But you don't want to hurt her again. That did not feel good in the least.

I extended my arm that was against the counter and brought the other hand lower, under her ass to support her, working my mouth away. "We have to stop, Grace."

"Mmm?" She continued kissing my neck, which was driving me crazy, so much so I thought I may rip her countertop off. "Why the hell would we want to do that?"

I closed my eyes. Thoughts of various things I'd like to do with her and to her made it increasingly hard to focus. "Oh, God. I'm not sure."

But she stopped, laying against my chest. "You're right." She blew out air. Releasing her feet and dropping to the ground. "Oh, my God, what was I thinking?"

I held her against me. "You were thinking the same thing I was thinking. How good it would feel."

"Yes, but he's my brother. I should be the one stopping it." She frowned. "Should it concern me you were the one stopping it?"

I chuckled. "I think you can feel how turned on I am."

She moved back, leaning against the counter and dropping her head. "I'm sorry. I shouldn't have started that." She pulled her tank back into place.

I snatched her shirt and my sweater from the floor. "Do *not* apologize for that." I dove in, trapping her against the counter again, throwing our clothes behind her and nibbled on her earlobe. "You gave me all sorts of things to fantasize about when I get back to the hotel." I nuzzled her. She smelled good. Like what it would smell like if a light breeze was blowing and we were crushing wildflowers under our sweaty bodies in a damned meadow. I was seconds away from abandoning my show of willpower and carrying her off to the bed-room.

"You have to leave?"

"I think I should. Don't you?"

Say no. I'm begging you.

Her gaze darted around the kitchen before coming to rest on my face. "Probably. But I don't want you to leave."

"I don't want to leave either."

She closed her eyes, then spun and took my sweater off the counter, handing it to me with a sigh.

I stretched it on over my head, watching her the whole time. I took her hand and kissed it. Then I moved toward the door, while still holding on to her. She stopped abruptly. "Zane?" When I turned I was surprised to see how pained her expression looked.

I pushed her hair back behind her shoulder. "What?"

"I probably shouldn't even ask you for this. You did so much al-ready."

Don't you know I'd do anything for you right now? I thought about saying it out loud, but I didn't want to freak her out by pressing her too far too fast.

"I...uh...I'm feeling kind of...raw right now. I haven't talked about that night in a long time. Could you maybe lay with me on the couch for maybe...fifteen minutes? I just.... Would you hold me?"

I pulled her into my arms for a moment. Then led her to the couch and lay on my side, scootching back as far as I could. She mim-icked my position, curling her hands under her face. I lifted onto my elbow and ran my fingers along her hair, again tucking it behind her shoulder. I leaned to put my cheek next to hers. I wanted to tell her I loved her, but I didn't want her to respond when she was feeling vul-nerable right now and it may paint her words. Still, the words kept ringing through my mind. She relaxed, but didn't close her eyes.

"Grace?"

"You have to go, don't you?" She started to get up, and I gathered her in tighter.

"No. But I think we might have a problem."

She rolled onto her back and studied me. "What?"

I again played with her hair, then kissed her softly on the corner of her lips before pulling back, my gaze raking her face. "I think I'm falling in love with you."

She lifted her palm to my cheek, peering at me with a concentrated look. She kissed me gently at first then slowly, deeply. We continued for some time, a controlled tease of mouth and tongue, sucking and nibbling on each other's lips. My arm began to cramp, so I tried to shift my weight without jostling her.

"Lay on me."

I tilted my head. "Do you think we should tempt fate that much?"

"I want to feel your weight on me. Then just five more minutes and you can go."

I shifted to cover her and renewed our kissing, keeping myself under control. It was totally new to me and fucking awesome. I didn't move against her body, though I wanted to. And it wasn't any five minutes either. I think it went on for at least twenty minutes, and still it was too short. We both knew when it was time to quit. She had one hand resting languidly on the back of my neck, the other held up to trace my lips with a finger. "I should let you go."

I fell back against the couch and she rolled, getting to her feet.

At the door I asked, "When can I see you again?"

"Do you have to leave town?"

"Not yet."

She smiled. "Tomorrow I only work a half day. Noon 'til four. I could make dinner for us?"

I patted the outsides of her arms. "Not after working all afternoon. How about some Arris'?"

She cocked a hip. “I thought you said it wasn’t as good as your St. Louis pizza?”

I kissed her. “I did. But you like it, so we’re having it.” I drew her in. “Will you sleep all right?”

“Yes. I’m pretty tired now. Thank you for staying.”

I separated from her enough to look down into her face. “I don’t know if you noticed, but it wasn’t like you had to beg me, beautiful.”

I had a weird feeling on the way to the hotel. I think people call it contentment and peace.

CHAPTER NINE

Zane

I texted her before I even took Whitney to breakfast. I imagined Grace in her kitchen, in her robe, stirring pancake mix, and it filled me with warmth.

GOOD MORNING, BEAUTIFUL! HOW ARE YOU THIS MORNING?

DID YOU SLEEP WELL? HAVING A GOOD START TO YOUR DAY?

I got her response within seconds.

SLEPT LIKE A ROCK, THANKS TO YOU. <3

I smiled, and put my phone down, then picked it up and looked at it again. She didn't say anything about how her morning was going.

Ehh. I'm probably reading too much into it.

After breakfast with Whitney, I gave her a kiss goodbye and watched her drive off, grateful for our time together, but missing her already.

I checked my phone. No messages from Grace. Not that I expected any, but... I shook my head at my own foolishness and decided to text her.

HOW'S JAMIE DOING TODAY?

I went back to my room, dug a spiral out of my suitcase and worked on a song idea. After about an hour, though, the room was making me crazy, so I went down and hung out in the wide open lobby, which worked for a while. The fountains provided the right kind of white noise to enhance my creativity. But she hadn't answered and it was like a pebble in a tennis shoe, irritating the heck out of me.

IS EVERYTHING OKAY?

This time I got a reply right away.

> SORRY. WE HAD A RATHER ROCKY MORNING HERE. LEXI, MY REGULAR SITTER, FELL AND BROKE HER ARM AND I HAVEN'T FOUND ANYONE ELSE. I MAY HAVE TO RESORT TO PAYTON, GOD HELP US. AND, ON TOP OF THAT, JAMIE'S IN MOURNING OVER WHITNEY BEING GONE.

I smiled. I could hear her voice in the words.

> WELL, I'M NO LEXI, AND I'M CERTAINLY NOT ON THE WHITNEY LEVEL, BUT I THINK I COULD BE BETTER THAN PAYTON. I'D LOVE TO SPEND SOME TIME WITH JAMIE TODAY.

There was a slight delay this time.

I DON'T THINK I CAN ASK YOU TO DO THAT.

I sent my reply.

> YOU DIDN'T ASK, I VOLUNTEERED. AND I'M SERIOUS, I'M LOSING MY MIND HERE AND WOULD REALLY LOVE TO DO SOME COLORING.

After a brief pause, I could see she was typing.

PAYTON'S ACTUALLY ON A BUSINESS TRIP (ONE HAS THOSE WHEN ONE'S A RECEPTIONIST? I THINK SHE HAS A GUY AT HER PLACE.) SO, I'M KIND OF DESPERATE....

I closed the spiral and got to my feet.

ON MY WAY.

SHE ANSWERED THE DOOR in a sexy outfit that was part suit, part dress. A solid blue/gray number with a flap like a suit coat, buttoning on the side with two large buttons. Her hair was swept up today with a few wispy curls falling around her face.

"Whoa." I took her hands, spreading them out wide so I could check out the attire. I whistled. "There are many facets to the woman who is Grace Clayton Prescott."

She blinked. "Did I tell you my full name at some point?"

"I think it was mentioned. Plus I did some stalking of you before I came to good ol' J.C." I gave her a kiss. "Something special going on at the shop today?"

"Actually, I'm giving a talk at the Chamber of Commerce about being a small business owner. I'm kind of nervous, to tell you the truth. I don't like being in front of people."

"Unless it's with a handsome hunk of a rock star like me, right?"

"Right. I hope there's one in the audience."

I chuckled. "You'll be great."

"Hey, Jamie." I called over her shoulder. "Is it time for Giant Fish Dude yet?"

He wagged his head. "Oh, Zaner. It's Big Fish Man, not Giant Fish Dude."

"Oh, yeah." I winked at Grace. She passed me a two-page, stapled instruction sheet. I glanced at it. "You are coming back, tonight, right?"

"Yes, I'm coming back. If you have any questions, my phone number's on the bottom."

I skimmed through the material. "I texted you this morning, remember?"

"Oh. Yeah. You're right."

"And, I'm not sure if I'll need the social security information listed in Addendum C." I smirked.

She put a hand on her hip. "Are we going to have to talk on the fire escape again?"

"Zaner!"

"What? I didn't do anything." I said to Jamie. Then I looked at her. "I'll take good care of him. I promise." I lowered my voice. "One pack limit to the cigarettes, only clear alcohol, and a maximum of two prostitutes at a time."

"You're going to go on the fire escape," Jamie warned.

I frowned, turning to him. He was shaking a finger at me.

I twisted back to face Grace.

"Did I ever tell you he has exceptional hearing?"

"No. But it's probably listed in the manifesto."

She grinned, coming closer. "You think you're so cute."

"I am, aren't I? I dressed to kill today in my white T-shirt and jeans."

She stuck a finger in my waistband between us, where Jamie couldn't see. "Don't underestimate the power of a tight pair of jeans and a snug T."

"Mmm." I kissed her, rubbing her arms. "Hey, Jamie, I'm walking your sister to the door real quick."

Her eyes sparked.

"You just want to kiss her some more."

I raised my brows and she pulled me into the hall. "How does he know so much?"

"It's a mystery, even to me. Now. You better give me a kiss to remember you by, not like those weak ones inside."

I held her hand up, and indicated I wanted her to spin under it, then I took her into a deep dip and laid one on her. When I separated from her, she kept her eyes shut for a moment. "That'll do," she said in a squeaky voice. She strutted her sweet suit-wearing ass down the stairs, knowing full well I was watching, then backed through the door while fanning herself.

That girl is a menace. She gets me revved then walks away. Well, she won't walk away tonight, I guarantee it.

When I went to twist the doorknob and let myself back in, the pitter-patter of little feet running to the couch caught my ear. I threw the door open and, strangely enough, Jamie was bouncing on the couch as if he just jumped on it. He quickly righted himself.

"Jamie, were you listening in on our conversation?"

He scratched his head. "Big Fish Man is in the Amazon today."

I squinted at him. "Uh-huh."

The kid's WAY smarter than I give him credit for.

I decided to let it ride for the moment and joined him on the couch.

About two o'clock he was climbing the walls. It was a good chance it had something to do with the three ice cream sandwiches he conned me out of. He was very convincing. If he could have remembered case law, he would have made a damn good lawyer. As it was, car salesman seemed to be his career path.

"Why don't we go on a little walk? It's nice out today."

"Can we go fishing, too?"

"Uhh...let me text Grace and see if she's okay with it." Thirty minutes later, when Grace hadn't texted back I figured she was in her presentation and turned the ringer off. "Does Grace take you fishing?"

He nodded vigorously.

I knew zip about fishing, but how hard could it be? "Well, she's probably fine with it, so let's go."

The fact I managed to hook myself—resulting in a scratch and a ripped shirt—before we even left the house, should have been a red flag. But Jamie was so excited, I couldn't let him down. I grabbed another T out of the back of my car where, thankfully, I had my second duffle bag. Jamie told me he knew his way to the park, but...not so much. Luckily an older gentleman steered us in the right direction and we soon had hooks in the water.

"Zane, can I ask you a question?"

"Sh-sure. It must be serious. You didn't call me Zaner."

He nodded solemnly. "How do you kiss a girl?"

"Whoa, whoa, whoa. This is a conversation you should have with your sister."

He wrinkled his forehead. "What does she know about kissing girls?"

Kid had a point.

"Grace likes it when you kiss her."

My gaze darted to him. "She does? Did she...uh...tell you that, buddy?"

"Nope. I can tell."

"Mmm. I see." I was pussyfooting around this one for sure. "Well, first off—and this is very important—you have to know the girl wants to kiss you."

He bobbed his head. "How do you know if she wants to kiss you?"

I wouldn't delve into the subtle nuances of body language with a seven-year-old, or however old he was. "Well...it's always good to ask.

Just, you know, say something like, 'I'd like to kiss you. Would you be okay with that?'"

"Okay."

I thought I was off the hook, like the fish in the pond who didn't seem interested in our Cheetos bait.

"So, if she said yes, how do you *do* it?"

"Uhh...." My palms began to sweat. "Well, I guess it's best to do it soft and gentle."

He smiled. "I can do that."

"Good. Who are you planning on kissing, by the way?"

"Somebody pretty."

Never hurts. I was fairly sure he was talking about Whitney, because earlier he asked what her favorite flower was. I was going to need to warn both her and Grace about this.

I felt pressure on my rod. I looked out over the water. My bobber was gone.

"Zaner. You've got a bite."

I'd never fished before, so I admit, I was pretty excited. "What do I do?"

"You set the hook."

"How do I do that?"

"Like this." He did a quick jerk on his rod, and I followed suit.

"Now what?"

He made a motion. "Reel him in. Reel him in."

I cranked on the handle, and Jamie jumped around near the water's edge.

"That's it. Keep going. You got it. Now, go slow, and put the tip of your rod down. Good. Good. Now lift it."

When I raised the rod, the most beautiful little fish was on the end. It was blue on top and the blue kind of melted into green. The middle was plain, but the bottom was gold. "Is it a rainbow trout?"

He shook his head with a somber expression. "Sunfish."

"Cool." I considered him. "You're a smart kid."

"I know."

And modest, too. I grinned at him. "Now what?"

"Now you take him off the hook."

"Oh, okay." I didn't want to seem like too much of an idiot, so I acted like I knew what I was doing. I grabbed the line and let the end of the pole rest on the ground. I tried to grab the fish, but he was flopping around. "Oh. Lively little sucker, isn't he?" Jamie looked at me with one eye squinted and the same side of his mouth screwed up as if he'd lost all confidence in me. I forced a chuckle and tried again, going in slowly. The damn thing writhed again when I got close, and his fins were sharp. I snatched my hand back, biting down on the expletive tickling my tongue.

"That's not how Gracie does it."

Thanks for telling me now, kid.

I frowned, determined to get this fish off on my own. Maybe if I attacked from the head to tail. This time not only did the fin get me, the hook did, too. I shook my hand. "Oww, oww, oww."

"That's not how Gracie does it," he said again in a singsong voice.

I cocked a hip, staring at him.

"Do you want me to tell you how she does it?"

"That would be nice."

"She loops the line over the rod and pulls the fish all the way to the top."

I held the fish on the opposite side of my rod and circled it with the line. "Like this?"

"Yep. Then bring it all the way up to the rod."

I followed his instructions, wondering how this would work, and if he even had it right. The next thing I knew, the fish was off the hook and floundering across the grass.

"Uh-oh."

What now? "What?"

"You're supposed to do it over the water. He'll die out here."

"Oh." I got near it and kicked it lightly in the direction of the pond. The stupid son-of-a-bitch thrashed around until he was back almost to where he began. Jamie wailed.

"He's going to die."

It's only a fish.

But I knew it was much more than that to him. I approached it again and tried to move it with my foot faster, so it wouldn't have time to squirm backward. On my second attempt the damn thing landed on my boot. I raised it, juggling it like I was playing hacky sack. Lifting and kicking at the same time I was able to toss him in a long arc to the water. He splashed and swam away. It was cool to watch him do it, since he was so near the surface.

"You did it, Zaner." He latched onto my side. "I'm so proud of you."

I ruffled his hair. I was certain he'd heard those words on many occasions come out of Grace's mouth. "I caught my first fish."

"You mean you never fished before?" he asked, wide-eyed.

"Nope. My stepfather wasn't much of a fisher."

And even if he were, he'd never take me.

"So that's why you're so bad at it."

I scowled. It seemed being with a kid kept you humble.

GRACE

I was walking back to my car, congratulating myself on getting through the talk without either passing out or throwing up, and he was there, leaning against it. My heart convulsed. "What are you doing here?" I scanned the lot to see if anyone else was around, but it was empty.

"I think the real question is why are you letting some strung out rocker watch Jamie?"

Anger edged out fear. "A. He's not strung out, and B. It's none of your business."

He clenched his hands, and the fear nudged out the anger again. He clearly had gone by my place and somehow found me here. "You are my business, Grace. And anyone who belongs to you."

"Why did you come here? Why, after four years, did you decide it was time to come harass me? Shouldn't you be at work?"

"You ask too many damn questions, Grace." He exhaled. "I got fired from my job when they found out I wasn't sick the day I came here. And I caught your little dance number on YouTube. In the comment section they mentioned you owned a flower shop in Jefferson City, so I came because I want you back. Then I find you whoring around with Zane Sanders." He took some steps forward. I retreated. His voice was razor sharp. "I mean, what the hell?"

"Brad, we ended things."

"No. You ran away."

"Yeah. After you hit Jamie. I would never let that happen again. *Never.*"

"I don't know who the hell you think you are. You can't run out on somebody and BOOM, it's over."

I was getting closer to the building. If I ran now, could I reach someone before he grabbed me?

A car honked and he turned his head. I took the momentary distraction and broke into a run. Before I took a half-dozen steps, my ankle rolled again. It hurt, but I knew whatever he would do would hurt more. The back part of the building was brick, but the front had windows. If I could pound on the windows....

I got one solid knock in before he grabbed me and threw me against the bricks. I screamed. Surely I was close enough for someone to hear. He covered my mouth with his hand.

What the hell are you thinking? It's broad daylight.

He always was aggressive, but he was careful in how he did it. This wasn't careful. We waited, but no one came.

"They probably thought a bird hit their window." He chuckled, his face so close I could count the veins in his eyes. "You'll pay for what you did to me. And it's gonna come at a high price. You can say goodbye to what you love most."

He shoved away from me and walked quickly toward the parking lot. I leaned against the building, a few tears of relief sliding out. I waited until my shaking calmed some, and walked to the car. I called a lawyer. I took the rest of the day off so I could meet him at his office and fill out the paperwork needed to file a restraining order. After I finished there, it was almost time for me to be off, so I went home a little early. I wanted to be by Zane. Even sitting on the couch next to him would make me feel more relaxed. But I wasn't going to tell him what happened. It was my problem and I would take care of it. I trudged up the stairs to my place, bone-weary. I took a deep breath and pressed on a smile. But when I went to put the key in the lock, I could tell the deadbolt wasn't turned.

Odd.

I opened the door and called out, "Hi. I'm home." They weren't on the couch. I wondered what they were doing. "Jamie? Zane?' When I got no answer, my heart began to race. I told myself not to jump to any conclusions, to relax, but even so, my calls became more urgent. "Zane? Jamie where are you?" They weren't in Jamie's bedroom. The place wasn't that big. Brad's words came back to me. *You'll pay. Say goodbye to what you love most.*

Oh, my God. He came here. I should have called and warned Zane.

When I rushed back to the living room I saw Zane's ripped and bloody shirt.

"Oh, God. No." He took Jamie and Zane. *Why? Why would he target them and not me? This has nothing to do with them.* I clutched the shirt to my chest and had to grab onto the back of a chair for support, because my knees went out from under me. *I need to call the police.*

I jumped when the door swung open. "Zane!" I was nearly hysterical. Jamie wasn't with him. "Where's Jamie? Where's Jamie?"

Zane turned and called down the stair. "Come on up, bud." He looked at me, then immediately set a pair of fishing rods by the door. Jamie bolted in the door behind him.

"Jamie!" I held my arms out and he rushed into them. I clutched him to me and closed my eyes. I had to pull it together. I didn't want to scare him, but I was shaking and having trouble breathing. Zane approached and I went crazy and shouted at him. "How could you do this to me? You took him without telling me?"

"I...we...I texted you. And I left you a note on the kitchen table. What's going on, why are you upset?"

"You—" My head was spinning. I was being ridiculous, but the adrenaline surging through my veins was making me lose it. "You can't just go somewhere and not let me know. I was scared. Damn it. I was scared."

He approached me like he was approaching a wild animal. "That's pretty clear."

Jamie pulled his head back and peered at me with wide eyes. "Gracie. You cursed."

"I know. I'm sorry." I looked up at Zane and couldn't hold back the tears anymore. I held my arm out to him. "I'm sorry. I shouldn't have yelled at you."

He got on his knees and put one hand on Jamie's back, one on mine. "Did something happen? Why are you home early? I'm sorry you were scared, but we're here safe and sound. Did you not trust me to take care of Jamie?"

"No. I thought he—" I stopped myself. "I...uhh—your shirt. Your shirt was torn and bloody."

"You thought he...who?" He stared at the shirt in my lap. "It's torn, yes, but I wouldn't say bloody. It has some spots of blood...I hooked myself, is all." He scrutinized me. "This reaction seems a little disproportionate to the circumstances."

I scrubbed the tears off my face. "I know. You're right. I'm sorry. It's just...it's been a long day." I got to my feet.

"What aren't you telling me?"

"Nothing. Nothing."

"You're lying, Grace." He was angry. "I only took the boy—" He went to gesture to the rods, but when he raised his arm, I flinched. It was a kneejerk reaction. My nerves were shot. "Why did you just do that?"

"I-I...." I didn't know what to say.

"Fire escape."

"Wh-what?" I sputtered. "You can't call fire escape. You don't live here."

He glanced at Jamie. "There's rules to this?"

Jamie shrugged. "We don't let Payton—"

He whirled back to me. "We can discuss this here..." he put his hand on Jamie's head to emphasize his point. "...or we can discuss it on the fire escape."

I studied Jamie, who was looking from Zane to me. I snapped my gaze back to Zane. "Fine." I fluttered my arm in the general direction of the TV. "Jamie, you can turn on the animal channel." When I took a step toward the kitchen, pain speared through me, and I took a breath in through my teeth.

Zane observed me with concern. "The ankle?"

I nodded, shuffling forward and grabbing onto the top of a kitchen chair.

"Should we wrap it again?"

I considered it. "Probably."

He pulled out a chair. "Let's talk in here. We'll keep it low."

I nodded and gratefully fell into a chair. Zane opened a drawer and took the Ace bandage out. He rooted around before addressing me. "Baggies?"

I lifted my chin. "Next one down."

I took a glimpse at the piece of pink paper on the table. It was from my grocery list pad.

> HEY! HOPE YOU HAD A GOOD DAY! I BET YOU KNOCKED THEIR SOCKS OFF AT THE CHAMBER OF COMMERCE. I'M LEAVING THIS IN CASE YOU DIDN'T GET MY TEXT AND YOU BEAT US HOME. WE WENT FISHING BUT WILL BE BACK SOON. ~ ZANE

He did leave a note. I was an idiot for freaking out.

He filled the baggie with ice, wrapped a towel around it, and came to the table. He pulled over another chair. "Here." He carefully raised my foot and put it on the chair. "Ooh. Yeah. It looks swollen. Let's ice it for a little bit then we'll wrap it." He laid his hands on my leg. "Are you okay? Do you want a glass of water?"

My throat was dry. "Yes, please."

He didn't say anything else until he gave me the glass of water. I took a long drink. He lowered his voice. "Grace...did you really think I would hit you?"

"No. No. It was...reflexive. That's all."

He leaned closer. "See, I don't think it's that at all. I think it's a learned response."

I didn't have the energy to argue with him. I sat staring at my lap.

"Has a man...hit you?"

"I don't really want to talk about this."

"Well, that's too damned bad, because we're talking about it. I bet it was that douchebag Brad, wasn't it?"

I raised my gaze to his without saying anything. He jumped to his feet. "That son-of-a-bitch!"

"Zane!"

"Why were you losing it today when we got home? Has he threatened you?" He came closer and hissed. "Threatened to hurt Jamie? You need to tell me, Grace."

Tears built again. "He said he would make me pay for leaving him. That he would take away what I loved most. And then when you weren't here...and your shirt...."

He came over to me and squatted, putting a hand on the side of my face. "Hey. Hey. It's okay. I won't let anyone hurt you or Jamie. You have my word. I'd die first." He ran his gaze down my leg. "How did you re-hurt your ankle? Did you see him today?"

I nodded my head rapidly. Now that he knew, I needed to tell someone. "He was waiting for me at the Chamber of Commerce."

"Did he touch you?"

I froze. I didn't want him to go seek some sort of stupid revenge.

"Grace, did that man hit you?"

"No. He didn't hit me."

"But he did touch you. What did he do?"

I glanced up. It seemed like Jamie was engrossed in his movie. "I tried to run away from him and twisted my ankle again."

"Mm-hmm. And then what happened?"

I sighed. "He grabbed me and slammed me against the wall."

He straightened and walked a few feet away, turning his back and putting his hands on his hips. He was staring at the ceiling for some reason. "I'll kill him."

Shit. "See, this is why I didn't tell you."

He spun on his heel and came back toward me. "If I ever see that man, I'll rip his head off and shove it up his ass."

"Uhh...interesting choice, but can you lower your voice? You're going to scare Jamie."

He stared at me with his hands on his hips, and without turning, called out, "Jamie. Are you scared, bud?"

"Nope. I want to rip his head off, too."

"Jamie!" I was shocked, but a little amused, too. "See what you're teaching him."

"I'll have you know I taught him all sorts of things. Jamie, how are you supposed to kiss girls?"

"Soft and gentle."

"See?" Zane said smugly.

"Or hard and dirty."

Zane's eyes widened. "He was listening to us. I did not teach him that. I swear."

I had to laugh. I really liked Zane's sexy nerdy look with his glasses, his jackets, his ties and the suspenders he wore yesterday. It was unusual in a community—the rock world—where the dress code was quite different.

Zane frowned, casting a glance toward the living room. "That little stinker." He pulled out a chair and sat, now animated. "You know what else he said to me today?"

I was relieved the subject changed. "What?"

"When I told him I've never gone fishing before, he—"

"Wait. You've never been fishing?"

"It's not like it's mandatory for every American citizen to go fishing. So when I said that he said, 'So that's why you're so bad at it.'"

I covered my mouth with my hand to hide my laughter.

"Oh, so you think it's funny."

"Yeah. Kind of."

He hung his head.

"I'm sorry. He can be quite blunt."

"No kidding." He lifted his gaze and studied me. "Listen. You had a long and sucky day. I'm calling for pizza, but we're talking about this later."

"I did file for a restraining order, after."

"You did?"

I nodded.

"Well, that's good. I'm staying here tonight, by the way. I'll stay on the couch, but no way am I leaving you guys alone here."

I reached for his face. "Has anyone ever told you you're sweet for a rock star?"

He chuckled. "No. No one's ever said that to me."

I gave him a quick kiss. "Well, you are.

CHAPTER TEN

Zane

We had a nice evening of pizza, puzzles, and the planet, and by that I mean Animal Planet. Working with Jamie on the puzzles was the first time I really saw his difficulties, beyond his general childlike behavior. Grace was so patient with him. She was amazing in any number of ways, and I was only starting to discover that.

I was still seething inside about that man laying a hand on her, but I tried to keep it hidden. The thought of her being afraid...it made everything inside me hot and tight. But, between that asshat Brad and myself, she'd certainly had enough drama lately. I didn't want her to have to worry for one evening, so I tried to make things as pleasant as possible.

While she was putting Jamie to bed, I cleaned up a little. I ran out of things to do before she got back, so when she came in, I was sitting on the couch musing.

"He probably nodded off before I even got out of the room. He was fighting it hard. I'll come sit by you in a moment. I only want to...." She surveyed the room. "Did you clean in here?"

"Yeah. A little."

"Well, I'll just...." She stuck her head in the kitchen. "You cleaned the kitchen, too?"

I rolled a shoulder. "There wasn't much to do."

"Well aren't you the best little rock star ever?" She crossed to me and sat on my lap. "You sure know the way to a girl's heart."

I smiled, kissing her. "I have other ways, too."

She touched her fingertips to my chin on either side. "Oh, I bet you do." She gave me one solid kiss, then eased back, running a finger along my lip. "Jamie's asleep now." She stretched back on the couch like we were doing a dip again. "You know what that means?" She crooked a finger at me and I climbed on top of her. "It means you can kiss me...hard and dirty." That wonderful, wicked, million-dollar grin spread across her face. She laced her fingers into the back of my hair and drew me into a searing kiss. And just like that, she had me amped and ready for anything she wanted, and I hoped she wanted a lot.

I scrounged up some willpower from somewhere, and pulled my lips from hers. "Are you sure you're not trying to make me forget about the talk we're supposed to have?"

"No, that's what I am trying to do. Is it working?"

"Damn straight it is." I buried my head in her hair, nuzzling her and she ran her nails down my back, finding the tail of my shirt and trying to lift it. I extended my arms to get to my knees and rip it off. I whipped it to the ground and fell back over her, running my tongue along her neck and cruising over her collarbone, down to the buttons on her shirt. I would make this last. I know most people would wait longer to be intimate with someone, but being without a woman for several days didn't happen with the life we led, and it felt like I'd waited a lifetime to be with Grace.

"Wait. We shouldn't do this." Who said that? Was it me? I sat.

"Oh, no, we should." She scrambled up and straddled me, sliding my glasses from my face and setting them on the end table. "We definitely should."

"What if Jamie were to walk in on us? We shouldn't do it here."

"But we should do it, right?"

"Hell, yeah." I lifted her from my lap, grabbed my shirt, then reached back to take her hand. "Come on."

We tiptoed past Jamie's door like cat burglars and went to the end of the hall. I took the knob to her room, but turned back. "I guess I should ask you if it's okay if I enter your bedroom before I barge in. Is it okay?"

"Oh, yeah."

I swept her into my arms, kissing her as I backed into the room. I got déjà vu from the night we brought her home, drunk, but this was a much better circumstance. I threw her on the bed, peeled off my jeans and joined her. I half unbuttoned her, half pulled the buttons out of their holes. She had a beautiful teal bra on, with black lace. Too bad she wouldn't be wearing it long. She was way more built than I had given her credit for. But it was simply a bonus. She could be as flat as my guitar, and it wouldn't matter. I got on my knees and she ripped through unbuttoning and unzipping her jeans and slid out of them. Holy shit, was her body perfect.

But I had to remind myself normal people took things slow. And I wanted her to know this time was different.

"Grace, I know I should take this slow. But I'm not good at this. I've never done it." I shifted so I was on my side, propped by my elbow. To be honest, I was nervous. Zane Sanders, gun shy. "But I want to try. I think we have something here. Something special. And I want to make sure before we do anything you could regret, that you're ready."

"I was ready the moment you pulled me out of that audience."

In some respects, that made me feel better. In others, it made me wonder if she was taking this as seriously as I was. I kissed her then ran my gaze over her body again. "You're so damned beautiful, Grace. I'm afraid to touch something so perfect."

She led me to her breast. "But I need you to touch me, Zane." She looked at me with such longing. "I need you."

I was determined this time would be different, because I was different. I was...happy with her. I slowly brought my head to her chest, kissing the side of her breast and pouring my heart into everything I did. It was more like worship than sex. My hand skimmed over her stomach. It aroused me, too. Velvety skin, the indention of her waist, her belly button...I could spend a half hour kissing her only there, but I sensed Grace's impatience. I wouldn't let her hurry me, though.

She moaned, her lips turning up when she asked, "Is this sex or torture?"

I brought my mouth to her ear and nibbled on her lobe. "Both."

"Ooh."

I took her mouth again. Soft, languid kisses meant to pull her to me little by little. At some point, she quit fighting me and gave in, synching with my rhythm. Kissing me in the same measured manner, a tease, but a tease with a promise to make good eventually. I nibbled along her jaw and she breathed softly, with her eyes closed. I cupped her breast, molded it with care then brushed my thumb over her silky bra, feeling her nipples, hard, beneath my fingers, separated by the fabric. I licked a finger then traced the top of her bra with it.

"Oh, my God." She grabbed my face and kissed me. "You're making me crazy."

I smiled. That's what I wanted. I wanted her to beg me to satisfy her and then bring her the most intense gratification to make up for the wait. We left the light on, which I was immensely grateful for. I released her bra where it clasped in the front and she shrugged out of it.

I reconsidered my idea of taking it slow.

I had to get those breasts away from me if I had any hope of staying in control. "Turn over."

She looked at me curiously for a second, then did what she was told. I straddled her, without putting my full weight on her and moved her hair to one side so I could kiss her neck. She moaned. I cruised along her shoulder blades to the small of her back, alternately sinking my teeth in and rolling my tongue over her skin. With each new place I discovered on her body, I wondered at the genius of a woman's design. All those luscious dips and curves, each one inviting me to taste her. I rolled her underwear off and pitched them aside then gave my full attention to her fabulous round ass, kissing and caressing it. She kicked her head back and clenched her pillowcase in each fist.

So you like that, do you?

I memorized each place I produced a reaction from her, and hoped I'd have many more opportunities to reveal new sensitive spots.

I moved to the side and urged her onto her back, starting again at her neck. "I could do this all night." I grazed the backs of my fingers across her stomach, playing her like I played my guitar. "Do you want more?"

"You're going to make me beg, aren't you?"

"Often and loudly. But not too loudly, because we don't want to wake Jamie."

"Of course. I'll keep my pleading low key."

I chuckled. I loved that she was playful. I moved on top of her, stretching her arms up to grip the ornate wrought iron headboard. "These stay here and here only." With a grin, I slid down her body, stopping to breathe on her nipples then lightly brush my lips over them, which made her writhe and whimper. Low laughter shook my chest. "I'm only getting started."

"You're evil."

I licked the inside of her thigh.

"Oh! And so good at it." One of her hands came to my shoulder. I captured her wrist. "Ah-ah-ah. Now I have to begin all over." She moaned. I kissed the inside of her wrist, then worked my way up to the elbow, which really set her off. I wrapped my fingers over hers on the bedpost. "Now keep it here. If you're good, I will reward you."

She squeezed her eyes shut and I took the opportunity to surprise her and closed my mouth around her nipple, sucking hard. She inhaled sharply. I released it and moved to the other side, lazily circling her nipple with my tongue, then lapping at it a couple of times before sucking.

"Oh, yeah. That."

This teasing her was equally torturous for me. I was so hard for her. I left her breast and she breathed in deeply, relaxing from her straining against me.

We can't have that.

I rolled to the side and she started to reach for me. I shook a finger. "Put it back." She did with a frown. I wouldn't make her wait much longer. Couldn't. I leaned over her to whisper in her ear. "I'm going to make love to you until your fucking legs are Jell-O..." I put my hand between her thighs and alternately stroked and slid my finger inside her. She was so ready for me I stifled a moan. "...and you can't even remember your own name." She sighed then panted, her face scrunched up as she recovered from the stimulation.

"Do your arms hurt? You can put them down now."

"When do I get to torture you?"

"Oh, believe me, you already are." I slid farther. "I want you, Grace. I want to fill you and please you, but first I want this." I dipped and flicked my tongue over her, then slipped my finger in again, moving it in and out more insistently.

She slapped her palm on my shoulder and dug her nails in. "Oh, God." Her panting increased, her calls pitching higher. Then she clutched my hair. "Oh, my gosh. That feels so good. ...Oh, Zane." She released, tilting her head back. I clamped my hand between her legs and moved my palm against her. I'd learned that prolonged things. "Oh. O-oh." I watched her until she came down, gasping for air, but with a smile on her face.

I reached for my jeans and pulled a condom out of my pocket. "This is always the awkward part."

She took it from me and sat. "It doesn't need to be." She put the end in her mouth and tore the packaging while looking at me. Who knew opening a condom could be so sexy? She removed it and grabbed me, carefully rolling it on then stroking me. I closed my eyes and breathed in. Yes, I wanted her to touch me, too. To know me. All of me.

But she was too good, and I didn't think I could hold on much longer. "Honey, unless you're ready for this to be over right now, you need to stop."

She smirked and slowly lay back. I straddled her on my knees but changed my plans and brought myself between her breasts. She shut her eyes and pressed her breasts in around me. I rocked against her, cozied in her bosom.

I sighed. "Oh, that's good."

This seemed to turn her on because she drew her knees in behind me and rocked her pelvis in time with me, both of us making noises of pleasure and desire. But I wanted to be one with her. I stopped my motion and fondled her gorgeous mounds, gently flicking her nipple while I squeezed her. I scooted back and she straightened her legs to accommodate me.

As I came to lie on top of her, I caught her off guard by taking a quick lick and suck at each breast, applying pressure with my teeth even as I brought myself up and into her. Then I had to stop so I could concentrate on how good it felt to bury myself in her. She sighed, too, then made some noises of surprise and pleasure as it seemed some new tremors ran through her. I kept my arms extended so I could watch her as I brought her to peak again, and moved my body forward, knowing the more contact I had with her, the more stimulated she would be. Instead of driving straight and hard, like I wanted to, I slowed again, dipping my hips and bringing them back in a fluid motion.

She arched her back, her need etched on her face as she called out to me and grabbed my ass, trying to bring me in even deeper. Slowly I increased the pace, writhing against her. I was barely holding on and wasn't sure if I would make it when she tensed around me and exclaimed. I rushed to finish so my completion would bring her to a still more exquisite ecstasy. Her muscles tightened, becoming like cables as she breathed through her climax.

"Oh! Oh, God, yes. Oh." She panted, melting into the bed, a puddle of relaxation in direct contrast to her total tension of moments before. She laughed, threading her fingers through my hair and pulling me to her chest. After a moment or two, she released me, still trying to catch her breath, and I withdrew from her—the breaking of our bond almost painful—and rolled off to the side.

I was breathing hard, also. We turned our heads on the pillows to look at each other. It was the first time I was driven to supply someone else's needs and it filled me with pleasure to know I had accomplished that.

"That was—" She broke into a huge smile. "Oh, my God...*amazing*."

I found the strength to rise a little. "You are amazing." I kissed her forehead and fell against her. This was new. This feeling of utter satisfaction—not simply physical. I was filled with warmth and a sensation of completeness. That hole inside of me, that edge of bitterness and the sorrow and anxiety of feeling lost and alone—she filled that, brought comfort to my soul, in a totally unfamiliar but welcome way.

Later, when we extinguished the light and pulled the covers up around us, I thought about how I could express what I was feeling to her. She was lying in my arms as I stroked her hair, my lips resting against her head. I had this overwhelming need to care for and treasure her. I never thought that could be me. I thought I was missing some essential gene.

She rolled onto her side, slinging her leg over me, lacing her fingers on my chest and planting her chin on them. "In the four years I lived here, I never once brought a man back to my place because of...what Brad did to me. I was scared, disappointed with life, disillusioned by what I thought was love." We left the bathroom light on with the door cracked, so I could make out her face. She was staring into my eyes, hers tearing. "You gave me the desire and the courage to change that."

It was sweet, and offered lovingly, but something pricked me about it. The "you gave me" and not "you're giving me." As if this was a one act show and I was about to exit stage left. Preoccupied by these thoughts I responded, "I'm glad I could be of assistance."

She chuckled, inching closer to kiss me. "You were of assistance. Numerous times, in fact."

Exhausted, we were both drifting off when Grace mumbled, "Zane?"

"Mmm."

"Are you laying like a four?" She tapped my foot with hers.

One of my knees was bent under my other leg which was straight. "Yes, I guess so."

"Me, too." Her words were getting slower. "We're a pair of fours." And she was out. Breathing evenly, with her foot touching mine.

I quirked a brow. "That's an interesting observation."

She rolled over and snuggled into my side. I played with her hair. I came so close to saying something, but the words stayed in my mouth. In the end I held her close and we fell asleep like that, with her draped across my chest, a smile on my lips.

Someone was shaking me.

Oh, shit. If she was all a dream I'm gonna be pissed.

"Shit. Zane, wake up. We can't let Jamie see you."

She was in full on freak out mode and it was adorable. "I shouldn't have done this." She covered her face with her hands and cried.

I sat and put my arm around her. "Come on, now. No one died. And no way will I regret a single thing I did last night. Not one second."

She stilled, brushing a tear away. "You're right."

She slayed me. "You know, honey...you're kind of high strung." I was trying to make her laugh.

"I know. I'm sorry."

"No, I like you that way."

She twisted her head to look at me. "You like that I'm a friggin' basket case?"

"Uh-huh. It takes the pressure off me to act sane." The light from the window made her hair glow. "You're fucking gorgeous in the morning." I furrowed my brow. "You know what? This is the first time I've ever woken up with a woman."

"Gracie? Where's Zaner?"

She stared at me with wide eyes, clutching the sheets to those fabulous breasts of hers. "I'm not ready to have that conversation with him yet."

"Okay. I'll go in the bathroom."

"Coming, Jamie."

When I came into the kitchen, Grace said a little too brightly. "Oh. Good morning, Zane."

"Yes, it is."

"Zaner!" Jamie jumped out of his chair and latched on to me.

I rubbed his hair. "How are you doing, buddy?"

"Good. Where were you?"

"Just in the bathroom."

"But I checked the bathroom."

Grace's gaze flew to mine, and I almost laughed at the look of sheer alarm on her face. "Oh. Then it must have been when I stepped outside to stretch. How many gajillion pancakes are we having this morning?"

"Six-hundred and sixty-three," Jamie responded brightly. He ran back to his chair. So far the only two gears I'd seen the kid in were full throttle and ignition off. I don't know how Grace did it.

"Whoa. Your poor sister's going to be worn out." He became engrossed again in his coloring. I stepped behind Grace and loosely held on to the counter on either side of her, leaning in to speak in her ear. "You're so not subtle."

She stuck her tongue out at me, and I had to laugh.

Jamie clicked his tongue. "Gracie," he said, warning her, "you're going to wind up on the fire escape."

The kid seemed to have a gajillion eyes in his head and supersonic hearing. Nothing got by him. He had to hear her moaning and calling out my name. The thought made me zone out for a minute as a few of the images flashed through my mind. I had to stop because I could feel myself becoming aroused. I stepped over behind Jamie to check out his work. It was a rain foresty scene. I shifted my attention to Grace after a minute or two. She was leaning against the counter, her stare unfocused, but the corners of her lips lifting. Our gazes connected and her smile grew. She had to be thinking about last night, too.

"Gracie, they're burning."

"What?" She turned. "Oh! Shoot." She spun with three blackened discs on the spatula she was holding, stepped on the trashcan's release, and pitched them. Jamie rolled his eyes then got back to work.

GRACE

Zane's phone buzzing made us all jump. He slid it out. "Jericho? At this time in the morning? I'm sorry. I better answer this."

"No problem." As he walked away, I watched his fine ass disappear. You'd think I had enough the night before.

I was actually a little sore. After Zane's excruciatingly slow seduction of the night before I'd fallen asleep on his chest. Somewhere around two a.m. I woke to Zane's head between my legs and we went for round two, which was harder and quicker and equally as delicious. He was incredible. In so many ways.

He was gone for quite a while. I didn't mean to eavesdrop on him, but I brought some scrambled eggs and bacon out for him so they wouldn't get cold.

"I know, man. All I'm asking for is a little more time. I'll finish it in time. I swear." He must have heard me, because he glanced over, changing the frown on his face to a smile. I set the plate and fork down in front of him. "Thanks, babe."

"You want pancakes," I whispered.

"Sure."

I went back into the kitchen and got another plate for his pancakes. He returned, setting his plate next to Jamie's and taking a chair. After breakfast Jamie was snuggled on the sofa watching a movie and Zane was helping me with the dishes. Sort of. He slid his hands around my waist and moved my hair so he could kiss my neck.

"I can't stop thinking about you."

"Zane, if I ask you a question, would you tell me the truth?"

"Depends on the question. And, by the way, this smells like a trap."

I spun, grabbing a towel so I could dry off. "Are we interfering with your work?"

"We who? Jamie and you? Absolutely not."

"Then, why did Jericho call?"

"Oh, he's being anal retentive." He stuffed his hands in his pockets.

I waited.

He rolled a shoulder. "The guys were hoping I finished the final song for our new album so we could practice it before the tour started and we could record it after it ends in a few weeks."

"And...is it done?"

A few noises came out of his mouth similar to language. "Practically."

"And by practically you mean...?"

He stared at the floor. "How's your ankle?"

I crossed my arms and narrowed my eyes. "Za-a-ane."

He shuffled his feet glancing down. "I have the chorus kind of written." He raised his head, wincing. "Damn it." His gaze shifted back and forth. "I have to go."

Even though I'd figured that out, is still hurt to hear it. I uncrossed my arms and turned back to the sink, trying to conceal how emotional I was. "I get it.

"No. You don't get it. I don't want to go."

I spun to study his face.

He shrugged. "I like it here."

Now the tears really threatened. "But you have responsibilities. You owe it to the band. And you owe it to your fans. And I don't want to get in the way of that." I exhaled, dropping my head as I realized the truth of my words. "You have too much talent for it to be squandered."

He put a fist under my chin and lifted it. "I don't want to squander this—" he gestured back and forth between us, "—either." He looked off to the side. "Let's go away for a couple of days."

"What?"

"Only a couple of days. Then I'll go back to the band and finish the album."

"But...." He didn't get that I couldn't leave at the drop of a hat. How I wished I could.

"You're worried about a sitter." He licked his lips. "I know you don't want to overuse Holly, but...I'd offer her any amount she wanted."

It would be good to get away with him. We had barely started to work things out between us. "She did tell me she was looking for some way to earn enough money to pay for her car repairs."

He jumped on it. "I'll pay for it all. Hell, I'll buy her a new car." He stepped up and put his hands on my shoulders. "I want to spend time with you." When I wavered, a smile shadowed his lips. He drew me in to speak in my ear. "Besides, I'd hate to forget all that information I learned last night about what turns you on."

Even though I knew he was playing me, I couldn't stop the quiver running through me. He held still, waiting. "Okay. I'll call her."

"Yes!" he shouted, squeezing me. "I just want a little more time with you before I have to leave."

CHAPTER ELEVEN

Grace

I couldn't believe I was going on a road trip with my own little rock star. Outside his usual environs, though, he was much more the regular guy than a rocker. Except when we karaoked. Totally a performer there. I smiled thinking about it and spaced out for a stretch. We were headed to Meramec Caverns. It was the only place he went with his family, and he visited it several times in high school with friends. It was funny to think since then he went all over the world with Just Short of Chaos.

Lights caught my attention. "Oh, no."

Zane sat up. "What?"

"I'm getting pulled over. Was I speeding? I don't feel like I was speeding."

"Maybe you have a signal light out or something."

"Well, we're about to find out." I lowered my window when the older, portly police officer approached. His younger, thinner partner got out, but held back on the rear passenger's side of the car. "Hi."

"Yes, ma'am. Can I see your license and registration, please?"

"Of course."

Zane fished through the glove box for me while the policeman waited. When I passed him my driver's license and the paperwork Zane gave me, I noticed the officer was staring at my chest. In fact, if he'd been a cartoon character he'd have been salivating. I frowned and pulled my dress in tighter and higher. Denied any view, he switched his attention to Zane, who urged his cap lower to avoid recognition.

"Umm...was I speeding, Officer?"

"Yes, ma'am. Didn't you see that sign back there that said the speed limit was dropped to thirty?"

"No. I didn't. I'm so sorry."

Zane cleared his throat and yawned loudly, stretching himself into a Y, hands above his head. When he caught me eying him, he mumbled, "Sorry."

When I twisted back, the officer was also looking at Zane, but he smiled and handed me back my stuff without writing anything on his ticket pad. "Just slow it down, now. Have a nice day." He marched back to his squad car.

My jaw dropped. "He didn't write me a ticket."

"No. Nice guy."

I checked my side view mirror. The man was reaching in his back pocket. He slid a wallet out and I could see him stuffing bills in it as he turned to open his door.

I gasped. "Did you bribe him?"

"Simply encouraged him to make the right decision."

"That's a bribe."

"I like to think of it more as...monetary persuasion."

"Still a bribe."

"Ya know," Zane leaned forward, peering out the windshield, "I think we're almost there."

"And I think you're changing the subject, Mister. If we were home, we'd be taking this discussion out on the fire escape."

As we pulled out, the police car followed suit, which wasn't remarkable. But when they continued to follow us for several miles, I worried we might have trouble. Maybe they were trolling for more money. I made certain I stayed within speed limits and used my turn signal appropriately.

I checked the rearview mirror. "Did it seem like that officer was—"

"Scoping out your tits? Definitely. If he didn't have that badge, I would have beat the shit out of him."

"Not to mention the gun," I said, trying to lighten the mood a little. I didn't want anything ruining our time together.

He nodded and cracked a smile, looking out his window. "Correct. The gun was also a deterrent."

I gave his hand a squeeze. "I'm sorry I was speeding and we wasted time being pulled over. And money. I'm usually not a speeder."

"Are you kidding? I thought you were crawling." He stared out his window again.

"Too slow for a rock star?"

"Too slow for a hundred-eighty-year-old nun."

I slapped his leg. "Hey."

He chuckled. "I was teasing you. You're much more like a ninety-five-year-old nun."

"Well, the reason I'm going slow now is because that cop's still behind us."

"I noticed," he murmured. A few minutes later he became alert. "This is starting to look familiar. You may want to be watching for a sign."

I glanced at the scenery. "Familiar? All I see is trees and more trees."

He didn't comment, but within minutes the GPS warned us of a turn, startling us as it hadn't spoken in a while.

I slowed. "Turn? Turn where? Into some trees?" But around the next bend I spotted a sign. "Meramec Caverns, here we come." Peeking in the mirror, my heart kicked up a notch or two. The police car followed. But I reasoned maybe that's why they never quit trailing us. This was their destination all along.

I parked, casting my gaze at my dress. For some odd reason, Zane asked me to wear a dress. Yet, I had to wear tennis shoes instead of heels. If he was taking me to a fancy meal, why couldn't I wear my heels? "Are you sure I can't wear jeans and a sweatshirt and change into the dress after the tour?"

"Yes, I'm sure," he grinned, but offered no explanation.

"I'm going to freeze my ass off," I mumbled. But I was smiling, too. Who didn't like a mystery destination? Although this is the first one I ever had....

He leaned over to give me a kiss. "I'll keep you warm, baby." I think we both had in mind what we were going to do in the privacy of our room at the bed and breakfast later.

"You better." For a moment, he took the kiss deeper and we had a mini make-out session leaving me wanting for more when he pulled away.

I exited the car and subtly checked the vicinity for the party who had trailed us when we came in.

"They're gone."

I guess I wasn't as subtle as I tried to be. I spun around.

He closed his door. "We lost them before we even came down the hill." He was referring to the winding path to the parking lot. He stretched then his eyes lit up. "Let's go." He grabbed my hand on the other side of the car.

This was the first time I spent a day without taking care of Jamie or the store. I love both...but the idea I was playing hooky energized me, and being with Zane made me happy. "Uhh...do you know if there are any restrooms?" We scanned the area. "Oh, wait. There's a sign. I'll be right back."

"I'll meet you at the cave entrance. I'll get the tickets."

"Let me give you some money."

He took off, waving his hand. "I got it."

I narrowed my gaze. This would not do. He needed to let me pay for some of it, at least. I had the money. But at the moment, the two Diet Pepsis I drank to keep me awake after a long night of making love to Zane were making me uncomfortable. He wasn't at the entrance when I got back.

Hmm...I wonder if there's a long line. Or maybe he decided to use the facilities, too.

After about fifteen minutes, when I was beginning to worry, he tapped me on the shoulder. "Sorry it took so long. I got you this." He gave me a blue Meramec Caverns zippered fleece jacket. "In case I'm not good enough to keep you warm."

I leaned in. "Oh, you're plenty good. Thank you. That was very thoughtful." I contemplated demanding I pay for dinner, but decided it wasn't the time. I donned the jacket, and not long after, our tour guide arrived. She started her presentation by telling us the caverns were a hideout for many. Reputedly Jesse James and his gang sheltered there, as well as runaway slaves making their way north. The original owner, who was described as quite the entrepreneur, even sold tickets for its use as a bomb shelter and made one of the wide open caverns a ballroom where he hosted dances. He was even said to be the inventor of the bumper sticker as he hired school children to tie signs to all the visitors' cars when they were on their tour. Personally, I'm not sure I would have been real happy about that.

All this was fascinating, but it wasn't until we were deeper inside that I really understood the full wow-factor of the cave. One doesn't often see a geological structure that's seventy feet high and sixty feet wide. The series of closely knit stalactites and stalagmites is called The Stage Curtain and we were entertained there by a spectacular light show.

At one point, Zane jerked on my hand. "There it is. Come on."

"There what is?"

He led me over to a small crevice in the wall. He checked around, and then stepped into it. “Uhh...I’m not sure we should explore on our own....”

“We’re not exploring. We’re there.” He shined the flashlight he bought at the gift store ahead of us. We were in an opening about six feet by five feet. The “hallway” of sorts we took in made a sharp turn making this “room” hidden.

“Oh. Did you carve your name in here?” I was excited to see traces of a younger Zane.

“Nope.”

“Oh...you discovered this place and wanted to show it to me?”

He squinted. “Yes and no.”

I waited. He set the flashlight on the ground. It was one of those big camping ones and the light fairly decently illuminated the place.

“I wanted to bring you here so we could do this.” He pounced on me, bringing his lips to mine and making our earlier make-out session look like the kind of kiss someone would give their Aunt Pearl. He took me from passive cave explorer to sex maniac in about two-point-five seconds. His body was rubbing against mine in exactly the right places. He took an arm, raised it over my head and held it, then coaxed the other up with it, grabbing both wrists in one hand. The rolling motion of his body against mine was X-rated. The things the man could do with his hips.... He finally freed my lips so he could glide his lips and tongue along my neck to my shoulder while at the same time, jerking my jacket zipper down.

“Holy hell, this feels good.” My eyes were closed, I was arching my back, I had basically lost my mind. He released my arms and they fell naturally to his shoulders where I clutched at him. I felt like if this man’s body left me at this particular point in time, I would die.

Then, in a flash, I realized what the dress was for. “Oh, no, Zane. We can’t do this.” I moaned. He hit that spot behind my ear when he nudged my head to the side.

I was telling him something. What was I telling him?

He patted the walls. "It's here somewhere.... Ah. Here. Come here." He shifted me about six inches to my right where the wall jutted out forming a chair of sorts. He lifted me a few inches and set me on it. "Perfect."

When his lips were off mine, I could think. "Zane. The main passageway is less than four feet away."

His grin gleamed in the flashlight's beam. "I know. That's the thrill." He kissed my neck again and writhed against me.

I had to smile. He just did that to me. "Is that what you call it?"

He rumbled with laughter, pushing my dress up and holding it, pressed between our bodies. His cold hands touched my hip and, a few seconds later, I heard the rip of my bikini underwear.

"Zane, we have to hurry."

"I don't think that's going to be a problem."

"What are you doing?"

"Hang on, woman. I'm getting a condom on."

"Oh, good, responsible cave sex."

"Yeah. Doing it caveman style."

Then he was in me, with that magical, fluid movement that drove me nuts. I closed my eyes, reserving all senses for other regions. He drove his hips harder and I banged my head on the rock.

"Oh, yeah. You're going to want to watch that."

"Me? You're the one who's thrusting."

"Ooh. Say that again."

"I want you...ooh...to keep thrusting."

I opened my eyes. A little boy was framed in the arch opening to our room.

"Mo-o-om!"

"Oh, shit!" I said in a panic.

"Oh shit!" he responded in disappointment.

They warned us not to touch the limestone. We were doing a little more than touching. He scrambled to get his zipper up. Then grabbed my hand and the flashlight. We reentered the tunnel leading in.

"Oh, my jacket."

"Leave it."

We bolted out of concealment and didn't slow. The kid who saw us was wide eyed—who could blame him?—talking to a woman who was squatting by his side. We probably had seconds before someone official chased after us. We ran across the parking lot, having to dodge one car. We glanced at each other when we got to the car, both gasping for air, both with big goofy smiles on our faces.

"You are so not telling anyone about this." I slid behind the wheel and backed out of my spot.

"Whoo." He patted my knee, leaning back against his seat and panting. "Totally worth it."

Ten minutes later, he had to rethink that when I saw the lights in the rearview mirror.

I peered at him. "He's probably looking for someone else. Pull over and he'll fly by. Only he didn't. Once again I saw the dirty old man police officer strolling up to my window. This time his partner came to Zane's.

"You need to step out of the car."

"What?" I wasn't expecting that. "Oh, okay."

"You, too, sir," the other officer told Zane. "Walk to the front of the car, please."

"Put your hands on the car and spread your legs, please." The way he said the end made me feel sick. I did what I was told.

"Sir, put your hands on the hood."

Zane turned his head. "What is this—" He wasn't able to finish his statement as his policeman shoved him.

Reflexively I took a step toward him. The man behind me grabbed me, bunched my dress in both of his fists, and threw me against the car. Hard. Like he almost knocked the air out of me.

Zane charged around the car. "What the fuck do—" He was slammed against the car with his arm twisted behind him at an awkward angle. "Come on, man. That's my guitar hand."

"Oh, is it?" The younger guy corkscrewed it harder and Zane squeezed his eyes shut. "Fuck!"

The cop leaned in, his face close to Zane's. "You want to add assaulting a police officer to indecent exposure?" He yanked Zane back from the car and rammed him into it again.

"Zane!" I screamed, nearing hysterics.

He looked at me, his cheek smashed against the side of the car.

"Please stop. I'm fine." I tried to control the trembling in my voice.

My officer moved closer. "You sure are fine." To my shock, he grabbed my breasts. Not a little, ooh-I-accidentally-touched-you kind of fondle, both hands, in full contact. "I bet with these tits it was very indecent."

Zane went nuts. He scuffled briefly with the police officer but Zane's knees were kicked from behind and he went crashing to the ground.

"Now I said get those legs spread." He kicked the inside part of each of my feet, forcing them out wider.

Cop or no, I wasn't about to let him play with my breasts. What unbelievable balls. I struggled against him, trying to land an elbow, but I couldn't get enough room to cause any real damage.

He twisted one arm behind my back and grabbed my hair. I could hear Zane fighting, and the ratchetting sound of cuffs, but my captor got his ugly face in my line of vision. He tsked. "Like my partner here said, you don't want to get a resisting arrest charge thrown on top of your indecent exposure."

"You're gonna see what fucking resisting arrest is," Zane spat.

The cop restraining him mimicked what mine was doing, grabbing Zane's hair in the back and pushing him again. "What? You don't like to see her being touched?" He brought his knee into Zane's back, and he cried out in pain. "You're gonna watch everything."

I blinked out a few tears, shaking all over.

My cop eased his grip a little as he reached into his pocket with his other hand. "Well would you look at what we found at the scene of the crime." He held out my underwear.

I closed my eyes. This was a nightmare.

"You know what that means? You're completely naked under..." He bent his knees so he could glide his palm along the inside of my leg slowly, lifting my dress at the same time. "...here."

I fought with everything I had, but it was useless. I ended up with my cheek against the window exactly as Zane's was. I peeked at him. His lip was cut and he was breathing hard.

"You better behave better than that. Take an example from your boyfriend there. He's being good." Zane was worn out and hurt.

"Okay," I said shakily.

"Now that's more like it." He let me go and the relief flooding through my arm was incredible. I rubbed it with my other hand. "Turn around."

Just do what they say and it will all be over in a little while.

I spun slowly. "Now. How about we reenact that little indecent exposure scene from the cave."

Zane called out my name. I glanced at him. The cop grabbed my face, squeezing it and jerking it back. "Don't look at him. On second thought, I think I want you on your knees like your boyfriend."

"Clint, anyone could see us here."

"True. How 'bout we take her to that old barn up Cherry Creek Road. I'll let you go first."

Oh, my God.

He hesitated. "My shift's almost over, and Mary's making pot roast tonight."

The older officer studied me one more time. I could hardly breathe. He scowled at his partner. "You owe me."

"Fine." He kicked Zane. "Get on your feet."

The older cop spat to the side. "Damn shame waste of a good hard on. Turn around." He cuffed me, leaning in to whisper, "I had so many more plans for you." I squeezed my eyes shut and fought off a wave of nausea. I started to get in the car, but as I went to pass him he hissed in my ear. "Wait." He tugged the zipper of my dress down.

"What are you doing?"

I looked to the other cop, but he was having a conversation with Zane.

"Shut up," the older policeman said through clenched teeth. He slid his sick hands over my skin to the front and grabbed me again, pinching my nipples, and rubbing his erection against my ass. "Fuck." He let me go, didn't bother to zip me, and began to push me into the car.

Then I heard the most glorious sound ever, a car.

"Fuck," Zane's cop said. "It's the chief."

A squad car was pulling behind theirs.

"We're screwed."

"Shut up. It's our word against theirs. Be cool."

Two policemen approached. The one who seemed to be in charge asked, "What's going on here?"

All of a sudden my guy was as sweet as cherry pie. "Oh, we got these two for indecent exposure down at the caverns."

"I tell you what's going on," Zane shouted. "Your officers here are molesting my girlfriend."

Chubby guy chuckled and said, "Oh. He's just mad 'cause he resisted and now we got him for that, too."

Zane spit out blood. "Bullshit!"

The policeman looked at me. "Is this true, ma'am?"

I nodded.

His jaw tensed.

"Oh, I may have maybe brushed her breasts when she was resisting. But it's no big—"

Zane interrupted. "It was no brush. He was all over her and he told her—"

The new guy held up his hand. "Stop there, please. We'll take your statements down at the station. Officer Randoza, will you please take that gentleman to our car. Ma'am, if you'll come with me."

"Gladly."

The other policeman went to Zane's side of the car and took his arm to lead him to their car.

As Zane passed the guy who had touched me he glared at him. "I'm going to have your fucking badge."

"Ahh. He's bull shitting you because he's pissed."

"We'll take statements from you two, also, but as of this minute, you are suspended pending investigation. We will follow you to the station."

Zane twisted to throw them a smirk.

When the man in charge was helping me into the car, he stopped. "Ma'am. Would you like me to zipper your dress?"

"What?" A vein in Zane's neck pulsed. "When did he unzip your dress?"

"Sir. If you could please get into the car."

"That son-of-a-bitch." Zane got in.

"I would appreciate it if you would zip that, please."

He did so, and helped me into the back seat.

Bumping against Zane's shoulder was a relief.

"Are you okay?"

It took me a second to find my voice. "Yes."

He stared at me. "God. I'm so sorry, Grace."

"This isn't your fault."

We were silent the rest of the way. When we got to the police station the squad car doors were opened. We looked at each other and both tried to smile to reassure the other. Once out, Zane didn't take his gaze off me and his officer had to move him along because he tried to plant himself so he could watch me.

Once inside, we were led straight to a small room with a table and chairs. They took our statements without commenting, other than asking for details to clarify things. Finally, the man who introduced himself as Chief of Police, David Lindstred, spoke to us. "I want to assure you if these allegations are true, they will be dealt with severely. Now, we're putting you in holding cells, because there's still the indecent exposure charge to work out."

"You aren't really pressing charges after everything they did to us, are you?"

The man held his hands out. "Sir. Like I said, we need to check into a few things. We have yet to decide on the charges."

Zane fumed silently.

There appeared to be three holding cells, one to the right of the door, and two, connected, on the left. I was relieved when they put us across from each other. In my cell, one person was in the back corner, curled into a ball on the floor with a jacket over their head. I stayed right inside the door. After about fifteen minutes I sank to the ground, my back to the wall Zane and I shared, I extended my legs so no one got a shot up my dress.

"Grace?" His voice came from the same level. He must be sitting on the floor, too. We had nothing to sit on. It was only concrete and steel bars, but it was clean and well-lit.

"Zane?"

"Are you okay?"

"Yes, are you?"

"Yeah." He sounded dejected.

I wanted to cheer him, if such a thing was possible in a jail cell. "That was like getting groped by Santa Claus."

Receiving no response, I thought he didn't hear me. At least a minute passed before he answered. "I'm going to kill him when I get out of here."

"And land back in here? Uh-uh." I glanced at the police chief who appeared to instruct a few of his officers on how to proceed. I knew they couldn't hear us. I turned to face the front of the cell, hoping he would hear me better if I did that. "Besides, I need for you to finish what you started." It was actually the last thing I wanted, but it was the first thing that came to mind.

Again a decent amount of time passed. "Well, how about I sneak up on him and put a pillowcase over his head and beat him senseless?"

I paused as if debating then sighed. "Tempting, but no."

An officer approached, so we went silent. He kept his eyes on me the whole time but went to Zane's cell.

"Time for your phone call."

As they shuffled him away he leaned back to tell me. "I'm calling Jericho. He'll get us out of here."

He was brought back within minutes. He was still handcuffed but they had taken mine off. We waited until the guard walked away. "That was fast."

"He didn't ask any questions. Not even what the charge was. He's in St. Louis...it takes normal people around an hour to get here, so Jericho should be here in about thirty minutes. Hang tight." He paused. "Do you get the sense something odd is going on here?"

Other than them talking about raping me like they were running a suit to the cleaners?

"Umm...what do you mean?" Simply hearing his voice was making me feel better.

"Like...they didn't fingerprint us, or search us, or anything. I think one of the guys recognized me. The tall one with the bushy mustache."

I located him. "Did you notice, they're glancing over here a lot and discussing something?"

"Yeah."

I studied all the men. Looked like your average middle-aged dads for the most part.

Zane spoke again. "They didn't even write up any paperwork that I could see."

"You sound like you're familiar with the process."

He hesitated. "A few drunk and disorderlies."

I smirked, watching the men mill about outside. "So nothing as cool as indecent exposure."

"Well...once."

"You did it with some other girl outside? Not in that cave, did you?"

"No. No woman was involved. It was actually the night we named the band. It's a long story, but the guys are bound to tell you it at some point."

"Hmm."

"Grace?"

We were already talking, why was he calling my name? "Yes."

"Are you sure you're okay? He didn't...hurt you, did he?"

"No, Zane. I'm fine. But, would it be okay if we canceled our reservations and went back to my place when we get out of here?"

"Sure," he replied quickly. "Anything you want."

When Jericho Tyler walked into the place, I rose from the floor, brushing my dress off. "He's here, Zane."

"Jericho?" Shuffling noises indicated he was getting up, too.

The jumble of officers, when seeing Jericho enter, scattered like thrown confetti. He approached the desk and the policeman now manning it.

"Mr. Tyler," the man said enthusiastically. "Nice to meet you."

Jericho spoke to the man in a low voice. He pulled out a wallet and some sort of exchange occurred which I couldn't see. Then the man turned to call someone over from the section of the office hidden behind a door to the left of the desk. Jericho swiveled, leaning his right arm and elbow on the desk and crossing his legs at the ankles looking from me to Zane. He shook his head with an expression on his face that was a cross between amusement and disgust. The officer he spoke to was now in a huddle with the police chief. Jericho yelled over to the group then straightened, walking slowly over to us. Again he gave me a once over and stared down Zane. Zane didn't make a peep. Returning his attention to me he altered his course slightly to come within feet of my cage. I think I took a step back. Jericho Tyler was much taller than I imagined. He wore some sort of silky, long sleeved loose-flowing purple shirt with a paisley print and black pants.

"What's a nice dame like you doing in a place like this?" he said in a passable Bogart voice. He gave Zane a withering stare, but his eyes twinkled and his lips were lifted. "Oh, wait. Yes. He put you here." Swinging his gaze back to me, he offered a charming smile. "Nice to see you again, Grace."

He remembered my name? "Oh, thank you."

"Man, am I glad to see you." Zane said.

"I wish I could say the same," he replied. "What the hell are you doing in here?"

"Umm...well...Grace and I were...you know...working on things between us, and—"

"And working on things between you required indecent exposure?"

"Umm...I'm afraid so." He sounded contrite.

The chief came out. "We are dropping all charges against you." He ran a card through a scanner thing and the door opened.

Jericho took both of my hands, bending to speak to me. "Are you okay?"

I nodded.

To my surprise, he put a comforting arm over my shoulder, and we turned to watch Zane's release.

He was outside his cell, holding his wrists out so they could remove his cuffs. At the same moment, the two officers who pulled us over were leaving the room where we made our statements, heading in our direction. As soon as his cuffs were off Zane rushed the guy who touched me.

"Oh, shit," Jericho said concisely.

Zane spun the man around and coldcocked him. The man staggered backward a little bit and Jericho led me out of the line of fire with a "damn."

Zane wasn't finished, but cops came from out of nowhere to subdue him, which was proving difficult as he strained against them, that vein in his neck sticking out again. The three or four men trying to hold him finally dragged him back a bit and, as he continued to fight, he was swallowed up by them.

"Hold it," the chief said. The restraining officers looked to him. He scrutinized the man whom Zane had hit.

He shifted his massive weight, scowling, and wiped the blood from his mouth matching the dried blood on Zane's. "I probably deserved that." The words seemed to struggle out of his mouth. He glanced at the chief, who stared him down then turned to Zane.

"Mr. Sanders.... Let him go," he barked at the pack of men wrangling him. Zane yanked his arms out of their grip. The chief stepped up to us. "I'm going to let that slide, considering the situation." He studied Jericho. "But you need to leave now."

Jericho cleared his throat, and Zane's gaze switched to him. Jericho jerked his head in the direction of the door. Zane gave fatso another glare, then stormed past Jericho, slamming through the door. Jericho moved backward, taking me with him. "Gentlemen," he said with a nod, then he whirled and quickly led me out the door. Zane's boots were ringing off the pavement.

Jericho let go of me. "What the hell was that for? It's not enough getting arrested?"

Zane's eyes flashed. "He fucking put his hands on her. He..." he gestured vaguely, "...freaking grabbed her tits and was going to do more—" He peered at me and closed his mouth.

Jericho hesitated a half beat then turned around. "Well what are we waiting for then?" He and Zane started marching toward the door. "Bastard," he muttered.

"Oh, no." I shifted over to block their path, my arms spread wide. "Not that I don't appreciate this show of valor..."

Jericho's jaw tightened. "We're not gonna simply let that slide."

"We gave them our statements." I switched to pleading, "Could we *please* just get out of here?" Tears sprang to my eyes.

Zane came over immediately, placing his palms on either side of my face and lifting it to kiss me softly. "Oh, honey. I'm sorry." He embraced me for a moment, laying his chin on top of my head when I pressed my cheek to his chest. A thought crossed my mind, and I drew back. "Was that your guitar hand?" I lifted it to examine his knuckles.

Zane pulled it away, shaking it. "It's fine."

Jericho was leaning backward with a huge grin, watching on with his arms crossed. "Guitar *hand*? Last time I checked, the instrument was played with two hands."

"Yeah, I know. It was an excuse I used to stop him from torturing me. Kinda backfired, by the way." He exhaled. "Thanks, Jer. I know it was a drive and disrupted your evening."

"Oh, no." He uncrossed his arms and lifted his palms in our direction. "This makes it totally worth it. That was almost like...domestic."

Zane fought a smile. "Shut up." We strode past his bandmate.

"I feel all warm and fuzzy now." He trailed after us.

"Shut up," Zane repeated.

"Wait 'til Rafe hears about this." He slung his arms over Zane's shoulders from behind.

Zane tried to shoo him away. "Get off me, bro." He ducked to avoid the hands messing with his hair. "And you're not saying anything to Rafe."

"Wanna bet?" Jericho countered.

"What did you say to them, anyway? Their attitude seemed to change when you arrived. I thought for sure I'd get an assaulting an officer charge."

I stopped. "Yet you did it anyway?"

Zane peered at me. "Like he said, he had it coming."

"Yeah," Jericho added. "I agree with that." He looked at Zane. "I just sort of casually mentioned that the bad publicity created by having a cultural icon in their prison might be more trouble than it was worth."

Zane snorted. "Cultural icon? Don't you think that's laying it on a bit thick?" He interrupted whatever Jericho was going to say. "However you said it, thank you. You saved our asses." Zane gestured toward a sleek, red Corvette parked haphazardly in front of us. "This your pile of junk?" He shook his head with upturned lips. He spun around, walking backward. "Didn't they have anything in blue?"

"No," Jericho admitted. "I had to settle for red."

"Oh, the suffering you do," Zane cracked. As they continued to rib each other, Zane reached for my hand, seeming lighter now. I smiled.

But after Jericho left, offering me a spontaneous hug and sympathy for what I went through and got in his car, it was suddenly quiet. We walked the rest of the way to my car, which was miraculously pulled out of impound. The keys were in the ignition.

"Do you want me to drive?"

"Yes, please." I started to walk to the other side of the car but he jerked me back into his arms.

His fingertips touched my neck under my hair, sliding up to lift it as he swallowed me in a kiss. For a few seconds his lips collided with mine frantically. He separated to look at me. His thumbs brushed over my cheeks, his gaze watery. "I was so scared of what they might do to you." He clutched me to his chest, shaking a little as he tried to reel it in.

My arms circled his waist and we stood that way for several seconds. Finally, I broke the embrace, peering into his face. "We're fine. I'm fine." I sniffed, giving him a weak smile. "Can we get the hell out of here?"

"Yes." He started to walk around to open my door, but I waved him off. "I got it."

I got in on the other side, and Zane peeled out of the parking lot. The more distance we put between us, the less tight I felt. I curled up on my side, facing the window. Zane reached over and adjusted the jacket I had over me as a blanket, but my eyes were open. I couldn't sleep wondering about what might have happened if that cop's shift hadn't been near the end or if his wife Mary had made pea soup instead of pot roast.

CHAPTER TWELVE

Zane

I sped through the dark, trying to keep pace with my thoughts. She was asleep beside me, facing my direction. Curled underneath my jacket, she looked like the little girl she'd once been. She was acting so brave, but I know she was scared shitless, like me.

What the hell is wrong with them? In what world is what they did to her all right?

I kept seeing her face as she struggled to hold it together. And I sat and did nothing, *nothing* to help her. I slammed the heel of my palm against the wheel. Then remembered I might wake her. She stirred a little, but remained asleep. I slowed the car. With her beside me I'd take no chances.

But despite my best efforts, the images flashed across my windshield. His hands grabbing her breasts, running up her leg and lifting her dress—talk about indecent exposure—him slamming her against the car. My jaw was so tight it ached, but not worse than my heart did. None of this would have happened if it weren't for me. What was I thinking taking her in that cave? I was thinking of myself and my damned libido. I was as bad as they were, using her to gratify myself. Shit. Maybe I bought in to all this rock star bullshit. Who was I kidding?

But, I knew that wasn't it. And I hadn't really thought about why I chose the caverns. In a way, it was me wanting to share another part of myself with her. One of the few good memories I had of growing up. So stupid. I glanced over at her again. Her face was so beautiful.

So peaceful. Then, passing under a street light, I saw the bruise on her cheek and it stabbed at my heart, emphasizing what a total uncaring jackass I was.

I vacillated like this for miles. I let her get hurt. I tried the best I could to defend her. I was using her for sex. It was so *not* about the sex. I could become a better man. I'd never change. I was a careless asshole. I never intended to do anything but love her. But, it was the story of my life. People I loved got hurt because of me. I thought about Devin. He didn't do drugs until I asked him to join the band and Rafe introduced them to him. I liked to blame Rafe, but it was on me, too. I stole a peek at her again then barely made a curve when I refocused on the road. I was recklessly endangering her life again. I drove more cautiously. If I was going to do one thing right, I would fucking get her home tonight without anything else happening to her.

Like the nightmares about Devin, this day would haunt me forever. The visuals wouldn't leave me. Her dress, unzippered. His evil face against hers, tense and threatening. Him fucking trying to look down her dress the first time he stopped us. And now, add to that seeing that bruise on her cheek while she slept. And the thing that would really weigh on me was the what-if. What if that guy didn't want to get home for dinner, what would have happened then? The thought made my heart beat faster and my stomach roll. I checked on her. I had to know she was there, safe.

I mean, what the hell were they going to do with us after...whatever might have happened? Did they think we wouldn't tell for some reason? Or did they have no intention of giving us the opportunity? Would we have ended up in a ditch somewhere, or at the bottom of a lake?

I decided to switch my thoughts to more pleasant ones. Like how I was going to sue the ass off those sons-of-bitches. I thought about how good it felt to punch that fucker. But even this was ruined by the thought it felt good only for me. She didn't need any more violence after what she went through. Once again I was thinking about only me.

I returned to our conversations—her talking about thrusting, smiling as we ran out to the car, wrapping her in my arms. All of those memories now ruined because of their connection to what happened afterward. When I planned it, I wanted this to be such a fun day.

I blinked and we were taking the exit to her house. She woke with the change of speeds. "Hey. How are you feeling?"

How do you think she's feeling, you moron?

Her voice was rough when she spoke, "Better." She glanced around. "We're here already? I'm sorry. I didn't mean to sleep that long. Did you struggle to stay awake?"

She was apologizing to me?

"Oh, no. You forget, I'm a wild rocker. Used to late nights."

She nodded, but didn't comment. No witty comeback. When we pulled in front of her place, I switched the ignition off but turned to her. "Grace, if you don't want me here tonight, I can take a cab home. Just let me come in and pay Holly. I'll pay her for the full time, plus a little extra."

She latched onto my arm. "No. Please. I need you beside me. Please don't leave me."

I put my hand over hers. "Hey, hey, hey. If you want me here, that's where I am."

She nodded her head rapidly. Now there was no need to be brave, she seemed a little shaky.

I gave her what I hoped was a reassuring smile. "Let's get you into a real bed."

We texted, so they were expecting us. Grace greeted Holly and Jamie mechanically, but they didn't seem to notice. And she didn't fight me when I paid Holly.

"Time for bed, Jamie."

My phone rang. "Sorry." I glanced at the number. A Stanton area code. It could be Whitney or Tatum or someone from the police station. "Umm...I better take this. I'll go out on the fire escape."

She nodded dully and trudged off behind Jamie. Then I remembered Whitney and Tatum's names would pop up if it was them. I tapped to answer the call as I walked to the kitchen and opened the window to the fire escape.

When I heard his voice, I froze.

"Well, Zaner. How the hell are ya?"

He was slurring, probably was drinking since late morning. Zaner? Whitney wouldn't voluntarily tell him anything. Maybe he overheard her talking to Tatum. Hearing voices, I finished climbing out the window.

"What do you want?" A lead weight grew in my stomach. What a great way to finish the day. A call from my dear old stepdad, Tony Salvetti. I swung around to sit on one of the steps, closing my eyes and pinching the bridge of my nose.

"Oh, now. Is that any way to talk to your stepdaddy? Hmm...talkative as always."

I exhaled. "Did you have a point, or were you simply calling to torture me?"

"Well who said it couldn't be both?"

I'd give him a minute to say what he needed to say out of respect for my mom, but after that I'd hang up.

"Can you tell me why the hell you took my daughter from me to babysit for your newest whore's little brat?"

My eyes popped open and I jumped to my feet. "Don't talk about her like that." I tried to keep my voice even, not wanting him to know he scored a point.

"Ohh. You actually like this girl, huh? Must be good in bed. Grace, I think her name is?"

"Don't—" I wouldn't lose it. "Don't say her name."

"Oh-ho-ho. Bothers ya, does it, when someone like me says her name? Grrace."

You won't bait me, you evil son-of-a-bitch.

"What's wrong, Zaner? Where is she now? Getting lubed up for ya?"

I'm done with this phone call.

But I didn't end the call. I didn't know what was wrong with me that I had to listen to the hateful words coming out of that man's mouth. Maybe it was because I was hating myself right now.

"You're no fun tonight," he said lightly. "What happened to the good ol' Zane? The fuck up who'll never amount to nothin'...."

So half of the globe knows who you are? You have platinum records hanging in your place?

"You always were a pussy. Playing piano instead of football. Burying your nose in books. Then you had to go and kill Devin Moore. Good kid, until he met you. You ruined him. You ruined him, and then you killed him. His mama's never been the same, ya know that?"

Mrs. Moore was the best. The absolute best. I'd hung out at Devin's house a lot to get away from Tony and she had always welcomed me. Not only welcomed me but showed interest in me and my music, even before Devin was in the band.

"I'm done with this." I was about to push end but he yelled out. I brought it to my ear in case it was about the girls needing something.

"You still there, Zane?"

"Yeah. I'm still here."

"Then let me end this conversation with a word of advice. If you really love that woman, you'll get the hell out of her life before you screw it up like you did Devin's. Stop thinking with your dick for once and let her go blow someone else. If you like her so much, I bet she's good at it. She probably can—"

I disconnected and sat on the stairs again. I put my head in my hands. It pissed me off that he was still able to get to me. At least I didn't let him force me into a tizzy. I could hide the pain from him now I was miles away from home. To think when my mom first got married, I was excited about it. After not having a dad all my life, I was going to have one. I didn't realize sometimes not having a dad is a blessing.

"Zane?"

I jumped, her voice startled me. "Are you okay?"

I cleared my throat. "Yeah. I'm fine."

"He's asking for you." She seemed more relaxed. Jamie grounded her.

"Okay. Give me one more second."

She turned away then spun back. "You're sure you're okay?" Her forehead was furrowed.

"Yeah, babe. I'm good. Just tired."

"Okay, well I'm getting ready for bed. You're coming in, right?"

I managed a smile. "Yeah. I'll be there."

She frowned, still trying to read me then walked away.

Tony was not an educated man. Dropped out of high school before his junior year. But he had one thing he was excellent at. Crushing me. He was smart enough to know if a grain of truth in something, people will swallow the lies with it. He was right about Devin. None of it would have happened if it weren't for me. And he was also right about me being a fuck up.

I should have never attempted to have a relationship. Not with my baggage. My lifestyle. I'll hurt her. Worse than I already did. And I can't live with that.

It was time for me to exit stage left.

But I wouldn't leave now. I promised to stay with her. One last night with her and Jamie.

Shit. I don't know if I can do this.

I took a deep breath. Waiting wouldn't make it any easier.

I stuck my head in Jamie's door. "Hey."

"Zaner!" he yelled. But I could only hear my stepfather's mocking voice saying my nickname. Not this loving little boy. He stretched his arms out to me. I walked slowly over to him—wanting to remember this—and bent to give him a last hug. I closed my eyes and held on a little longer than necessary. He turned on his side, putting his hands palm to palm, as if in prayer, and slipping them under his cheek. I sat on the side of his bed, awkwardly giving his hip a couple of pats.

"So Jamie...you know your sister is a wonderful woman, right?"

He nodded. He looked tired.

"And as brother and sister, you watch out for each other, don't you?"

"Gracie makes me pancakes."

That made me chuckle. "Yes, she does. And you say they're better than mine...."

"They are."

"Okay." I rubbed my chin. "You remember what I told you about kissing girls? That you need to be sure they want to kiss you before you do it. That's very important."

"Got it, Zaner."

I love the way he says that.

What other pearls of wisdom did I want to dump on him? I wanted to make certain he didn't grow up hating himself like I had.

"You are a really good kid, Jamie—" And that was the end of that. I gave him another hug to hide how emotional I was.

"I like when you tuck me in." It stung.

You deserve better, kid.

"I like tucking you in, too."

I got to my feet and was about to leave when he threw out, "You can do it all the time when you're part of the family."

For a second I wasn't sure I'd heard him right. "What do you mean, bud?"

He yawned. "When you and Gracie get married."

Wait. "Did she say something about getting married?"

He closed his eyes. "No. But when two people kiss a lot, they get married. And you and Gracie kiss *a lot*."

I couldn't speak over the lump in my throat, and even if I could, I didn't know what to say. At the door I looked back. He was already snoring.

"Good night, little dude," I whispered. I closed the door and laid my forehead on it.

Holy fuck. If this is killing me, how will I ever say goodbye to Grace?

I tried to gather my strength and composure. I walked toward her room like Jamie was holding onto my legs. But when I opened the door and saw her, I rushed to the bed. She was laying on top of her quilt in a short, silky, teal blue nightgown.

She smiled at me. "He asleep?"

"Before I even hit the door."

She chuckled. All I could do was stare. She patted my side of the bed. "Well, come on, slow poke."

"Oh." I stripped off my clothes, down to my black briefs.

She watched, her eyes intently focused on me. She bounced across the bed and pulled the covers back before sliding in. "Zane? Aren't you coming?"

"What? Oh, sorry. Spacing out." I slipped under the sheet. "Like I said, I'm tired tonight."

"I'm sorry I made you drive and didn't even keep you company."

"No. It wasn't bad. It hit me after. When we got home." *Home?*

We turned on our sides so we were looking at each other. She swiped her hand across my forehead, snagging a lock of hair and smoothing it in place. "Are you sure you're okay?" She wrinkled her brow. "You're acting kind of...I don't know...weird."

"It's just...." I exhaled. "It's been a long day."

"You can say that again. I never thought I'd be arrested for indecent exposure. You're a bad influence." She was teasing, but the words were so true. "That kid who saw us is going to need some serious therapy."

I propped myself on my elbow. "Grace, can I tell you something?"

"Of course."

My brain was screaming, *I love you! I love you!* I wanted so badly for her to know it. But that wouldn't be fair. "You're an amazing woman. The way you take care of Jamie...running your own business...losing your parents at eighteen but pulling your shit together for your little brother.... I can't tell you how much I..." *love* "...admire you."

"I'm no hero, Zane. I simply did what I had to do."

"Maybe, but you did it well. Jamie's a great kid."

"Thank you. Yes, he's pretty special. But it wasn't my doing. He—"

"You don't give yourself enough credit." I brushed the hair away from her face and cupped it, wanting to memorize everything about her. The way she laughed, the way she moved, her sense of humor, her voice, the way she looked tonight, that nightgown set off by her creamy skin.

"Zane?"

She sounded funny. I studied her. "What is it?"

She put her hand on my cheek and caressed it. "I want you to make it all go away. Like only you can do for me."

I made love to her, pouring all of myself into every touch, every movement, every kiss. She fell asleep with a smile on her face. The moonlight, or streetlight, whatever it was, bathed her in a pearly glow. "I love you, Grace," I whispered.

I left about two in the morning. Driving away from her, I seriously thought about steering my car into the side of the bridge spanning the Missouri River. But that would hurt her, too. I put my elbow on the doorframe, my hand planted flat, across my forehead, and let the tears fall. Why couldn't I do anything right?

CHAPTER THIRTEEN

Grace

The morning sun was glorious as it filtered in through my filmy curtains. I flipped over to snuggle in with Zane, but his side of the bed was empty.

It's so strange how early he gets up, considering he's a rocker.

I threw the covers back and hopped out of bed. It was amazing what a good night's sleep would do. Rejuvenating my spirits and putting what happened yesterday into a different day. Everything always looked better in the morning. I grabbed my robe and flew out of my bedroom. When I got to the kitchen, Jamie was sitting at the table with a plate on a placemat in front of him, a fork in one hand, a knife in the other, gripped in his little fists, ends on the table.

"Whoa. You're ready, aren't you? Did you not allow Zane to make them because he burnt them the last time?"

"Zaner's not here."

"He's not? I wonder if he went out to get donuts or something. Well, I'll make you pancakes, and if he comes back with donuts, we can save your pancakes for tomorrow. Does that work?"

He nodded vigorously.

I finished the pancakes, and Jamie was digging in. Since we were supposed to have stayed at the B&B overnight, I had the day off. It was our last day to be together before Zane picked up the rest of the tour. Since Zane wasn't back yet, I decided to hop in the shower. When I walked into the bathroom, I spotted a folded over piece of paper stuck to the mirror. The page was torn from my magnetic shopping list pad on the refrigerator.

Aww. He left me a note. How sweet.

I pulled it down. All it said was, "I'm sorry. I can't do it. This was a mistake."

Can't do what?

Confused, I stepped back out to the living room, bringing the note with me. "Jamie, did Zane say where he was going when he left?"

Without looking away from the TV he answered, "I haven't seen him."

"Hmm." I stared at the paper again, but I still had no clue what he meant. "I'm jumping in the shower."

Jamie made no acknowledgement he heard me.

I wonder if Zane's planning something special for our last day.

Cautiously excited, I stepped into the shower. I didn't hear his voice when I came out, but he was probably watching TV with Jamie. When I entered the living room, however, he was nowhere to be seen. "Did Zane get back?"

"Nope."

"Only a half hour more of TV," I warned. I found my cell and texted Zane asking him where he was. A half-hour later, I still hadn't received a response. I was perplexed and didn't know if I should start a project, or if he'd want to go somewhere when he returned. Jamie was coloring, so I decided to check Zane's tour dates. That way, when he got back, we could figure out when we could get together on the road. Then I'd have something to look forward to that would get me through missing him. Chicago or Memphis seemed the best bets, but I was leaning toward Chicago, since it was the earliest, and I wouldn't have to wait so long.

It made me think about how seamlessly Zane had slipped into our lives. I felt more alive when he was around. For the most part, I was living life as a continuous list of chores. Get up, feed Jamie, walk him to the bus, open the shop.... I mean, it was pleasant enough. It wasn't drudgery.

I liked the job I had, both working with people, and flowers. Making arrangements satisfied my inner artist. It was kind of like a puzzle to solve, which colors harmonized best together, what vase should I use, does this seem full enough? And people came to purchase flowers either happy or hurting. Preparing for a wedding, date, anniversary...whatever happy occasion made better by the beauty of flowers. Or they were preparing for a funeral, to visit a sick friend, to brighten someone's day who was down. And I enjoyed helping both parties, sharing and hopefully adding to their joy, and sharing and hopefully decreasing their pain a fraction. And most of the people who came in were givers, people who thought about others, and those were the kinds of people you wanted near you.

And sharing my life with Jamie—he was what really brought joy to my days. I was blessed by helping him with his struggles and celebrating all the little joys he discovered. He could get happy about the simplest things, like pancakes day after day. How could you not want to be around someone like that?

But both the shop and taking care of Jamie could be difficult at times. Staffing difficulties, screwed up deliveries, inventory, balancing the books, creating marketing ideas.... And while Jamie was happy much of the time, the times when he wasn't could be very challenging. My job and home life both fulfilled me and drained me. But without realizing it, I had lost myself along the way somewhere. I forgot about my needs—the fun of a date, or a trip with someone I loved, the sensual pleasure of the bedroom, someone to share my trials with and my celebrations. Zane nurtured me and filled me. He treasured me for me and wanted to make me happy, take care of my needs, help me to both enjoy life and to endure it.

So where the hell was he?

He'd filled a hole I didn't know I had. But now I was aware of that hole, and I needed it filled. I was becoming restless and frustrated waiting for him without knowing why I was doing it. As the day slipped away, I only became more baffled, and concerned. Did Brad come here and do something to him? By this time he should have discovered and answered my texts.

Sitting on the couch as the sun's rays stretched across my hardwood floors, for the tenth time, I stared at the handful of words on the page that were my only clue. I puzzled over those ten words until my head ached. *I'm sorry. I can't do it. This was a mistake.* Sorry for what? For what happened yesterday? He couldn't predict or prevent it. He couldn't do what? What did I ask him to do? What was a mistake? That was the sentence worrying me the most. They were the words I gave him when he wanted to start a relationship. As the day wore on, I began to wonder if they were the words he was giving me to end it. At one point I walked into the bedroom to find my purse and froze, realizing his bag was gone. Why would he take his bag with him...unless he didn't mean to return? I let the idea into my head a little at a time. A passing thought at first, then my only thought. I forgot about feeding Jamie lunch until almost two o'clock in the afternoon. I spent a good chunk of my hours on the couch, with the note in hand, staring at the sun's rays, inventing different scenarios to explain his absence.

Where are you, Zane?

An ache started to grow. And not only did I have to deal with how his disappearance was affecting me, I had to deal with Jamie's mounting frustrations and concerns for the same reason. Along with the ache came the first spark of anger.

If you were leaving us, surely you could do better than ten fucking words, Zane.

Ten fucking words to sum up all we had? And the same ten fucking words to explain why that was gone. When I got to the point when I was about to scream or dissolve into tears I called Payton.

We sat on the fire escape. Jamie was in bed, and I was afraid to face my bed.

"And this is all? This is all he left you?" she said for the fifth time. "Only this? Nothing else?"

She wasn't helping.

When she arrived and we decided to go out on the fire escape to talk and drink, I went to the refrigerator and saw the cider he got me. And that six-pack is what did me in. Seeing it, I broke into tears. Drinking it fought off the tears for a time, but the buzz would end, leaving me empty. And eventually, Payton had to leave. And while it helped at first to have someone to share my righteous indignation, to be truthful, after she left, I was relieved.

Now I was sitting in the corner of the stairwell with the note in one limp hand, the last of the six-pack Payton bought for us in my other hand, rolling my head against the bars behind me to stare at the moon, as I stared at the sun earlier. In the end the ten words on the page became two words—where and why.

Where are you, Zane? And why did you leave me?

About a week after he left, I received a strange phone call.

"Yes, may I please speak with a Ms. Grace Prescott?"

"This is Grace."

"Hello, Ms. Prescott." He spoke very formally. "My name is Bernard Weinstein and I am an attorney representing Zane Sanders. I still can't believe I'm saying that. Anyway, Mr. Sanders instructed me to let you know about the case against the two Stanton police officers who assaulted you. Mr. Sanders' suit was dropped due to some recent news. Apparently, the two men—if you want to call them that—were arrested for the rapes and murders of five women and three men who went missing in the area. The FBI's investigation of the disappearances had pretty much come to a standstill until your lawsuit came to light and—long story short—since then the evidence has snowballed against the policemen and they will probably spend the rest of their days in prison. Mr. Sanders dropped the suit against the city of Stanton as the police chief was very cooperative with us and the FBI in our efforts to punish the men responsible for assaulting you. So, I said a lot. Are there any questions I can answer for you?"

"Umm...Zane wanted you to let me know this because...."

"Well, he told me he wanted you to feel safe and know the men did not get away with the things they did." An awkward silence followed while I tried to understand why Zane would do that after he left me. "Ms. Prescott? Are you still there?"

I cleared my throat. "Yes. I'm still here."

"Well, like I said, this is a lot to take in. I mailed you a short letter with my contact information should you have any questions at a later date. You should receive that today or tomorrow. Feel free to call me. Mr. Sanders has paid a retainer fee so you will not accrue any charges."

"Okay. Well, thank you very much for all you did."

"It's my pleasure. Take care now."

I hung up and sat on the couch for a long while trying to understand Zane's actions, but I couldn't figure it out.

Another piece of the puzzle that is Zane that I will think about tonight when I'm not sleeping.

ZANE

I was as miserable as I ever was in my life. A different kind of despair than when my mom died or losing Devin. I wanted her so badly my body literally ached all over.

Two weeks had passed since I left and the tour led us to Chicago—far too close to her. In fact I was thinking of organizing a European tour simply to get physical distance between us. Tensions were beginning to mount. The band was getting fed up with my attitude.

I didn't even think about how difficult it would be to sing those songs, the ones we danced to, the one we sang to, our songs. That first night after I left her, when I sang "Dancing Into My Heart" I froze on stage for the first time in my life. The music brought back the physical sensations. I remembered the line where I pulled her out of the crowd, the chord playing when she spun under my arm, the rhythm when we kissed. They were some of my worst performances, and some of my best. As usual, my music both pained and saved me. The harder songs were a godsend. I could pour myself into them, expressing the rage, anguish, and heartache. At the same time, I poured myself out of them with my sweat, leaving me cold and empty. I closed the concert to thunderous applause that meant absolutely nothing to me.

Tonight wasn't unlike all the nights previous. I walked off the stage and didn't stop walking. I didn't talk to anyone, just went straight to my dressing room. In the shower, the hot water melted me. I'd stand with my hands against the wall, steam rising around me, and I would let it all out. Let myself feel the pain I kept at bay throughout the day. When the water finally ran cold I'd get out, towel myself off, and go through the motions of getting dressed. Tonight, in Chicago we had what we liked to call a layover. We wouldn't travel until tomorrow. A fire pit we kept stored on one of the trucks along with our other equipment was out near the buses. Lawn chairs circled it. The flames were both blurry and mesmerizing. Six empty beer bottles sat at my feet—an accident waiting to happen—a fifth of scotch was in my fist and I was drinking straight out of it. This concert was the hardest by far. I don't know what it was. Being closer to her, I guess.

I needed to get things back to normal. The old normal, not the normal with her—pancakes, laughing, making love, repeat. The old normal was sing, drink, sex, repeat. I hadn't been with anyone since that last bittersweet night with her. Had no desire to be.

I could feel them watching me, and it didn't help. They were wondering what I would do next. So was I. The self-destructive behavior was escalating and leading to a Zane fuck-up of major proportions. Slouched in my chair, I was staring at the fire, taking a drink of my alcohol poison from time-to-time. A girl sat on Rafe's lap, Jericho already took one to a bus, and Dex was having an animated conversation with one about some stupid video game they played. More girls sat in chairs, some standing. Their shadows swayed in front of me.

"I can rock your world," one said, bending over so I could see her cleavage.

I waved a hand like I was shooing away a fly. "Leave me the fuck alone."

Most of them figured out I wasn't going to fuck them tonight and quit trying to talk to me, steering clear of the asshole lead singer. Fine. They weren't what I wanted anyway. I could hear conversations around me, but it was like they were held underwater. A roadie to my left was trying to score with one of our leftovers. Dex and the girl were prattling on and on about bosses, AK47s, health packs, and some other such crap. Rafe was too far away to make out what he was saying—or I was too drunk, or a combination thereof—but I could hear the cadence and timber of his voice, and her response in a higher register.

I felt absolutely dead inside. I needed to do something life affirming. I staggered to my feet, grabbed one of the girls nearby, and headed toward a bus. I didn't even know which one it was. The blonde? The brunette? It would be a blonde in my mind, and not one who was here.

Rafe got in my way. "Hey, man. You don't want to do that."

I shoved him in the shoulder, hard. "Get the fuck out of my way." I wasn't sure those were the words that came out, but they were the ones I was trying to say.

"Zane, what the hell are you doing?" Dex called out.

Rafe responded. "Leave him alone. If he wants to be a self-destructive asshole, let him be one."

I nearly stumbled, but the girl helped me keep my balance. "Are you okay?"

I grunted.

"Wrong bus, asshole," Rafe offered, but I didn't give a fuck. It didn't matter. I didn't care who, where, what, when, or how. I only wanted the pain to end. At least for a moment. Somehow I made it in the bus and through the door, but I guess I left the girl on the other side. I opened it again, snatched her hand, and moved forward, falling into a cabinet, burying its knob in my shoulder.

"Ouch. Fuck." I found a couch. "Come here."

The girl came over, and I pulled her onto my lap. I kissed her, kneading her boob like I was milking a damned cow. My kisses were sloppy, lacking any finesse whatsoever. But they didn't care. They never cared. They simply wanted to get laid by a rock star.

Well, I'm that, baby. So bring it on.

I wouldn't be fucking her anyway. I would be making love to Grace. Images of our time together warped reality. It was her hair I was burying my hands in, her I was tasting on my lips. I yanked down her top and tried to lower my head to suck her tits, but I hit it on the table. "Fuck!" It hurt enough already. "Come on, honey. Bring it over here." I was annoyed. I shouldn't have to work for it this hard. She straddled my lap, bring her hard nipple right to mouth level. And I suddenly felt like crying.

No, shit. I can't lose it.

"Take the rest of your shit off."

Good little slut who she was, she complied, coming back to me. "You like what you see?" she said in what I'm sure she thought was a sultry voice, but it just sounded stupid.

I tried to put a finger on her lips, but I think I palmed her face. "Don't talk."

She exhaled. "Whatever you want." I'm pretty sure she was getting pissed, but she wouldn't let that stop her.

She came over, unzipped my pants, stroking me. I laid back on the cushions and sighed. "Yeah. That feels good." She was working away. "Mmm. God, yeah." I had to feel something, even if it was solely physical sensation. I unzipped my pants all the way and she slid to the floor in front of me. Trying to focus my eyes, I looked at her. "Grace?"

"Grace? Who's Grace?"

I put my hand on her cheek. Her skin was soft. "Never mind. Keep doing what you're doing." As she opened her mouth to swallow me down, her image became clear for an instant. I pushed her away. "No. No. This isn't right."

"Well, we don't have to do it that way. I know other things." She slid her palms along my thighs. Her touch felt like spiders crawling on me. In a panic, I tried to stand, knocking her head into the table. "Ouch. What the fuck?"

"Get up. Get up." I grabbed her jeans and threw them at her. "Get the fuck out of here."

I moved to the other side of the bus and slumped in the seat, as far away from her as possible.

Oh, my God. What was I about to do?

It didn't matter. Grace was out of my life. For all I knew, she could be doing some guy right now.

But I knew she wasn't.

I wanted her so bad. Needed her so bad. But I loved her. I had to stay away. I was a mess. Always was. Always would be. Maybe at some point I could be with another woman, but I knew that point was a long ways off.

The window next to me was open. The cooler air felt good on my flaming cheeks. My head lolled to the left, and I was gazing out the window. Shadows swayed around the fire like some ancient tribal mating dance. I blinked and things became clearer. Jericho was returning to the fire with his arm over a girl's shoulder. They all looked my way.

"Shit," Rafe said, loud enough for me to hear.

Jericho took a step forward. "Oh, shit."

Dex's mouth was hanging open. "Fuck."

I shifted my gaze to the right to see what they were talking about, but I only saw the girl getting dressed. I didn't want to see that. I slowly turned to look out the window again. My head felt like a bowling ball rolling around on my shoulders.

Dex shouted, "Grace, wait!"

But Rafe stepped in front of him and was holding him back. "Let her go. He deserves whatever circle of hell she's going to put him in."

Dex shoved him in the shoulder. "I'm not worried about him, you asshole, I'm worried about her." He started to move past him, but they all froze, Rafe twisting to peer over his shoulder.

Worried about who? Wait. Did he say Grace?

I jerked to attention, pulling the curtain back to widen my range of vision. Grace was reaching for the bus door handle.

"Oh, no. No." I couldn't let her.... "Hurry," I hissed. "Grace is coming." I went over and tried to hurry/help her.

"Again I have to ask, who the hell is Grace?"

The door opened. I was holding the arms of the girl who was sliding on her skirt. The expression on Grace's face knifed me.

"Grace. No, no, no, no, no. Wait." I tied to rush toward her, but my heel got caught in the straps of the girl's bra and I went down, hitting my head on something on the way to the floor and splitting it open.

The last thing I remember was Rafe's voice as things were fading to black. "Crying was a good choice, Grace. Yelling at him would hurt less."

GRACE

Two weeks had passed since Chicago, when I came face-to-face with my own stupidity and naivety. Man, I had bought everything he'd sold me. Handsome, successful, tempting rock star. All it took was one unguarded moment to show me who he really was. In true Grace fashion, I stuffed all of my feelings of humiliation, anger, betrayal and grief way down inside me. Folded neatly, tiny and tight, put on a shelf and shoved to the back, where I'd never find them again. I threw myself into my work, and taking care of Jamie. I stayed awake late at night working on some new marketing strategies for the shop. I hadn't gone back to my bed. Couldn't. I'd work on my laptop until I couldn't focus anymore, curl up on the couch and go to sleep. I didn't even cover myself as a form of punishment.

I wanted to punish myself for being such an idiot, convincing myself we had a future together. What a joke. But nights...nights were the hardest. When my brain was too tired to protect itself from the memories. The false memories of what I imagined we could be together. I mean, who the hell was I to think we had some special "magic." Like we were different from anybody else? I thought I abandoned fairy tale thinking when I was young. But I guess I wanted it too much.

Still, the memories seemed real enough. I'd wake from fevered dreams and want to cry myself back to sleep, but wouldn't allow myself. I needed to grow up. Other people had it much worse than having their heart broken by a rock star. It was almost laughable...only I couldn't laugh anymore. It seemed when I denied myself my negative emotions, the other emotions went with them. As far as the future, I decided celibacy was far underrated. I got along fine in life without anybody by my side. No parents, no grandparents...no one special.

So I became a kind of shell Grace, like the shell Zane I had believed in. Sleep deprived, emotion deprived, carrying on like I always did. Taking care of business, that was Grace. I found myself very distracted. As if blocking out thinking of him, and any feelings associated with him, created a kind of static in my mind. I kept messing up orders, forgetting appointments, and losing things. People had to tell me something half a dozen times for it to sink in. But I was smiling and walking through life as if my time with Zane Sanders never happened.

That was why I was caught totally off guard when someone knocked on my door and I opened it. I couldn't even form a sentence.

"Hi, Grace. I'm not sure if you remember me. I'm Rafe Santiago."

I nodded.

"May I come in for a few minutes to speak to you? I won't take a lot of your time. I'll say my piece and go."

Sure. Why not? I won't believe a lying word your rock star mouth utters, but go ahead and throw it out there if it makes you feel better.

That was what I thought. I didn't say anything. Merely turned around and walked away, leaving the door open.

He stepped in behind me and closed the door. He was in a suit, of all things. Probably expensive because it fit him like it was made for him. "Uhh...I should probably mention...your neighbor may have gotten the wrong impression."

I remained silent, standing behind the recliner, keeping its bulk in between the two of us.

He seemed unsure of whether to keep going on or not. Stood with his mouth hanging open like he was waiting for someone to throw popcorn into it.

"Yeah. She..." He pointed at the door like whoever he was talking about was still out there. "...pretty brunette, short..."

Payton.

"Anyway, she said something like, 'Wow, Grace is banging two rock stars.' I didn't have time to correct her because she sped by and ran down the stairs."

Definitely Payton.

And she probably wasn't gone. She was probably either trying to listen on the fire escape, or with her ear pressed to my door. He waited for a response, and not getting one, slapped his palms together and sort of swiveled on his heels.

"So, I said I wouldn't take much of your time. Uhh...would you mind if I had a seat? This feels a little uncomfortable standing like this."

I was surprised by how overwhelmed I was by my feelings, which I thought I trapped pretty well. I searched for my voice but couldn't get much force behind it, although I did manage to say, "Sure. Have a seat." I waved at the couch, but noticed my hand was trembling and brought it to grasp the top of the recliner, turning my eyes away because seeing him hurt. He reminded me too much of Zane.

Jamie chose that minute to barge into the room. "Gracie, my room's all cleaned. Can I have my ice cream—" He saw Rafe and froze like I had.

Rafe rose. "Hi. You must be Jamie. My name is Rafe."

"Cool." He ran into the kitchen. I'd have to find out if he was upset later.

Rafe looked at me with raised brows. "Did I...not handle that right?"

I cleared my throat, shifting my weight. "I'm sorry. He got a new coloring book."

"Oh." He seemed to absorb this for a second. "Huh. First time I lost to a coloring book." He gave me a charming smile. I cast my gaze down, staring at the crisscrossing weave of the recliner. He sat back and clasped his hands. "Uhh...I wanted to talk about...Zane."

"What about him?" I threw out like a shield. Then I had a sudden thought. What if something happened to him and they had sent Rafe to tell me about it. "He's...he's okay, isn't he?"

"Well, to tell you the truth, no. He's sick over what happened."

I blinked, fighting back tears, but said nothing. I guessed he decided sitting was equally as uncomfortable as standing in our house because he got to his feet and moved over behind the chair opposite me, putting two chairs and a coffee table safely between us. He spun around slowly to face me, pinching his bottom lip. He sighed. "Zane's always been a bit self-destructive. He probably wouldn't like me telling you this, but his stepfather was a real asshole. I mean a *real* asshole. The guy is this freakishly fit construction worker type who never finished high school. He takes great pleasure in tearing Zane down. Like, completely destroying him. He told him he was a pansy for playing guitar and writing music, hell, for reading freaking books. He took every opportunity to make Zane feel worthless."

I blinked harder. I didn't want to care about whatever shit happened to Zane, but I couldn't not. The idea of someone treating him like that broke my heart.

"If you ask me, it's because he's jealous. He could tell Zane was special, talented, and it irked him." He leaned forward, resting his arms on top of the chair. "That's why Zane got into drugs. As a means of escape. To quiet the voices in his mind telling him he wasn't worth a damn. He got drunk last night and talked finally, about what...happened between you two and—"

Anger flashed quick and hot. "What happened between us? Nothing happened between us." He seemed shocked I had something to say about it after all. "He just made love to me one night and left the next morning without saying goodbye. He—" My voice caught, but I fought through it. "He left a three-sentence note taped to my bathroom mirror."

Rafe lowered his head, pausing, my words hanging in the air for a moment. He sighed. "I won't try to defend what he did. Or presume to tell you how you should feel about it or what you should do about it. I only want to make sure you have all the pieces of the picture."

I took a chance and looked him in the eye. Bad idea. His deep brown eyes were full of kindness and sympathy. The kind of shit that could break you down.

He glanced over my shoulder at Jamie coloring in the kitchen, and dropped his voice. "I guess Jamie made some statement about being family." That surprised me. "It freaked Zane out. It's not that he doesn't want you guys to be his family—I think he wants that very much—it's just he doesn't feel he deserves you. And he doesn't think he can do what's best for you, love you properly. Be a decent role model for Jamie. And—" He stopped, considering, and exhaled. "Well, I'm in this far, I might as well go all the way. He blamed himself for what happened to you...on your trip...." He shifted his gaze away with this, clearly uncomfortable talking about it. "And, on top of all that, his stepfather called him that night. It was like the perfect fucking storm."

"I-I remember he got a call. He was acting strangely that night."

"All those cutting remarks from his youth that ripped him up, and some new vile things the S.O.B said, all of that factored in to him leaving you. As goofy as this sounds, he thought he was doing it for you." He stopped, watching me.

"You're pretty astute, for a guy. And I don't mean that as an insult...."

"I took psychology before I dropped out of school to join the band." He smiled. "It's useful at times." He laced his fingers, swallowing. "Grace, he really cares about you. He's been...a mess, since he left you. And I've seen him a mess before and nothing compares to what he is now. Especially after...you walked in on him."

I passed a hand over my forehead and spun away from him, wrapping my arms tightly around myself. Seeing him and that half-naked girl....

"Grace?"

I didn't turn.

"Grace, I really need you to look at me for a moment."

I slowly turned to face him, fighting my eyes up. He had come all this way to talk to me. The least I could do was listen.

"I need to beg your forgiveness, as I begged Zane's. I saw you coming that night. I could have spared you a whole lot of pain...but things have been strained between he and I since Devin's death and...I guess I was still holding on to some resentment. It was totally selfish and uncaring, what I did. And I wish I could take it back. I'm truly sorry."

The only thing I could do was bob my head slightly. It wasn't him I was mad at.

He walked toward me and I shrank. I wasn't scared of him physically—although he was an impressive figure—I was afraid of what he might say next. I was barely keeping it together. "Grace," he repeated softly. "Nothing happened between him and that girl. He wanted something to happen, he wanted to chase away the memory of you, but, even as drunk as he was, he couldn't do it. He was sending her away when you walked in."

That did it, the tears spilled over and tracked down my face. He stepped even closer and wiped my tears away with his thumb before pulling me into his chest. "I wanted you to know that."

I nodded. Stiff in his embrace at first, but releasing the pain little by little and dissolving against him. I sobbed a couple of times, but the last thing in the world I needed was for Jamie to see me upset. He counted on me to keep things together in his world. I pushed away from Rafe, embarrassed.

"Are you okay?"

I nodded, not looking at him.

"I need to ask you one more thing. Please don't tell Zane about this. It goes against bro code and is totally uncool."

That made me laugh a little.

"There, that's better." He rubbed my arms then broke contact. "Well, I'll get out of your hair." He turned to walk to the door.

"Rafe?"

He twisted back.

"Thank you."

That huge smile came back. "No problem." He walked out the door and closed it softly behind him.

I closed my eyes. "Jamie?"

"Huh?"

"I think I'm going to rest. I have a headache. You can watch Animal Planet."

"Yea!"

Sometimes I wished I could be more like Jamie. Then nothing would happen an ice cream sandwich or a stack of pancakes couldn't fix.

CHAPTER FOURTEEN

Grace

After I put Jamie to bed, I was alone with my thoughts. A storm was bearing down on Jefferson City, but I had a thing about storms. Beauty shone in the turbulence. I loved the deep rumbling of thunder competing with the crash of lightning for attention. The bolts of electricity split the sky, and could light up a room, all a part of nature's big light show, the thunder serving as the orchestral background. I loved the way the storm clouds rolled in with authority, like some blustering boss. And after the drama things would quiet and the world would be bathed clean.

I sat in the window to the fire escape letting the energy outside fill me. I closed my eyes as wind blew the rain in, misting my face. When I opened my eyes the lightening zigzagged through the trees in the park across the street and it captured a shadow in the alley. Did I see something? With the next bright dart, it was clear someone was there. I stood, a chill running along my spine. Was it Brad? Who else was crazy enough to stand in the rain in an electrical storm? But something about the way they stood....

"Zane?"

He ran forward, jumped, and caught the rungs of the ladder that pulled down at the end of the fire escape. He charged up the stairs then stood frozen across from my window, his legs spread wide. I was paralyzed, couldn't move, couldn't speak, couldn't take in a full breath. A tremendous bolt of lightning snaked through the sky, and the thunder following shook the glass in the windows. His gaze was drawn skyward, and without him staring at me, I found my voice.

"Come in. Get out of the rain." Leaving the window open I turned my back and walked over to the counter, crossing my arms and leaning against it. He stepped inside and stood where he landed. He wasn't wearing a coat, simply a blue Oxford with the sleeves rolled, a gray suit vest, and a metallic blue tie, with jeans. Even soaked to the bone he looked amazing. He held a bedraggled bouquet of lavender roses and Peruvian lilies and perhaps some purple statice, it was hard to tell in the state it was in.

"Umm..." He held them out. "These are for you." I didn't move, so he laid them on the end of the counter opposite me. "They were much nicer before...."

He ran his fingers through his wet hair, pushing it off his face, and I noticed a fresh scar on his forehead, an inch below his hairline. I ignored the little dive my heart took. "I, uhh, came to the front door, but I guess you didn't hear me."

"I was putting Jamie to bed."

"Oh." His expression brightened. "How is he?"

I sighed. "Well, he's been better, Zane."

Instead of deterring him, the bite of my sarcasm seemed to loosen his tongue. He held an arm out in front of him, palm down. "I know. I know I hurt you both."

I realized I didn't want to hear it. Didn't want to hear how sorry he was, his excuses, and his bull shit. I moved so suddenly he took a step back, hitting the window frame. "I let you in because it's raining and I didn't want you to get struck by lightning. I would do that for a stray dog or an alley cat in this weather. But I think you should leave now." I marched out of the kitchen to the front door. He followed, dragging his feet. I opened the door for him. But he had to come close to get out.

He stopped when he was even to me. "Grace...if you could listen for a minute. One minute is all I'm asking."

I stared at him, so many conflicting feelings battling inside me, like the wind and rain outside. I closed the door softly. I didn't look at him, because when I did I wanted to run into his arms. "You came a long way...I can give you a minute."

"Thank you." He stood with his mouth open for a second. "I don't know what to say to you."

"Then this was an incredible waste of time and energy." I twisted the knob.

He threw his arms out. "Wait!" When my eyes flashed to him, he softened his voice, bouncing his hands. "Please. Please, I'm begging you...."

"What do you want, Zane?" My voice shook.

He turned around, walking in a slow circle, shaking his head. "I rehearsed what I wanted to say the whole way here, but now it seems lame." He stopped, focusing on me intently. "Grace," he hunched his shoulders, "I love you. I love you so damned much...."

A tear popped out when I blinked. "Well, Zane, you have a funny way of showing it."

"I know. You're right. I blew it big time. But I did it for the right reasons."

I put a trembling hand to my forehead.

"I wanted more for you and Jamie. You deserve so much more. But, being without you...." He swallowed and looked to the side for a second. "I knew it would hurt, but I had no idea how much."

I thought of so many biting responses to that, they log-jammed in my mouth. "What...." I walked over and threw myself in the chair. "What do you want from me, Zane?"

He walked quickly over and got on both knees in front of me. "I want forgiveness. I have no right to ask for it, but.... Grace, I was scared. I didn't think I was enough."

"Did I ever make you feel that way?" My voice was choked. I covered my mouth.

He touched the outside of my knees. "No, honey. Never." He hung his head for a second then lifted it, staring straight at me. "I've always had a hard time believing in myself."

I thought about what Rafe said about his stepfather and my heart went out to him. I couldn't do it. Couldn't stay mad at him even after seeing him with that girl. I loved him. Love doesn't choose who to love. It doesn't always make sense. It isn't always pretty. And you can't kill it, because it's still underneath. I ran my fingers down the side of his face. "I know."

He put his hand over mine, holding it, and squeezed his eyes shut. Then he turned and kissed my palm tenderly. "I will spend every second of my life making it up to you, I swear. That girl. That girl you saw me with. I didn't do anything with her. I was drunk. And I'll admit I took her to the bus...it could have been any girl there. I didn't care. I don't even really remember what she looked like. But, I did...I wanted to fuck the shit out of her. I wanted to forget about you and the pain and all my mistakes, but..." Tears fell, running down his cheeks. "I couldn't do it, Grace. I couldn't do it because it wasn't you, and you were what I wanted with every fiber of my being. I want to stay here. I want to fight for us. I want to be a better man for you. And—"

I took his face and I did what I was dying to do since I saw him on the fire escape, I kissed him. Then I threw my arms around him and sobbed.

"Oh, my God." He pulled me off the chair, and into his lap. "I'm so sorry, Grace. I never wanted to hurt you." He got choked up and couldn't speak any more.

"Zaner?"

I don't know how long he was standing there. Zane wiped his tears and motioned him over. "Come here, buddy." Jamie ran to him.

Zane hugged him, squeezing his eyes shut. "I'm sorry I was gone for a while, but I'm here now and I won't ever do that to you or your sister again. Can you forgive me?"

Jamie leaned away to peer at him. He nodded solemnly and laid his head down again. Zane held him for a second then asked, "Can I tuck you in?"

Jamie turned to me. "Are you okay, Gracie?"

I smiled. "Yes, Syrup, I am." He grinned, got to his feet, and held his hand out for Zane.

"I'll be back in a couple of minutes."

Zane went with Jamie, but was gone for a bit. I rose and went to Jamie's door. Zane was on his knees beside the bed stroking Jamie's hair. It appeared as if Jamie was sound asleep. I leaned on the doorframe with a sigh, and the wood creaked. Zane turned then pushed to his feet, gave Jamie one last glance, and came to me. He took my hands, and started to move toward the living room, but I stopped him. Without saying anything, I led him to the bedroom. I had to be with him again, had to share that oneness with him that gave me life. After tonight I knew there was no looking back.

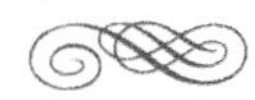

ZANE

I had been so nervous when I drove to her place. I knew this was a do or die moment for us, and that scared the shit out of me. I was asking her for a lot, and ready to offer a lot in return. When she led me to the bedroom, I was surprised. This was way more than I could hope for.

She stopped beside the bed and spun to me. "You're soaking wet." She loosened my tie, and peered up at me. I bent my neck and she lifted it off, carefully laying it over the trunk at the foot of her bed. Maintaining eye contact, she unbuttoned my vest and slid her arms around me. The gesture was so sweet, so simple, but everything we did now was done deliberately. I drew her in, kissing her hair. We stood for some time like that, holding each other.

Without raising her head, she undid a couple of buttons, and spread the sides of my shirt open, laying her cheek on my bare chest. It felt so right, like that spot was created for her. But I needed to know she was as sure as I was. I put a fist under her chin and gently lifted her face.

"We don't have to do this if you're not ready. I understand if I have to prove myself first."

She laid her hands flat on my chest beneath my shoulders. "Oh, I wasn't hesitating, I was taking my time. I want this, Zane. I want you."

The words burnt their way into my heart flaming my desire for her. I bent and took her lips, the kisses slow, deep and full of my love for her. That electric energy between us hadn't waned. If anything, it was more intense now because we knew what was at stake. We knew the pain of being apart, and we didn't want to have to experience that again. I wanted her to take the lead this time, and she did. She finished undressing me then placed a pillow on end against the headboard and had me sit there. Then with the light still on, she undressed for me, causing my blood to burn. No doubts would linger this time; nothing was hidden away. We were both literally and figuratively baring ourselves. She came to me and straddled my lap, taking me into her. She rode me in sensual waves, arching her back at one point with her hands behind her on my legs. Again it felt like she was giving herself to me. She was offering me undeserved blessings. She was offering me Grace.

In the morning, I got up with Jamie, giving her the opportunity to sleep in. I made him some halfway decent pancakes. When I was away, it might sound silly, but I often made pancakes and felt connected to them, thinking they were eating them, too.

"Jamie, can we have a serious talk? I think it might even be a fire escape talk, although neither of us is in trouble. It's just an important conversation."

He shrugged. "Okay." We climbed out the window and sat on the top stair leading down.

"So...I think you kind of guessed this but, I'm in love with your sister, pal."

He rolled his eyes. "Duh."

"Okay. So I have a serious question for you. I want to ask you if you would be okay with me marrying her at some point?"

"You're getting married?" he shouted.

"Sh-sh-sh. It's a secret. I want to surprise her. Can you keep it a secret?"

He nodded.

It was one of those beautiful crystal clear mornings where sitting in the sunshine felt like hanging out with a good friend. I scooted down so I could stretch my legs out and lean with my elbows on the stair behind me, letting the sweet rays warm me. Jamie shifted to do the same, only his arms were about at his ears. It was so cute.

"Will that make you my dad?"

"Not exactly. It would make me your brother-in-law, but I'd live here with you like a dad would."

"Hmm." He furrowed his brow and became quiet.

"Is something wrong, bud?" I thought he'd agree to give me her hand, thought he was in my back pocket, but now I was nervous.

He shook his head no, but it was clearly not the case.

I jostled him with my elbow. "Come on. I told you I love your sister, you have to tell me what you're thinking."

He remained silent, sitting up and planting his elbows on his knees, his chin resting on top of his fists.

"Is it because I was gone? Are you still mad at me for that?"

"No," he said matter-of-factly. "I forgave you for that."

"Oh. Okay." Now I definitely was anxious. Maybe he thought I wasn't good enough for Grace. "Well, I appreciate your forgiving me."

His forehead remained scrunched and his expression downcast.

I sat forward so I could see his face better. "You know, sometimes it helps when you're troubled to share that with a friend. I'd like to be that friend for you."

He twisted toward me and closed one eye, squinting with the other, then he stared at the step below.

"Do you think Gracie won't like me anymore when you get married?"

"What? No. Of course not. You're her brother. As far as I see, you are the most important person in her life. That won't change because I'm in the picture."

He didn't seem convinced. I needed some way to explain it to him. And it came to me. "Jamie, you like ice cream sandwiches, right?"

That at least got a smile. He nodded his head vigorously. "And you like pancakes."

He concurred.

"Well does liking ice cream sandwiches make you like pancakes any less?"

"No. They're different. You have one in the morning, and one at night."

That made my mind jump to *Jamie is the pancake, up early, and I'm the ice cream sandwich, hers at night.* I couldn't help the tremor of desire that thought gave me. "So, let's say I'm the ice cream sandwich and you're the pancake. Grace won't love you, the pancake, any less because of me, the ice cream sandwich. Do you understand?"

He nodded, smiling now.

"So...will you give me your permission to ask your sister to marry me?"

"Yeah."

Shoo.

I elbowed him again. "You know, you missed an opportunity there. You could say you'd give me permission, but only if you got an ice cream sandwich."

He smiled brightly. "You have to give me an ice cream sandwich if you want to marry Gracie."

"What?"

"Two ice cream sandwiches."

I frowned. "Hmm...you catch on quick, kid. What do you say we go get those sandwiches?" We got our treats and ate them on the staircase. I made Jamie swear not to tell Grace, but I had my doubts about whether that would happen or not.

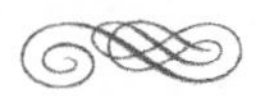

GRACE

Late summer was typically a slow time for the shop, and this August was no different. With more time on my hands I usually focused on ramping up our marketing. This year, though, I decided to take on the task of revamping our website, and it was going along pretty decently. Dex, who was a computer whiz, actually was able to help me out a bit, and the site was really coming along.

One of the advantages of the down time was it was easier for me to take off here and there and spend some time with Zane who was in the studio recording a new album in St. Louis. This was the longest we'd been apart, and I hated it. It seemed like life was what I did with Zane. Everything else was what I did while waiting for Zane to be home.

But tonight Payton was keeping me company. She insisted I needed to watch a romcom with her on Netflix. But she was acting so goofy, it was really distracting me, and I was losing the plotline. I stood, and she jumped to her feet next to me.

"What are you doing?"

"Just getting a glass of water. I'll be right back."

"Water?"

I smirked. "Yes. It's this new wet stuff. You should try it."

"No! Wait!"

I stared at her.

"You...you can't miss this part. This is the best part. I'll get the water for you."

When she came back I asked her, "What's so good about this part? Am I missing something?"

"What? Oh, it must be later."

She sat next to me again, but kept slapping her leg. I couldn't take it. "Payton! Could you please stop doing that? Every time I try to take a drink I end up spilling all over myself because you're playing the bongos on your thigh." I wiped my mouth with the back of my hand.

"Okay. Geesh."

"Did you have an extra shot of expresso in your Starbuck's this morning?"

"I'm not sure. I got some new thing called The Defibrillator."

I rolled my eyes and stood.

"Now what are you doing?" she huffed.

"I'm going to the bathroom. I'm pretty sure you can't do that for me. Just pause it."

When I got back, the movie was still running. "I thought you were pausing it? What happened with his mother-in-law?"

"Huh? What?" She was texting with somebody. "Oh. I don't remember."

"Can we rewind it then, please?" When I saw what I missed, I frowned. "You don't remember her mom found out they weren't really married? That's kind of a crucial plot twist, don't you think? How long ago did you watch this?"

"Uhh. I don't know." She looked at her phone and mumbled, "A couple of months ago."

"Who are you texting with? Are you seeing someone new?"

"Yeah."

"That's cool. How'd you meet him?"

"How'd I meet him?"

"Yeah, like was it an online thing...?"

"Yeah. That's it. I met him on Tender."

"Do you mean Tinder?"

A smile spread across her face. She picked up the remote and stopped the movie. "It's not that good a movie."

I sat with my mouth hanging open. Then a loud noise came from the alley. "What's that?"

"I don't know. Maybe you should go check," she said, beaming and squeezing her hands together.

But I figured out what I was hearing was some pretty loud electric guitar. I got to my feet slowly and crossed the kitchen to the window. Through the grates of the fire escape I could see a bunch of musical equipment scattered about. Who would set up a band in an alleyway? Kind of a strange venue. I climbed out and crossed to the railing to get a better look.

"Hi, babe." Zane was grinning at me. And it wasn't only Zane, it was Jericho, Rafe, and Dex, too, all at their respective instruments. The couple upstairs were crawling out their window, too.

"Holy shit! It's Just Short of Chaos! In our alley," she squealed.

"No, it's— Holy shit. You're right."

I smiled. "Uhh... what are you doing down there?"

He shrugged. "I thought we'd get in a little practice."

"Umm." He wore a gorgeous metallic blue blazer, over a black shirt and pants. "You always dress this nice for practice?" People were gathering on the balconies of the building behind them.

"No. Only on special occasions. Like when Dex has to have a root canal."

"Ugh. Don't remind me," Dex groaned.

Even from as far away as I was, I could tell his eyes were twinkling. "What are you up to Zane Alexander Salvetti?"

Rafe laughed. "Oh, dude. Now you're gonna get it. She used your full name."

Zane didn't take his eyes off me. "I thought I'd play you a little song I wrote."

"Ya know, I probably could have gotten the idea if you simply played your acoustic."

"Oh, no. For this we needed the whole crew." He spun around. "Ready, boys?"

They nodded.

Whirling back to me, he held four fingers in the air and counted down silently.

The music started with some very simple guitar chords, which were none the less pretty, and Zane's fantastic voice hopped in right away.

"I am the moleman
All covered in dirt
My special talent
Is making you hurt.
I dig and I claw
But only for me
Your light cannot reach
The devil in me.
The rock that I sing
Bites, razor sharp
It's hard and it suits me
In the dirt, in the dark.
But now I see your face

In every note of this song.
Please give me the grace
To help me go on."

He sang it like he was solely singing to me, although people were forming a crowd at the end of the alley now, too.

"It's dark in the bus
But not as black as my heart.
Because the way I need you
Rips me apart.
You danced into my life
Grace, and right from the start
Your light and your goodness
Enlivened my heart."
Now I see your face
In every note of this song.
Please give me the grace
To help me go on."

When I figured out he was singing about us, it felt like my heart was in his hands and was never safer. "Oh, Zane," I breathed, my fingers splayed on my breast bone.

"The dark overtakes me
I'm drowning in sin
And every bottle of Jack,
every tumbler of gin
Oh, give me the Grace
To be a better man
Love me to life
The way only you can.
Show me the light
And I will not blink
Give me the chance
Despite what they think.

I see your face
In every note of this song.
Please give me the grace
To help me go on."

The music swelled for the bridge, and Zane ran and jumped on the ladder, pulling it down and climbing it while still singing. I twisted to watch him through the grid work as he scrambled up the stairs. When he hit the first landing, he held onto the rail and swung around the corner, timing it to the music. He had a real knack for that.

"I don't deserve you, forgive me anyway
I don't know if I can change, but, God, please let me stay.
I know the man who I am
when I am with you
Is better by far,
And way overdue.
You're strong and your beauty shines from within.
Bringing light to my world and all that I've been."

He was on the landing below, singing to me. He walked slowly, looking at me the whole time. Then he took my hand and held it for me to twirl under and swayed with me in his arms, like the night we first met.

"We're lying like fours
Asleep in our bed
The warmth of our lovemaking
Cradles my head.
You give me the grace
Despite all I do
You gave me a chance
To show I love you.
I am the moleman
All covered in dirt

I feel all your pain
Know every hurt
But the dirt I loosened
Will help us to grow
I swear I love you
Far more than you know.
I see your face
In every note of this song.
Because you gave me the grace
To help me go on."

With the last notes he dipped me.

"If I kiss you, are you going to run away?"

I put my hands on his cheeks. "Not a chance."

Everyone applauded.

"You wrote that for me?"

He grinned. "Well, I certainly didn't write it for Jericho."

Jericho's voice came through the speakers. "Didn't mention my name even once. I checked, twice."

"Thank you," I yelled to them.

They nodded. I looked at them each in turn, Rafe last. Rafe cleared his throat and jerked his thumb in Zane's direction. I spun to find him on one knee, holding a ring.

"Holy shit."

Our audience laughed. Zane glanced at the band and switched off his head mic. The band's, however, were still on.

"He shut off his mic," Rafe said incredulously.

Jericho frowned. "Not fair."

And of course, Dex had to throw his two cents in. "Now we won't know if she says yes or not."

"Keep dreaming," Rafe murmured.

"Grace. I did a big public thing here, but I don't want you to feel any pressure. If you want to say no, we'll act like it's a yes, so you don't feel uncomfortable." He sighed. "You offered me grace once, and now I can't believe I have the balls to ask you again, but here I am. I love you more than any man could. Maybe not better, but definitely more. You took a chance once and let me pull you on stage to dance. I'm asking you to dance with me forever. Grace Clayton Prescott," he took a deep breath, "would you do me the great honor of becoming my wife?"

I could see in his eyes he was unsure about what I would say. He still felt himself unworthy of me because he made a few mistakes, but he was a good man. He may be unsure, but I wasn't. "Zane, I love you with everything in me. Yes. Please make me your wife."

Zane sprung to his feet and dug his fingers in my hair at the back of my neck as he kissed me.

Rafe's voice rang out. "I'd say that's a yes."

Cheers rose. Something knocked into our legs, which turned out to be someone. Jamie was squeezing us as hard as he could. Zane squatted. "She said yes, buddy."

"I told you she would." Jamie looked as happy as I had ever seen him.

Zane engulfed him in a hug.

When they parted, I tapped Jamie's shoulder. "You knew about this?"

He nodded, grinning ear-to-ear.

"And it only took four ice cream sandwiches to get him to agree to let me marry you."

Payton gushed, both hands over her heart. "Aww. You asked Jamie for permission? That's the sweetest damn thing."

I squeezed myself next to him. "She's right. It is."

He was going to kiss me again, but the band clambered up the stairs and clapped him on the back.

"Way to go," Rafe hollered, he crossed to give me a hug.

Jericho squeezed Zane's shoulders. "Congratulations, man."

Holly stuck her head out the window. "Rafe?" She passed him a glass of champagne. Lexi was holding a tray full of flutes and they were passed around.

"Where did that come from? Was Holly in on this, too?"

Zane nodded. "I needed a lot of help."

Rafe held his glass in front of him, his other arm still over my shoulder. "Grace, as of this moment, you are now an honorary member of Just Short of Chaos. You're one of us."

"Yeah," Jericho interrupted. "Even if you dump his ass, you're still one of us."

"And, if you dump his ass, I'm available," Dex added.

"Dex," Zane growled.

"What? Did I say that out loud?"

All three of them answered. "Yes."

"Aah. Sorry about that." He looked at Rafe. "Carry on then."

Rafe raised his glass. "To Grace and Zane." Most of the people stayed and clapped their support. "Champagne is on the house in apartment..." He eyed me.

"3B."

"Apartment 3B." When we climbed back through the window, I was amazed to see champagne flutes covering my table and counters. In the living room, a banquet table was set up and people in uniforms were bringing in chafing dishes and vases of flowers.

It was a pretty rowdy night, and I came to know what being just short of chaos was like. We were exhausted when everyone left and agreed to clean what little the caterers had left in the morning. Lying in bed together, after so much noise and action, the quiet was welcome. As I was drifting off to sleep, Zane tapped my foot with his.

"Are you laying like a four?"

I smiled. "I am."

He turned his head to look at me. "Wanna do that forever?"

"Sounds like a plan."

NOTE FROM THE AUTHOR

Thank you for reading ROCKED BY GRACE, part of my LOVE AND CHAOS SERIES. I hope you enjoyed it. Now that you've read the book, won't you please consider writing a review? Reviews are one of the best ways readers discover great new books. They don't need to be fancy or long, just a sentence or two honestly describing your opinion of/experience with the book. I would sincerely appreciate it.

Want more from M.J. Schiller?

Page forward for an excerpt from ~

ROCKED BY LOVE

LOVE AND CHAOS SERIES, BOOK TWO

ROCKED BY LOVE
CHAPTER ONE

Rafe

Perhaps diving into the crowd wasn't one of my best ideas ever. But when the muscle bound security guard standing *right in front of them* was doing nothing, I had to take matters into my own hands.

Seriously? How can you ignore something happening a foot away from you? Pussy.

I'd noticed the tall guy being an ass to the girl earlier in the set, so I had my eye on them when it happened. Jericho and I were playing back to back when he, the equally muscle bound man in front of the security guard, started getting physical with his girlfriend. The look of terror on her face was enough to set me off, so I hit an off chord to get the rest of the band's attention.

"Hey! If you want to hit someone with long hair, why don't you come up here and take on one of us."

"Uhh...Rafe...?"

I forgot that he was the only one of us with long hair now. Still, Jer followed me to the front of the stage where I whipped off my guitar and headset, handing them to him. If I'd thought about it and not solely reacted, I might have come up with a better solution. For the most part I thought trading violence for violence was something only idiots did. But sometimes an ass kicking is what's called for.

"What's your problem?" he barked back at me.

"I'll tell you what my problem is pal," I was so mad I was spitting. "My problem is it makes me sick to watch a two-hundred-fifty pound loser shoving around his hundred-pound date."

"She's mine, I can do with her what I want."

That was it. I lost my mind. Rage propelled me and I jumped off the stage.

Now, *I* wasn't the fighter in the band—that'd be Zane, for the most part—but I could hold my own. We'd been in our share of fisticuffs over the years, mostly in the sleazy holes we played in when we were starting out. We'd had drunk guys harass us—which Zane took exception to, igniting a fight—or we'd have brawls start off on the floor in front of us, see some guy out numbered or out classed, and felt the need to get involved. Learning to hold my own required me getting the shit beat out of me a time or two, but when push came to shove—literally—I was forced to learn how to defend myself, and forced to learn it quickly.

It was a decent leap from the stage, so the first pain I got was from the shock of hitting the ground. Security was looking like they had no fucking clue how to handle it when a rock star confronts a dick in the crowd, so they sat there shuffling their feet. The asshat wasn't even paying attention to me. I could have totally taken advantage of that, but I'm a gentleman, so I didn't. He was again yelling at the girl and had clamped onto her elbow. She was cowering and trying to placate him, and when he drew his arm back, another girl grabbed onto it. So there was one brave hundred-pound girl taking on this steroided out bastard while a whole platoon of security people sat with their thumbs stuck up their asses.

When I reached them, the guy had shaken off the girl who came to her friend's assistance, which landed her on her ass and fueled my anger even more. Now she was shrinking back and he was advancing on her, while her friend looked on, shell-shocked. Everyone else in the vicinity acted like they were protecting their girlfriends and had opened up a decent size hole so the action was front and center. A not quite waist high metal barrier was between us, but the guy could finally hear me, so he took his attention away from the women he was battering for a second.

"Hey! What the fuck did I tell you?" I seethed. I'd like to say my high school hurdling aided me in getting over the partition, but I attacked it more like it was a pommel horse. I planted my hands on the top rail and pushed off, swinging both legs to the right to clear it. It wobbled, but remained upright. He was again towering over the girl on the ground, threatening her, and she was scooting backwards on her elbows while not taking her eyes off him. She looked more pissed than scared, though. I stepped between them and used two hands to shove him back so I could make some room to demolish the guy, or be demolished, which was the more likely outcome. But I'd always found bullies backed off when they were met with any resistance, and I was hoping it would be true in this case, too.

"What the fuck?" he shouted, and took a swing, which I easily ducked. He was probably drunk off his ass. I came back up and landed a left hook and followed immediately with my right, tagging him good with an uppercut. He stumbled back and teetered for a moment like he might go down. Shaking his head, he roared and charged me, knocking me to the ground not far from the girl, who rolled away. This is what I didn't want. Without my legs I couldn't get much force behind my punches and he had the advantage. Now that he had a real opponent, the guy's anger became explosive. Luckily, he didn't get time to land more than a few punches before security swarmed. It took a half dozen of them to wrestle him off and drag him away. I scrambled up. Fans were clapping me on the back and cheering. I offered the girl on the ground a hand. She had dark brown, long wavy hair and green eyes that had spit fire earlier but now were smiling. I pulled her to her feet. She was tall, I guess about five-eight, though heels can be deceptive.

"Are you okay?"

She brushed herself off. "Yeah, thanks."

We turned to check on her friend, but she was gone.

"Where'd your friend go?"

A guy spoke up. "She followed that douche bag out."

The brunette slapped her forehead. "Unbelievable. Un-fucking-believable."

I put a hand on her arm. "As hard as it is to watch, some people can't be helped."

She gasped. "Your hand."

I looked down. Blood was dripping onto the floor from my knuckles.

Jericho yelled from the stage. "Hey. Muhammad Ali. Wanna get your ass back up here? We have music to play."

"Coming."

The girl called out as I turned. "What about your hand?"

I shrugged. "As long as I can hold a guitar pick." I flashed her a smile. "Gotta go." I twisted to walk away, but she grabbed my arm.

With her free hand, she slid the sheer scarf from her neck. "Here." She quickly wrapped it around my cuts.

"But your scarf."

"No big deal. I can get another." She tucked the end in. ""There you go."

I worked my fingers to see if I still had mobility. Hurt like hell, but the wrap was the perfect light, stretchy material for the job. Kept me from bleeding all over the place, but I could still use my hand. "Thanks."

"Thank you," she said sincerely.

"Need help up, buddy?" Jericho said pointedly. He extended his hand. The security people had moved the little barrier and were waiting for me to get through before swinging it back in place. I walked through the opening and gave Jer my "good hand." He yanked me up and handed me my guitar, wearing a bemused expression.

"I was going to jump down and help you, but you seemed to be handling it okay. Your mouth's bleeding, by the way."

I wiped at it. "Yeah, thanks. You're real friggin' helpful."

He grinned. "I try to be of service."

"Sure you do."

Zane addressed the audience. "So, you guys get a twofer tonight. A fight and a rock concert. Let's hear it for rock star/prize fighter Rafael Santiago."

I was settling my head mic on, suppressing a grin. "You guys are enjoying this, aren't you?"

Zane nodded. "Immensely."

Dex chimed in with, "Made my night."

ALSO FROM M.J. SCHILLER

ROMANTIC REALMS COLLECTION:

TAKEN BY STORM[1]
AN UNCOMMON LOVE[2]
LEAP INTO THE KNIGHT[3]
LADY OF THE KNIGHT[4]
A KNIGHT TO REMEMBER[5]

ROCKING ROMANCE COLLECTION:

TRAPPED UNDER ICE[6]
ABANDON ALL HOPE[7]
BETWEEN ROCK AND A HARD PLACE
ROCK ME, GENTLY[8]
MIDNIGHT MELODY[9]

1. http://myBook.to/TakenByStorm
2. http://mybook.to/AnUncommonLove
3. http://myBook.to/LeapIntoTheKnight
4. http://myBook.to/LadyOfTheKnight
5. http://myBook.to/AKnightToRemember
6. http://mybook.to/TrappedUnderIce
7. http://mybook.to/AbandonAllHope
8. http://mybook.to/RockMeGently
9. http://mybook.to/MidnightMelody

REAL ROMANCE COLLECTION:

UPON A MIDNIGHT CLEAR[10]
THE HEART TEACHES BEST[11]
DAMAGE DONE[12]
HOMETOWN HEARTACHE[13]
TAKE A CHANCE ON ME[14]
BLACKOUT[15]

DEVILISH DIVAS SERIES:

TO HELL IN A COACH BAG[16]
DAMNED IF I DO[17]
THE DEVIL YOU KNOW[18]
SATAN, LINE ONE
PITCHFORK IN THE ROAD[19]
SIN WORTH THE PENANCE[20]
HELL HATH NO FURY[21]

---

10. http://mybook.to/UponAMidnightClear
11. http://mybook.to/TheHeartTeachesBest
12. http://mybook.to/DamageDone
13. http://mybook.to/HometownHeartache
14. http://getbook.at/TakeAChanceOnMe
15. http://mybook.to/BlackoutMJSchiller
16. http://mybook.to/ToHellInACoachBag
17. http://mybook.to/DamnedIfIDo
18. http://mybook.to/TheDevilYouKnow
19. http://mybook.to/PITCHFORKINTHEROAD
20. http://mybook.to/SinWorthThePenance
21. http://mybook.to/HellHathNoFury

ABOUT THE AUTHOR

Bestselling author M.J. Schiller is a retired lunch lady/romance-romantic suspense writer. She enjoys writing novels whose characters include rock stars, desert princes, teachers, futuristic Knights, construction workers, cops, and a wide variety of others. In her mind everybody has a romance. She is the mother of a twenty-four-year-old and three twenty-two-year-olds. That's right, triplets! So having recently taught four children to drive, she likes to escape from life on occasion by pretending to be a rock star at karaoke. However...you won't be seeing her name on any record labels soon.

About the Author

M.J. Schiller is a lunch lady/romance-romantic suspense writer. She enjoys writing novels whose characters include rock stars, desert princes, teachers, futuristic Knights, construction workers, cops, and a wide variety of others. In her mind everybody has a romance. She is the mother of a twenty-five-year-old and three twenty-threee-year-olds. That's right, triplets! So having recently taught four children to drive, she likes to escape from life on occasion by pretending to be a rock star at karaoke. However...you won't be seeing her name on any record labels soon. You can find her at: mjschiller-author.blogspot.com and on Instagram, Twitter, Facebook, Pinterest, and many other places. Thanks again for reading!

Read more at www.mjschillerauthor.blogspot.com.